CW01560534

CURSE OF THE FAE LIBRARY

A Paranormal Women's Fiction Novel

DM Fike

Avalon Labs LLC

Copyright © 2024 by DM Fike

All rights reserved.

The characters and events portrayed in this book are fictitious. Any similarity to real persons, living or dead, is coincidental and not intended by the author.

No part of this book may be reproduced, or stored in a retrieval system, or transmitted in any form by any means, electronic, mechanical, photocopying, recording, or otherwise without written permission from the publisher or author, except as permitted by U.S. copyright law.

Cover Design by Avalon Labs LLC

For Clark. May you always enjoy telling stories.

BOOKS BY DM FIKE

Magical Midlife Mom Series

Magical Midlife Librarian Series

Magic of Nasci Nature Wizard Series

CONTENTS

PROLOGUE

CLIO SCRAWLED HER SIGNATURE with a flourish. She returned the quill feather to its pot and blew on the letter to dry the ink. How many had she written over the years?

She heated the stick of marron wax in a golden spoon. She was a fool to keep hoping, but even old fools have dreams. She poured the liquid carefully over the envelope, then pressed down with her seal. The letter *C* popped out of the grooves.

After the wax seal had cooled, she retrieved her pen to carefully write the address. She'd accidentally written the town before the street once and had flipped two numbers in the postal code. She made sure to get it right so those irritating people that worked for the human letter service wouldn't scold her again.

Clio shoved the letter into her desk drawer for safekeeping until her next trip off the island. Wringing her aching, knobby hands, she wondered how many more letters she'd be able to write. Her arthritis, along with the rest of her body, wasn't getting any younger.

Unease ran through her. She needed to train a replacement, but how could she do that when the only viable candidate didn't even know this place existed?

A sharp cry came from outside. A glance at the window showed that it had grown dark, mostly from the gathering clouds outside. The dragon probably wanted to be let inside. Others had called her a fool for indulging the young beast, but she knew the dragon would do her no harm.

Clio placed her hand against the ropey branches that weaved together to form the wall. The boughs twisted as they parted, entwining together again to create a railed staircase that led downstairs away from her living quarters.

Lightning flashed outside the circular windows as she carefully trod down the narrow staircase. No wonder her arthritis was acting up. A storm brewed outside, shaking the branches of the tree against the windows. The darkness had become so intense, she couldn't see anything except the silhouette of leaves when a second bolt lit the sky. At least the lights in the sconces turned on automatically, burning bright until she moved out of range and another would take its place.

As her slippers hit the marble floor, a thud reverberated through the high-ceilinged main hallway. She walked toward the sound, near the front entrance, as fast as her old legs could carry her. The thudding intensified when she didn't reach it fast enough.

"Hold on to your scales. I'm coming." She raised her voice, even though it was unlikely anyone could hear her through the thick bark.

Once in the enclosed front entrance with its reception desk and bell, Clio once again splayed her gnarled fingers across the vine-like surface of the wall. The ropey branches obeyed her command, receding to open a doorway leading into the gathering storm outside.

Clio winced as nearly horizontal rain pelted her robe, the thin material soaking through within seconds. Yet, the dragon was nowhere to be seen.

"Agatha!" she yelled. "Stop messing around. Get in here!"

In response, a short burst of flame lit up in the distance, past the moat, followed by what sounded like a shriek.

"Agatha?" Clio's anger melted away into worry.

Nothing replied.

Clio's pulse quickened. The dragon could be in trouble. She hobbled out into the storm, pushing back a flood of fear as rain obscured her vision. Mud squelched into her slippers. She lost her connection to her magic as she scurried across the moat to the other side.

"Agatha, where are you?" Clio squinted into the dark.

A flash of lightning split the sky, illuminating the path that wandered up toward the ridgeline. Angry eyes flashed in the center of the silhouette.

"No!" Clio cried. She lifted her arms against the flames.

The oncoming inferno engulfed her.

CHAPTER 1

M OVING BACK HOME WHEN you're twenty-five years old sucks, but it completely obliterates your self-esteem when you're forty.

I paused with my car idling in the driveway. I caught a glimpse of my reflection in the rearview mirror, tired brown eyes staring back at me. I brushed a strand of medium-length dark brown hair back over my ear, not that it would stay there. Who was I kidding? I wasn't here to impress anyone, especially not in the wrinkled T-shirt and shorts I'd worn while traveling all day from Redding, California.

I withdrew the keys from the ignition and opened the driver's side door, stretching my legs for the first time in two hours. Then standing, barely tall enough to peek over the car's roof, I surveyed my childhood home. My brother Jason had fixed the place up significantly in the last few years. He'd repainted the aging shutters around the front window, had a new roof installed, and even planted a scraggly maple tree to replace the birch that had been eaten by borer beetles. Still, the single story, three-bedroom house surrounded by the forests of Otis,

Oregon remained remarkably the same. I could imagine either my mother or father spotting me at the kitchen window and running to open the front door for me.

At least that was one good thing about my recent failure. My parents weren't around to witness it.

I felt sick as that awful thought flickered across my mind. Even after licking my wounds from the divorce, I would have gladly traded my pride for another day with Mom or Dad.

A different face peeked out above the sink. Instead of going through the front door, the garage creaked open, slowly revealing a sturdy man starting with his work boots, then his jeans and long-sleeved checkered shirt, and ending at an Oregon Ducks baseball cap. Age had weathered my brother, giving his tan skin a tougher sheen and streaking his short black hair with bits of gray. But his goofy smile matched the teenager I remembered, who enjoyed tinkering with Dad on classic cars and skipping school to shoot hoops with his friends, much to Mom's chagrin.

"You got here faster than I expected," Jason said as way of greeting.

"I didn't get caught behind any slow drivers on the mountain roads coming out of Salem."

"That's a minor miracle."

"That's me. Lucky Rosalind Baldwin. Crashing at her brother's until she can find somewhere else to go."

His smile disappeared behind a hint of pity. "You can always stay here if you need to."

"I know," I said, wishing I hadn't given in to melodrama. Just because I was coming home like an unemployed college student didn't mean I had to act like one. "And I'm grateful."

"I bet you're starving too. I made spaghetti."

"With meatballs?"

"Is there any other way?"

I gave him a fierce hug. "You're the best."

He slapped my back soundly. "Of course, I am. I was always the favorite child."

I playfully pinched his shoulder as I pulled away from him. "Whatever. That was definitely me. I never got arrested by the cops."

"It was one midnight race through town with a couple of buddies. No one, not even the retired sheriff, will ever let me live it down."

"That's life in a small town. The rumor mill needs fuel, and there's nothing more juicy than half the high school basketball team getting put behind bars."

Jason laughed, then glanced behind my shoulder. He grimaced at my cheap sedan. "You know this model gets broken into all the time, don't you?"

"Thank you, Mr. Mechanic."

"I'm serious. I can't tell you how many customers have had them broken into."

"That's why I was able to buy it for so cheap. A girl on a budget needs wheels."

Jason walked toward the vehicle. "Let me bring your stuff in, just in case."

"In case what? Ms. Blume next door moseys over in her walker and steals something?"

But he insisted on unloading my stuff, so I helped him haul the few precious boxes of worldly possessions I owned into the garage before going inside to eat.

Jason had perfectly recreated Mom's delicious homemade spaghetti, right down to the breadcrumbs in the mouth-watering meatballs. I savored each bite, a tiny time capsule that transported me back to my youth.

"Have I told you I love you?" I asked him between mouthfuls.

"You mean you love the recipe."

"I can love both things. They're not mutually exclusive."

Jason had never left Otis, not even after graduating. He went straight from high school to Dad's garage, learning the ins and outs of our father's business. Jason blended into the small town, only a stone's throw away from the coast, as if he were one of the Douglas firs swaying in the forests towering over the valley.

I envied how easily he had found his place in the world. Despite my age, I hadn't decided what I wanted to be when I grew up. It's not that I hadn't tried. I loved learning. In college, I took introductory classes in everything from English literature to physics, fascinated by them all, but the minute I started getting into the minutia of a field, my interest waned. I bounced from major to major so much that I'd ended up with a bachelor's degree in general studies.

My professional life hadn't fared much better. Project manager, graphic designer, saleswoman . . . I never held down a job for long. I changed so often, I stopped listing most positions on my resume so I wouldn't scare potential employers. I also bounced around from city to city, hoping to connect with a physical location.

And yet here I was, back at Otis and starting over again.

My phone buzzed in my pocket. I retrieved it, hoping it was Lindsey, my best friend growing up. I doubted it would actually be her, though, since she should be on her way to India as a flight attendant right now.

Instead, the phone screen displayed the last person in the world I wanted to talk to.

Jason noticed my face crumple and asked, "It's Mikey, isn't it?"

"He goes by Mike now," I said, defending my newly minted ex-husband out of habit.

"I could call him another four-letter word if you'd like."

"Please don't." I pushed back from the table.

"You're not answering that, are you?"

"I have to. The last time I didn't, he was calling to ask if a box I'd labeled 'Important Documents' in huge red letters was important. He ended up throwing away my college diploma."

Jason's hand tightened around his fork, ready to stab something other than pasta. "I could take care of him for you."

"We've been over this. Our society frowns upon murder."

"I wouldn't get caught. One of my buddies was in the army. He knows people."

"It's still a no." I scurried out of the dining room and down the hall into the spare bedroom before Jason could provide another "helpful suggestion." Even though his overprotective nature made me roll my eyes, I was grateful that he cared.

I needed all the help I could get dealing with my scummy ex.

After closing the door, I answered. "Hello?"

"Rosie?" Mike said in his nasally voice, using his nickname for me that I now hated with a passion. "About time you picked up."

I squashed a rebuke that I was no longer at his beck and call. Antagonizing him would only instigate another argument, and I couldn't stomach another fight. "What do you want?"

"I can't find what you did with our previous years' tax info, so I can't file for this year."

"It's June. You should have done that in April."

"I filed an extension," he shot back in anger. "Don't treat me like an idiot, Rosie."

Me treat him like an idiot? That was rich since he was calling me to find something I'd left in a very obvious place. "Have you checked in the 'My Documents' folder of your computer?"

I could hear him clicking around. "It's not there!"

"It's filed under a subfolder," I said slowly, not bothering to explain if I just threw everything under one folder, it would be impossible to find anything. "It's under one labeled 'IRS.'"

"So that's where you put it," he said with disbelief. "I was looking for a 'Taxes' folder. You should have made it more obvious."

He could have also filed his own taxes instead of having me do it for the four years we were married, but that would have been beneath Mike Newman, city councilman and rising political star. He couldn't be bothered taking care of the "details" in his life while he focused on his illustrious career.

"Mikey, honey?" I heard a sickly-sweet voice in the background. Apparently, someone had permission to use his old nickname. My stomach turned at the sound of Bella Worthington's voice, his new fiancée and the person who had broken up our marriage.

No, that wasn't fair. Mike had destroyed our marriage when he'd had an affair with Bella, a woman fifteen years his junior. I should have known when he hired her as a "political consultant" that something fishy was going on, but I'd been none-the-wiser right up until I found them conducting a "work meeting" in our bedroom, naked and intertwined with each other.

Mike infuriated me, but truthfully, I was equally mad at myself. I'd been about as successful at picking romantic partners as I'd had finding a career or a city to settle down in. Every single man I'd ever dated—from my high school sweetheart onward—had been highly ambitious. I had exes that founded thriving startups, researched the cutting edge of their scientific field, and one that even competed in the Olympics. Once their careers took off, our relationship would be put on the back burner, and he'd inevitably break up with me.

I'd believed Mike would be different. He'd been a humble psychology professor. It was only after the honeymoon that he'd shown an interest in politics, and honestly, I'd encouraged him at the beginning. But once he delved into that world, he scaled back to part-time work so he could focus on "fixing our community." We spent less time enjoying each other's company, and more time talking about his political ambitions. In the last year, we barely spoke at all except to further his career. Even if Bella hadn't come along, we'd been mentally separated for a while.

That didn't make the affair sting any less.

"Who are you talking to?" Bella's voice was getting louder on the other end.

"Nobody." I heard scuffling as Mike frantically moved the phone around.

Bella's next words were muffled but audible. "You're talking to your ex-wife!"

"Babe, it's about taxes."

"But I thought you said you wouldn't call her again."

"Gotta go," Mike said, so loud that I winced. Then he abruptly cut the line.

I plopped down on the bed, tossing the phone onto the comforter next to me. There weren't many things that Bella and I would ever agree on, but I did wish Mike wouldn't call me ever again. I'd be happy to forget about him and his new fiancée.

The long drive from Redding must have taken a lot out of me because I slept without waking up once. I hadn't done that in months. Maybe it was because moving back to Otis finally cut proximity to Mike. Or maybe being back in the spare bedroom—which once upon a time had been my room, despite

Jason using it to store his dusty guitar cases—came with some familial peace.

Either way, I didn't actually get out of bed until ten o'clock, which never happens. By the lingering smell of old coffee in the kitchen, Jason was long gone. He generally went to the garage early in the morning, like Dad always had. He'd be back for a break within the next hour or so.

Which meant I had something to do.

After a quick shower, I got dressed in my comfiest shorts, the one with the tie band instead of a button and zipper, and a comfy T-shirt that only showed off a smidge of my love handles. I wasn't aiming to impress anyone today. Then I ambled out into the kitchen to see what I could make for lunch.

Jason may be a bachelor who could cook for himself, but even after all these years, he hated doing the dishes. He left dirty pots everywhere, along with a sink full of plates and silverware that preceded my arrival by several days. I filled half the sink with soapy suds while unloading the dishwasher. It was the least I could do since I'd become my brother's roommate for the foreseeable future.

Once I'd cleared away the dishes and started simmering a batch of tomato soup on the stove, I tackled the messy stacks of paper on the counter. Jason threw receipts, mail, and any other scrap paper in one huge haphazard pile. I separated them first into things to keep—like customer invoices he'd need for his financial records—and obvious bits to recycle, although I would ask him first before I tossed anything away.

About halfway through the substantial stack, past an entire tree's worth of credit card offers, I uncovered a generic white envelope. At first thinking it was yet another advertisement, I threw it on the "recycle" pile. It landed face down, revealing a maroon wax seal with the letter *C* raised amid two fancy flourishes.

Curious, I read the front again. To my surprise, it wasn't addressed to Jason but to me. I didn't recognize the flowing cursive handwriting.

There was also no return address.

I was about to open it when the side screen door slammed open.

"Do I smell tomato soup?" Jason called, tromping in with his greasy mechanic uniform.

I tossed the envelope aside in lieu of lunch. "You do, and I'll make grilled cheese sandwiches to go with it."

Jason noticed the stacks of paper on the counter and groaned. "Did you really have to start cleaning right away?"

"I was just tidying up," I protested.

"Like you 'just tidied up' the garage after Dad died? I couldn't find my favorite toolbox for a month."

"If you didn't have seven thousand things lying around, it wouldn't be a problem."

"I have a system, and you ruin it when you move stuff around." He grabbed the stacks of mail and threw them back together in one huge, tilting pile before I could stop him.

"Hey, I was sorting through those!"

"I'll do it myself later."

13

"When? Next Christmas?"

He shrugged as he filed past me toward the hallway bathroom. "I'm a busy man."

I thought about being contrary and re-sorting the stack, but my rumbling stomach demanded lunch first. As Jason washed up, I made the promised cheese sandwiches.

Our bickering was forgotten as we dug into another old favorite meal. Jason told me about his morning. A customer came in with a car that wouldn't start. Turns out, her teenage son believed the gas tank was where *all* fluids went into a car, so he'd poured a bunch of oil down there. We both had a good laugh.

"So how much did you charge for that?" I asked.

"Nothing. Money's tight for their family, so I drained the gas pump and sent her on her way."

"You're so sweet."

He leaned back in his chair. "Don't I know it."

"And so humble too." We'd finished the soup, so I gathered up the dirty bowls. "Are you going back to the garage this afternoon?"

"Yeah, I'm working both shifts today." He eyeballed me suspiciously as I filled up the sink again with suds. "You're not going to spend the day cleaning, are you?"

I flicked a bit of bubbles into the air. "Don't you like having clean dishes?"

"Sure, but you won't stop there. If I leave you here alone, you'll rearrange my tools again, and who knows what will go missing this time."

I furiously scrubbed at a tomato stain. "I need to keep my hands busy. It helps me feel useful."

"Well, then let me suggest something you can dig your fingers into." Jason pushed back from the table and walked to a rack of keys on the wall. He selected a flat football keychain with two keys. "You can go over to my storage unit and do whatever you want with the stuff inside there."

I gestured for him to leave it on the counter while I finished up the dishes. "Why let me rummage through your storage unit but not touch anything here at the house?"

Jason gave me a sheepish grin. "Because it's not really my stuff. It's Mom's and Dad's old things. I've been running out of space in the house but didn't have the heart to get rid of anything yet, so I packed it away."

I lapsed into silence as a wave of fresh grief hit me. It was ridiculous really. Mom had died in an accident right after I graduated high school, and Dad had lost his battle with cancer almost five years ago. I should have been past this.

Except I knew I never would be. Maybe the bouts of raw grief would become fewer and further between, and I'd get better at handling them, but I'd never stop missing them. My love for them could never truly fade away, no matter how much time had passed.

Jason must have understood because his voice got softer. "Sorry. I didn't mean to upset you."

"It's okay. It's tough being an orphan, even though we're adults."

"Yeah, that's definitely my least favorite thing about growing old."

"Do you have a favorite thing?" I teased, hoping to lighten the mood.

He pretended to give it careful consideration. "It's pretty fun that I can relate to the actors in prescription medicine commercials now."

"How about all our prom hits being on the 'oldies' radio channel?"

"Yeah, that's cool. But what I'm really looking forward to is that male pattern baldness. I'm about the age Dad was when he started losing his hair. Wait until you feast your eyes on my chick magnet combover!"

As we burst into laughter, a warm gratitude settled over me. Mom and Dad may have been gone, but I still had my older brother. As adults, we sometimes went weeks or even months without talking, but when we got together, it felt like absolutely no time had passed at all.

I dried my hands on the kitchen rag and snatched the football keychain. "You're in luck. I've decided to check out the storage unit instead of messing with your stuff today."

"Great. Just don't feel obligated to throw anything out. I know it was too hard for me."

"Well, I'm not you," I said with confidence. "I've moved so often, I have no problem getting rid of stuff. I'm not a hoarder like you." I went toward the spare bedroom to grab my messenger bag.

"Don't you need the storage unit's address?" he called after me.

"It's Otis, Jason. Unless you hauled everything to the coast, there's only one place you could have gone."

CHAPTER 2

O TIS'S ONLY STORAGE FACILITY was located behind a local marketplace that, for no logical reason at all, sold the world's best slushies. The bland beige buildings with green sheet metal stood behind an old wooden fence that badly needed a paint job. I drove through the open gates and parked near the office.

Before I could even exit my car, a spry old man wearing a track suit and ballcap walked out to greet me. "Well, if it isn't Ms. Rosalind Baldwin."

I smiled, happy to hear my maiden name used after the divorce. "Hello, Mr. Dalton."

Mr. Dalton had been my high school PE teacher. He had retired from making surly teenagers run laps right after I graduated and bought the old storage business to run instead.

"You must be here for your brother's unit."

"I am. I have a key, but I'm not sure what number it is. Do you mind looking that up for me?"

"Sure thing."

He gestured me into the office. It had very little furniture, only one desk with a computer and two chairs on either side of it. A scrawny, young man in jeans and a T-shirt sat in front of the computer. His glassy eyes blinked awake when he saw Mr. Dalton approach.

"Rosalind, meet my grandson, Mr. Aydin Dalton."

I waved politely at Aydin, who only nodded back. Aydin was the offspring of Mr. Dalton's son, Thomas, who had sat behind me in algebra.

"Aydin's learning the ropes so he can run the place a few days a week for me during summer break," Mr. Dalton said. "Aydin, can you find the unit number for Mr. Jason Baldwin?"

"Sure." He languidly clicked away at the keyboard. After a very long pause, he said, "Number 521."

"Thanks," I said, heading for the door.

Before I could leave, Mr. Dalton said. "Aydin can escort you."

"I'm sure I can find it."

"Aydin will be happy to help."

Aydin didn't look happy as he slumped out of his chair. He meandered out of the office, not bothering to see if I'd follow. I went after him, ignoring Mr. Dalton's consternation at his grandson. That was the expression he used to give students before he made them do extra push-ups for goofing off.

Despite Aydin's lack of enthusiasm, he walked surprisingly fast. I had to almost jog to keep up with his much longer legs. It wasn't until we turned down a second aisle of storage units that I finally called out to him.

"You run on the track team or something?"

"Huh?" he asked, finally slowing down as if realizing I was behind him.

"You're walking pretty fast."

"Oh," Aydin said. "I guess I just needed to stretch my legs."

"Not a lot of opportunity for exercise in the office, huh?"

He snorted. "Yeah, no."

Maybe I should have kept my nose out of it, but I couldn't help but add, "You don't seem too excited to be here."

"I'm not," he said bitterly. "I'd rather be at the Oregon Shakespeare Festival."

That threw me for a loop. The repertory theatre on the coast was renowned for its excellent performances. I hadn't expected a jaded kid like Aydin to have much interest in it. "You're an actor?"

"I did drama this year," he said, a spark lighting his eyes. "I did mostly stage work for the fall production, but I actually got to play Horatio in *Hamlet* for the spring play." He puffed up his chest and projected his voice. "Good night, sweet prince, and flights of angels sing thee to thy rest!"

I hid a smile. "Sounds very Shakespearian."

"Yeah," he said with a faraway look. "It was amazing. My drama teacher said I was a natural. She's the one who suggested I do an unpaid internship with the Oregon Shakespeare Festival. She knows some people and can make it happen."

"What's holding you back?"

Aydin shook his head. "My dad doesn't understand. He doesn't believe you can make a living on stage."

"That's not true," I said. "My first college boyfriend became an actor."

"Really?" Aydin perked up.

"He was majoring in accounting when I first met him, but the boy was miserable. He took his first acting class our sophomore year. I convinced him to keep going, and he eventually switched majors."

"I bet he had some support."

"Are you kidding me? His parents hated it. They quit paying for his housing. That didn't stop my boyfriend. He got a part-time job and kept acting. The last time I heard, he landed a lead role in one of those permanent Broadway shows on the Las Vegas strip."

"Wow! That's amazing!" Aydin's eyes lost some of their sparkle. "That doesn't mean I'll make it."

"True. There are no guarantees in life. Sometimes, you try something and fail miserably. The only way you'll know for sure is if you try."

"You sound like my mom," he said. "That's what she says. She thinks I should do the internship, even if I just do grunt work. But Dad insists I should make some money here at the storage units to save for college."

We'd reached unit number 521.

"It's nice having the cash," I admitted. "But there are some experiences you can't buy. You're lucky your teacher can get you an internship at the festival. Not everyone has that opportunity."

Aydin shrugged. "I guess so. Anyway, here's the unit. You have a good day."

He left at his former breakneck pace before I could thank him.

I faced the unassuming metal door. I considered going back to the car and driving it to the unit but figured I could do that after I'd taken a look inside.

After unlocking the padlock with the larger key on the ring, I rolled the garage-style door upward with all of my meager upper body strength, revealing a space as large as the spare bedroom back home.

It turns out I hadn't mentally prepared myself for my family's old junk. Waves of nostalgia washed over me as I spied different items: a glazed blue gardening pot that my mother had planted marigolds in every year; my dad's old table saw that he'd used to build my childhood bookshelves; a large photo frame engraved with leaves shoved behind a stack of boxes. I pulled the frame out so I could see Mom, Dad, Jason, and me smiling underneath our long gone birch tree. I vaguely remember taking the picture during my kindergarten year. It had hung over the fireplace most of my childhood.

I pinched myself to stop the tears threatening to form. "This is going to be tougher than I thought," I whispered. Then I rolled up my sleeves and dug in.

So much for me not being a hoarder. After three hours of shifting through the storage unit, I'd barely filled half of a banker's box to donate. Even then, I wasn't sure I wanted to give away my mom's worn paperback murder mysteries. I had fond memories of her curled up on the couch, reading stacks of them at a time. What if the donation center threw them away?

"I'm as bad as Jason," I said as I shoved the books back into another box to keep. At this rate, the two of us would be buried with all this crud.

Taking a break, I leaned against the door frame for support, glad that despite the summer sun, a breeze kept things cool. I stared at the mountain of my parents' belongings still left to go when something caught my eye.

Behind an old DVD shelf and beneath a papasan chair that had lost its cushion, the corner of a sturdy gray box poked out. Moving the wooden frame aside, I discovered a fireproof safe. It wasn't that big, maybe half the size of a toaster oven, but it weighed almost as much as the tubs of books I'd been lugging around (and not putting into the donate pile) all morning.

"What did Mom and Dad put in here?" I complained as I hauled the safe to the brighter entrance for a better look. "Bricks?"

The simple safe had no labels or any indication of what might be inside. It was also locked up tight, with a weird circle-shaped hole instead of a standard keyhole. Recognizing that shape, I retrieved the football keychain and found the second, smaller key had the same form factor. The key slid right into place, unlatching the thick door.

23

I pulled out a white brick on top and did a double take. "I was joking about the bricks," I muttered as I examined the strange markings all over it. The etchings had no discernable pattern, sometimes swirling, sometimes slashing across the surface.

Beneath the brick were many letters neatly folded into generic white envelopes, all with no return address. The hair stood on the back of my neck when I noticed one addressed to me, just like the one in Jason's paper stack. I flipped it over, finding a familiar maroon wax seal with the letter *C*.

Breaking the seal, I pulled out a letter written on heavy paper with a slightly bumpy texture. Someone had written on it in scrawling black ink, their penmanship matching the flowing script of the address. It read:

Dearest Rosalind,

You have no idea how saddened I am to hear that our beloved Sophia is no longer with us. Even though I never understood her desire to live a normal human life, you must understand that I loved my daughter with every fiber of my being. I wept for many days, knowing that the two of us would never reconcile in this lifetime.

I do not want that tragedy to befall the two of us. I want nothing more than to meet my only granddaughter, who by now must be a beautiful young woman of her own. Please do not forsake me as your mother has all these years. Come visit me at your earliest convenience. All you have to do is return the stone to the fairy ring, and I will explain everything to you.

Your Ever Doting Grandmother,

Clio

My heart pounded in my chest. Mom had always told me that her own mother was "dead to her." I'd always assumed she had passed away.

But this letter was dated after my mother died. My maternal grandmother had been alive my entire life.

I stifled a flash of anger at my mother's deception. I had no idea what kind of person my grandmother had been, but she seemed pushy, even in an old letter. Mom probably had a reason for cutting off all ties.

A flash of blue amid the other white envelopes in the safe caught my attention. I snatched the smaller envelope, recognizing my dad's bold penmanship. He'd written "To Rosalind" on top.

My heart skipped a beat as I tore open the envelope and read the handwritten letter from my father inside.

Rosalind,

If you're reading this then I'm probably gone.

First, I love you and Jason so very much. Your mother loved you both too, with all her heart. Don't blame her for keeping this all a secret. She had her reasons, and it was not my place to circumvent them.

I met your mother by chance in the woods. Do you remember that weird archway on our favorite hike near the house? It was more than a family hiking spot. It's where your mother and I first met. Sophia never told me where she actually came from, only that her mother was very strict and would never approve of our relationship. The day Sophia decided to stay with me, she took a brick from that structure as a memento of her past and told me she would never look back.

It wasn't until after we'd been married a few years that her mother showed up on our doorstep. She begged Sophia to return with her, but your mother refused. She'd just given birth to Jason. She made the old woman promise never to come by again, and true to her word, she never did.

But the letters began arriving instead. Sophia never opened them and made me promise to do the same. She also made me swear I would never tell you about your grandmother for as long as I lived. After your mother's death, the letters became addressed to you.

I thought about telling you the truth so many times, but I had never broken a promise to Sophia. Plus, I was a little angry that your grandmother seemed disinterested in Jason altogether. Now that I am no longer alive, though, you are free to find out the truth for yourself.

I've kept all the letters your grandmother sent and your mother's brick memento in here for you. You and you brother can choose to do with them what you will. I know you might be curious, but be careful. Sophia fled from her mother for a reason. If you or Jason do ever end up meeting your grandmother, remember that she might not be all that she appears.

Love you, sweetheart,

Dad

I reread the letter twice. I had to wipe away tears to keep them from dripping onto the blue paper. It sounded so much like him, as if he were in the room with me. I wanted to shout at him that he should have told me all of this sooner, that Mom's promise for secrecy should have died with her.

But I also knew that would have gone against everything my dad stood for. His word was his bond. At least Dad had found a loophole so he could give this all to me after he passed on.

Now I had to figure out what to do with this information. I had a grandmother out there, but should I find her? Mom certainly hadn't wanted me to meet her. And even if I did want to chat with Grandma Clio, there was no way to find her. None of the envelopes so far had any return address.

Maybe there were more clues inside the rest of her letters.

I spent the remainder of the morning sifting through the contents of the safe. The envelopes dated back to before I was born, at first addressed to my mother but eventually directed at me after her death. They all pretty much said the same thing. Clio wanted either my mom or myself to return some stone to the fairies and reclaim our destiny.

"No wonder Mom ran away from home," I grumbled. "Grandma Clio sounds like a nutcase."

Perhaps it was just as well that I had no way to meet Grandma Clio. I shoved everything back into the safe. After all the envelopes had been safely tucked inside, I hoisted the brick, its weight heavy in my hand.

I was about to place it back in the safe when a sudden thought occurred to me. What if that archway where my parents had met wasn't an archway at all? When Clio wrote about a "fairy ring," I imagined a bunch of rocks arranged in a circle on the ground. But what if this brick was the "stone" and that archway was a "fairy ring?"

"That's ridiculous," I said to myself, moving to stash the brick back in the safe. "My mind's making connections that are not there."

But I couldn't bring myself to let go of the brick. It was a hunch, and a pretty silly one at that, but when I locked up the storage unit a few minutes later, I had the brick with me, stuffed in my messenger bag.

CHAPTER 3

H UNCHES ARE STUPID.

Decades ago, I had loved the trail near our house that wound up the mountain deep into the woods beyond. I'd been meaning to come back for many years, to glimpse the familiar pathways and taste the salty sea air wafting inland.

Instead, I huffed up the incline, wheezing and gulping from the water bottle I'd stuffed in my messenger bag. I regularly did yoga, but the incline proved more brutal than my half-hour routine. I wiped sweat from my brow as I searched for landmarks to my destination. At last, two cedar trees that shared a trunk appeared, the first marker that would take me off the main path toward the archway.

I'd hiked here often as a kid. My dad had discovered the trail after he'd bought the house, years before he met my mother. He liked to take us up here to "shake out our wiggles" when we became too rambunctious at home. He'd chase us through the forest until we'd make it to the archway. My mother rarely came on these excursions.

Now I wondered if her absence was related to the archway.

The sky let out a rumble above me. I'd become so focused trudging upward that I hadn't noticed the gathering clouds. Splashes of drops turned into a light drizzle. I hadn't brought a jacket, so the water splashed on my clothes.

Wonderful.

At least the next two landmarks came quickly: a speckled boulder the shape of an avocado and a bubbling stream that sprouted out of the mountain itself. The archway was close. The messenger bag strap dug into my shoulder with the brick weighing it down.

Thunder rattled louder now, the rain coming down in steadier streams. My shoes sank into random mud patches, firm only where it remained dry under the shade of old growth trees. Between my wet socks and protesting thighs, I wanted to forget the whole "fairy ring" thing.

But my determination returned as I rounded the crest of a hill onto a flat open meadow, the trees parting for me. Across the field, an archway sprung from the swaying grass, composed of two hefty columns of white brick. The curve of the arch, called an "extrados" if I remembered correctly from my college architecture class, was made of individual bricks in the same pale stone. Blooming red and purple wildflowers created a path directly to it.

A strange hum undercut the rain as if welcoming me forward.

"Whoa," I breathed in awe. It was a lot more spectacular than I remembered from my childhood.

To avoid trampling the flower petals, I walked in the soft green grass toward the archway. As I got closer, I noticed the inlaid bricks had been carved with symbols. If this had been built as an actual doorframe to a building, half of the symbols would have been covered up by the surrounding walls. The archway seemed more like an art piece than a construction project. The only thing missing was a single brick on the left column, creating a gap that allowed a view of the other side.

Just the right size and shape as the brick in the messenger bag.

I almost pulled it out before something else caught my attention. Near the tall grass growing at the base of the columns, there were rougher etchings, clearly not the same as the pattern on the rest of the stone. I pushed the grass aside to reveal a rough inscription scratched onto its surface, probably by a pocket knife.

L+S.

A lump forward in my throat. Linus and Sophia, my parents' names. I traced the letters with a fingertip, as if I could connect with them back through time. I missed them so very much.

I reminded myself I wasn't here to reminisce. I was here for answers. Retrieving the brick, I compared its patterns to those etched on the column. Their swirling and slashing patterns appeared identical.

My heartbeat quickened. Maybe this wasn't a dumb hunch after all.

Holding my breath, I slid the brick into the left column gap.

Seconds passed, then minutes. Nothing happened. Rain continued to pour, soaking into my skin.

I blew out a sigh. What had I expected? My grandmother to magically appear before me? The ground to open up and swallow me whole?

Angry at myself for acting so foolish, I pushed the brick back through the gap and shoved it into my messenger bag for the walk down. I made it all the way to the end of the wildflower path before I realized I didn't need to haul the heavy brick down the mountain. It obviously was meant to be here, so it might as well stay.

I considered dropping it in the mud but decided it should go in its proper spot. I marched back over to the left column and unceremoniously shoved it into place.

Immediately, the carvings in both my brick and its twin on the right side began to glow.

I shrieked as more symbols in the archway lit up as if a switch had been flipped. Blue light pulsated up and down the columns, casting a halo over the entire field. When sparks began to shoot off the archway, I ran all the way back to the tree line to hide behind a hemlock.

What had I done?

I peered at the archway from behind the shaggy tree. The sparks had stopped shooting. I tiptoed back to the archway, noticing I'd inserted the brick in a different orientation. It looked upside down to me, but apparently that was the proper way to align it.

I also noticed the bricks weren't the only things glowing around the archway. A different sort of light shot out from between the columns.

Sunbeams?

I blinked on purpose, once, twice, but the sunshine stayed. Also, a brilliant blue sky, but only between the archway's columns.

"This can't be real," I breathed, but the clear sky didn't waver. In fact, the forest disappeared altogether inside, exposing instead a white, sandy beach.

I made a full 360-degree circle around the archway. The beach scene remained firmly between the columns, like a surreal digital photo.

The archway had turned into a portal to some tropical paradise.

"Maybe it's an illusion?" I always talk to myself when I'm alone, but this time it felt justified since I was either crazy or the world itself had gone mad. I timidly stretched out a hand between the columns, yanking it back when a warm breeze blew across my bare arms.

All my senses were screaming that this was real.

The sensible thing would have been to go get Jason and make sure he saw the same thing. But I was tired of relying on him for everything. Besides, if I could walk through to the other side, I wouldn't need his help to determine if it was real.

So I closed my eyes and walked forward.

The rain quit pelting me as I stepped onto the beach. I instinctively tilted my head toward the warm sun as I reopened my eyes. Ocean spray swept past loose strands of my hair. Swaying palm trees marked the boundary of a jungle beyond.

A strange sound like an animal clearing its throat caught my attention. A flock of a dozen bright red birds broke out of the leafy canopy, twirling around each other like miniature flamingos except their bills were a long, thinner black.

"Scarlet ibis," I said, remembering reading about the birds in a travel article about Trinidad once. Was I in the Caribbean? Pulling out my cell phone, I held it to the pristine sky but couldn't get a signal. Figures.

I looked back over my shoulder at where I'd come from. An archway, made of weathered gray stone, loomed behind me. It still rained in the meadow. To make sure it wasn't an illusion, I poked my head back through just as a bolt of lightning threw the storm into sharp relief. Squealing, I ducked back onto the more welcoming beach.

The portal was real. My grandmother had said she would explain everything if I returned the stone to the fairy ring. Glancing down the beach, I saw it curve inward toward a path that led into the thick jungle.

Could Clio, my maternal grandmother, really be at the end of that path?

I needed answers so badly, but a part of me still wanted to run back home and tell Jason. I imagined leading him up the trail and knew that the minute he spied the glowing archway, he wouldn't let me explore it. He'd insist on going alone to keep me safe.

But this hadn't been meant for Jason. The letters had all been addressed to me. Deep in my gut, I knew that this was my journey to take, not his.

I had to go forward. I had to know where this would take me.

I pointed a finger at the archway leading back to the Oregon forest. "Don't go anywhere," I commanded. Its glowing symbols didn't seem inclined to disappear.

Hoping I wasn't making a huge mistake, I walked down the beach toward the path. Every step coated my sneakers in sand, the grains nestling into my socks and rubbing against my skin. I finally kicked off my shoes and stuck the nasty socks inside. I shoved the shoes into my messenger bag, wincing at the thought of sand getting all over my wallet, but I couldn't deny the relief of drying my wrinkled feet.

The path cut a narrow lane through the dense bush of the jungle, clearly manmade. Animals scurried in the gloomy underbrush, although I couldn't see any of them. I steeled myself, pushing down fear as I stepped onto the path.

Pebbles poked my waterlogged soles. I considered putting my shoes back on but decided against it given how wet they were. As my eyes adjusted to the dimness, the path became overgrown, weeds creeping in at the edges. I had to climb over mangrove roots as the trail followed a swamp, buzzing insects bouncing over the water. A cream-colored boa watched me curiously as I darted past. I gave him a friendly wave, knowing he wouldn't harm me, but nearly jumped out of my skin when something splashed to the water's surface. It turned out to be a fish eating a bug.

"Grandma Clio's got a lot of explaining to do," I complained.

Fortunately, after a ten-minute walk, the swamp gave way to a drier forest. Unlike the old growth pines of the Pacific

Northwest, leafy trees and shrubs swayed all around me, allowing sunlight to trickle in between their layered heights. A teeny mouse ran across my path, pausing only to twitch his nose at me before retreating into the foliage.

"Be careful of snakes," I called after him.

Suddenly, the path split into two. I ultimately decided to take the wider path to the left, figuring it would be a main roadway. I made note of a half-bent sapling as a landmark, so I'd know where to go if I needed to backtrack. Our dad would have been proud of remembering that wilderness safety tip.

The path split off twice more, widening each time. I made note of new landmarks, even as my sore muscles ached from yet another uphill incline.

My fear morphed into irritation as I kept going nowhere into unknown territory. "How much farther, Grandma Clio?" I asked the forest.

As if in reply, I turned a corner and the path receded. A circular swatch of forest gave way to cobblestone flooring the size of a baseball diamond, the sun shining almost painfully bright on the stones without tree cover. Six more archways stood in this makeshift courtyard like a miniature Stonehenge, made of the same rough gray stone as the one on the beach, although none of their symbols glowed. I crept in for a closer look and found out why. Someone had removed a brick from each of them, disrupting the pattern etched in the stone.

"Do these lead to six more places?" I wondered.

A roar answered from the sky.

Terrified, I dove back into the forest tree line, crouching underneath a large monstera plant with their finger-like leaves. Despite the gaps, the overlapping wide leaves shielded me from aerial view.

Which was a good thing considering what flew overhead.

A dark beast soared over the cobblestone courtyard. I couldn't get a good look at it without exposing myself, but from what I saw, it flapped wings with no feathers, so it could not have been a bird. It was too large to be a bird anyway. It hovered overhead for a few beats, its body completely blocking out the sun.

It flew off as quickly as it had appeared, roaring again.

I stayed hidden long after the native birds gave themselves the all clear and began chirping again. What *was* that thing? Normal animals like boas I could deal with, but that thing was definitely not normal.

My urge to return home finally outweighed my curiosity. I would have retreated right then if the beast hadn't flown off toward the beach. Running away only to get ambushed did not rank high on my list of outcomes.

That left me with the only other path that led out of the cobblestone courtyard, the one that went opposite from where I'd come from.

"Great." My hamstrings protested against the slope. "More uphill."

As the incline steepened, I wondered if I should have faced the flying beast. Here I was, a divorced 40-something with no real goals trudging through a tropical forest because my grandmother had told me how to activate a "fairy ring." A near-hysterical choke escaped my lips. What if I'd finally succumbed to stress and had a nervous breakdown? What if none of this was real, and I was sitting in a psych ward somewhere?

At least I was reaching the apex of the trail. I crested a ridge and peered down below.

I'd been to the Grand Canyon once, and the sheer awe of witnessing such a fantastic natural wonder had nearly knocked me over. This experience was ten times that. I had to sit down in order to drink it all in.

The forest had parted to reveal an expansive crater, perhaps created by a meteor or volcanic eruption. An impossibly gigantic tree, almost like Jack's beanstalk, rose from the center. Its topmost boughs scraped the sky well above the rim where I stood. Other mature trees grew around it, but they might as well have been dandelions next to a redwood. The giant tree was also separated from the others by a moat with a sturdy wooden bridge to get across.

Those details alone would have made the tree a jaw-dropping sight, but on top of all that, the tree had windows. Real glass windows, from small picture windows to grander arched windows to even a few bay windows jutting out of the trunk. And the pièce de résistance was a circular stained glass window, the mosaic of reds and oranges of a setting sun contrasting with striking blues and greens of a foaming sea.

I'd discovered a tree castle.

CHAPTER 4

I STARED AT THE tree castle dominating the crater, questions forming in rapid succession. Where in the world was I? What was that monstrous tree with windows? And what kind of scary creature flew above the forest?

Grandma Clio had a lot of explaining to do.

Once I recovered from shock, I practically ran down the hill. The path had smoothed over from so much use that it didn't even bother my bare feet, and going downhill was much easier than going up. I lost sight of the tree castle as the path dipped back into the woods, but I would catch occasional glimpses of its upper boughs through the foliage. I recognized many exotic plants like the pink-blooming ipe tree and the purple-tentacled passion flower, but I rushed past them all to get to the heart of this incredible paradise.

I slowed to a more modest pace as I reached the moat and walked carefully across the bridge. I needn't have bothered. The wooden planks felt warm and sturdy beneath my bare feet, and the guard rails were so high and solid that it would take an athlete to scale them. Still, as I peered through the slats, I didn't wish to drop into the murky waters below.

It wasn't until I'd made it to the other side that I realized the tree castle did not have any sort of entrance. The path led straight to the tree and then stopped at its roots. I looked around everywhere, but besides an enormous grilled, circular window above where only the birds could reach, there was no way inside.

I cupped my hands around my mouth. "Hello?" I called out. Maybe someone on the other side of the glass would hear me?

When no one answered, I searched the tree itself for any clues. Giant roots wove together to form an ashy brown trunk, moss clinging to any crevice it could find. Higher up in the tree, the bark smoothed over, strips of it even flaking off to expose a pristine white surface underneath.

The tree was another rare plant, eucalyptus regnans, a type of ash tree native to Tasmania. It should not have existed with all the Caribbean flora. But then again, a tree with windows didn't grow natively anywhere.

How else could I get inside? I rapped a knuckle against the bark. It seemed silly to knock, but I had no idea what else to do.

The moment my skin touched the tree, I felt something whisper in my skull. A foreign presence. Watching me. I jolted backward in shock.

"Hello?" I called out again, holding my hand to my chest. "Who's there?"

But the sensation had gone away, and I could no longer feel anyone.

A strong breeze swept through the crater, the leaves of the ash tree swirling in a frenzy above me. A single feather-shaped leaf broke off, falling down in swoops and arcs toward me. I caught it as it floated past me.

That strange presence resonated through the leaf, similar to before. I almost dropped the leaf but held on. A kind of joy, not my own, coursed through my veins. The excited presence welcomed me.

Not just any presence. The tree's presence.

I stared into the tree's boughs, fighting dizziness when viewing it from this close of an angle. "Are you talking to me?" I asked the tree, incredulous. "Do you know me?"

The tree's branches continued to sway, only this time, there was no accompanying breeze. She—somehow I knew the tree was female—urged me to touch the bark again.

I let go of the leaf, and the tree's foreign thoughts faded away, leaving me empty, as if I'd lost part of myself.

I was communicating with a tree. I had officially lost my mind. But was it any weirder than stepping through a magic portal to a tropical island?

I might as well finish what I started. I placed my open palm against the tree trunk.

The ash tree shivered beneath my skin. I gasped as the rope-like tendrils making up the bark slithered around my hand. Inch by inch, the bumpy surface parted, opening up like someone drawing back a curtain. An opening emerged beneath my startled fingertips, creating a doorway into the tree, easily twice my own height.

I stepped forward, bare toes gripping cold stone. The grilled window above illuminated a perfect circle with a cross in the exact center of the floor. The walls and the high ceiling of the hexagonal room were made of ropey bark, a metal chandelier hanging off one sturdy branch. Besides an empty reception desk next to a larger open doorway, the room was bare.

I crossed the entryway to peer into the next area, but I couldn't make out anything in the gloom.

"It's too dark to see," I muttered.

In response, a sconce flickered to life on the wall beside me, lit by a single candle. It set off a chain reaction that created a runway of dancing flames leading down a long hallway.

"That's a neat trick," I said to the tree, sensing her presence somewhere in my mind.

The tree's thoughts beamed happiness. It warmed my entire body like a pleasant hug.

Besides the sconces, the hallway was bare, no doors or adornments of any kind despite having the same stone floor as the entrance. The only thing that broke up the monotony were small windows curving upward in a strange pattern before disappearing into the leafy eaves above. The long hallway ended in a set of closed double doors, easily as tall as the entryway and three times as wide. It didn't take a scientist to realize that this much space couldn't actually exist inside of an ash tree, even one this big.

I searched for a handle on the massive double doors but couldn't find one. I touched the dark wood, and to my delight,

the doors cracked open, sending a streak of light into the hallway.

"Thanks," I told the tree.

She responded faintly in affirmation, as if tired.

"Don't worry. I can open the doors the rest of the way."

Easier said than done. I tried to push one door open, but it
was so heavy, it didn't budge. I had to throw my entire weight
body against it just to open wide enough for me to pass through.

As I slipped inside, I wondered what I would find. A ball-
room? A throne? Maybe a trove of treasure?

It was better than all that put together.

I forgot to breathe as I walked into the world's most fantastic library. As I stared at it from the bottom-floor atrium, I
counted six stories of bookshelves, all exposed like the backside
of a dollhouse. Some shelves were made of branches and held
traditional books, others were made of metal and held rolled
up scrolls, still others were made of glass, and a few I swear
with straw. Interspersed ladders allowed access to taller places.
Randomly placed staircases, both spiral and straight, allowed
people to flow between floors. Reading nooks—small desks,
large tables with chairs, cushioned couches—made up the rest
of the available space. One bay window offered rocking chairs
next to a cozy-looking fireplace.

It was the craziest collection of styles, books, and decor I'd
ever seen in my life. And topping it off with the proverbial
cherry was the stained glass sunset window, shimmering high
above me as a centerpiece of the atrium's sky-high ceiling.

I had to explore every last inch of this library. I went for the obvious choice first. Directly in front of me and up a small flight of stairs on a stage was a gigantic pedestal. A leather-bound book lay open on top of it. The book must have been as wide as an eagle's spread wingspan. A strategic beam from a skylight fell directly on its exposed pages.

I peered at the open pages. Only one sentence was written on the top of the left page.

What knowledge do you seek?

Frowning, I flipped back a page, but it had the same wording. Forward, the same thing. No matter where I turned in the book, it only had that one question. I shut the front cover of the book, but it had no words on the outside, even the spine.

There was a quill feather in an ink pot nearby. "Okay," I told the book, grabbing the feather. "If you want a question, I'll give you one."

I tried writing a question, but the quill tip contained no ink. I dipped it into the pot, but it was empty.

Instead, I rummaged around my messenger bag and retrieved a sand-covered pen. I wiped the particles off on my pants' leg as I contemplated my question. Should I ask about Grandma Clio? This crazy tree? The portal that brought me here? I had so many questions.

"Don't you dare defile the Grimoire with your nasty pen!" a hoarse voice shouted before I could decide.

I jumped in surprise. An elderly man with wispy white hair had entered the room behind me. He wore blue trousers and a long gray coat fastened together with brass buttons. Despite his age, he scurried up the steps on spry legs. The tip of his bulbous nose barely reached my shoulder, but he still managed to scowl down at me, waving a knobby finger.

"How'd you get in here?"

"I-I . . ." I didn't have the words to explain the strange set of circumstances that had led me here. "I was . . ."

He didn't wait for me to articulate. "The library's closed! Off limits! Locked up! You are trespassing!"

"I didn't mean to," I said, finding my voice. "I was looking for Clio."

"Is this some kind of sick joke?" He squinted hard at my face. His eyes widened in shock. "Who in Queen Mab's court are you? A changeling?"

"I'm not a changeling," I said, even though I had no idea what that was.

"I won't stand for any tricks," he said, raising his hands into little fists. "Just because I'm a hob doesn't mean I won't use my magic to defend myself. I'll drop a shelf on you. Or slap you around with a book. See if I won't!" His hands actually lit up, as if his finger bones were made of glowsticks.

I tried to shrink to appear less threatening to this old man. "I swear I'm not here to hurt you."

"Then how did you open the library?" he demanded.

"She let me in."

He narrowed his eyes. "Who's 'she?'"

"The tree," I said, knowing how insane I sounded. "She not only welcomed me here, she encouraged me to come in."

"Impossible," he spat. "Only a muse could—"

An ear-splitting roar cut him off, accompanied by an angry wind gust. It knocked the heavy doors inward so quickly that they actually bounced off the frame and opened wider.

The silhouette of wings swept down the hall toward us. I couldn't see much of its body, but it had bright yellow eyes that honed right in on me.

The old man paled. "You let the dragon in!"

"'D-dragon?'" My heart leaped into my throat.

"RUN!" the man screamed. He bolted toward the door.

I had no idea why anyone would run toward a dragon, but I sprinted in the opposite direction, toward the bottom floor of books. I hoped I could find a hiding spot somewhere in the shelves.

As I bounded behind a bookcase for cover, another loud roar erupted across the library. Shaking, I peeked around a corner to get my first real glimpse of the dragon, hovering not far from where I'd just stood.

It was a lot smaller than I originally thought, maybe only as big as a horse, but that didn't make it less terrifying. The beast had iridescent black scales that shimmered blue and purple in the light. Yellow, cat-like eyes surveyed the scene. Its vast wings jerked with a snap, cutting the air like a whipcrack. Sharp talons scraped the hard floor in a spine-tingling staccato.

It tilted its head back and released a stream of fire from between its sharp teeth like a flamethrower.

Fear twisted my gut. I had to get out of here before the dragon burnt me to a crisp. Maybe I could hide here until the coast was clear and sneak back outside.

Unfortunately, the old man had already taken that escape route. He slid behind the dragon and raced into the hallway. Once safely behind the dragon, his glowstick hands lit up. That light transferred to the double doors and they both slammed shut, startling the dragon. It aimed its flaming stream toward the door. When its attack did nothing to the wood, it let out a bellow of frustration that rattled my teeth.

I was locked inside a library—full of highly flammable books and scrolls—with an angry fire-breathing dragon.

CHAPTER 5

PANIC THREATENED TO OVERWHELM me as the dragon sniffed the air. Could it smell me? When it began scurrying around the pedestal like some sort of lizard, I huddled behind the bookcase.

I had to stay calm. I took deep breaths and tried to recall the steps from a past workplace emergency training course. First, I had to assess the problem. Gather information and figure out what was in my control. And above all, I needed to get to safety.

Too bad the course hadn't covered what to do when confronted with a dragon.

I dared a second peek around the corner. I did my best to ignore the skulking dragon because that certainly wasn't in my control. I couldn't risk the time it would take to open the heavy doors again. That just left the windows. I couldn't reach any of the atrium's windows because they were too high up. This floor, frustratingly, didn't have windows, but I might be able to get to another floor and find another way to escape.

It wasn't a pretty solution. I wasn't too keen on breaking a bone jumping out of a window, but I liked my odds a lot better than squaring off against a dragon.

I traveled down the aisle of bookcases, searching for a staircase that would get me off the ground floor. I paused for a few heart-pounding minutes, waiting for the dragon to move so I wouldn't be in its peripheral vision. It kept sniffing the air and started . . . cooing? Almost like a baby bird. It would have looked cute if it didn't also belch another string of fire. But it eventually turned around enough that I could zip across to the other aisle without being seen.

From there, I spied a spiral staircase near the fireplace, not visible in the dragon's line of sight. Reminding myself to breathe so I wouldn't pass out, I silently padded up to the second floor and relaxed a little. The dragon couldn't spot me quite as well from up here.

To my dismay, this story also lacked windows. I also discovered how mazelike the layout was. Not only were shelves placed willy-nilly, there wasn't an immediate staircase up to the third floor. I'd have to search to find one.

I checked all along the back wall first, nervous when I heard the dragon cooing and clicking around downstairs with its talons. There was no staircase back here. Forcing myself to inch back toward the atrium, I found not one, but two spiral staircases leading up. Both of them happened to be in clear view of anyone, or anything, in the atrium.

I was so screwed.

I pushed hysteria aside. I needed to gather more information. Where was the dragon? I crept up to a bookcase bordering the railing and peered down. To my surprise, the dragon had slunk to somewhere underneath me on the first floor. Although I didn't know its exact position, I could hear it rustling underneath me, the sound of its bulky body thwacking against bookshelves.

I wasn't about to squander my good luck. I made a quick run for the nearest staircase. In my excitement, I forgot to soften my steps, and my bare feet slapped against the hardwood.

The sound echoed like a gunshot in the near silence. The dragon's movements also stilled.

I stifled a gulp, standing on the bottom rung of the staircase, completely out in the open. If I accidentally made more noise, the dragon would home in on me. I'd be literal toast. On the other hand, the dragon could now be silently stalking back toward the atrium, and I'd never see it coming.

I froze, logic not giving me any good options.

I might have stayed there forever if one of the heavy library doors hadn't cracked open. Had the old man decided to rescue me?

Instead, a much younger, and much stronger, guy paused at the library entrance. Despite wearing a loose-fitting plaid shirt, his torso appeared ready to bust out of it, along with tufts of his chest hair at the collar. Jeans and boots completed the outfit. His dark copper brown sideburns matched the tone of his eyes and framed a square face. He scowled, looking ready for a fight.

Hope stirred in my chest. This guy looked like some modern-day warrior come to rescue me. Maybe I wouldn't die.

That spark vanished when the man did. One minute he was crouched near the door, peering in, and the next, he simply wasn't there.

I stared at where he'd been, confused. Was my adrenaline so high that I was imagining handsome strangers coming to my rescue?

At least I didn't imagine the door opening. The dragon darted out of the first-floor shelving, bounding back into the atrium and snarling at the door.

It had its back to me. I padded up the stairs as quietly as I could. Once at the top, I ducked behind a 3rd story honeycomb-like shelf housing a bunch of scrolls. I peered through the gaps just as the dragon whipped back around and roared. The flames reached all the way to my level, warming the temperature several degrees.

I swallowed a dry knot in my throat. I had to get out of here. Scrambling through the network of cubbies that held scrolls, I noticed natural light. I dashed toward it and found a series of floor-to-ceiling windows lining the far wall.

Finally, an exit point.

I pressed both palms against the cool glass. My excitement died as I took in the details. The windows were thick, double paned, and worst of all, not meant to be opened. Even if I managed to break one, which could take some time, the dragon would hear me. Plus, the ground below looked so far away. Would I even survive the fall?

But what other option did I have? I scoured the third floor, finding another staircase going up. The higher I went, the more likely I would die if I had to jump. If I really planned on leaving through a window, this was my only choice.

I grabbed the back of a sturdy wooden chair. It might do the trick, but it was heavy. I dragged it toward the windows.

"What are you doing?" a voice whispered.

I let go of the chair, a startled shriek escaping my lips.

The dragon, which had been scuttling around downstairs, went silent.

"Shush!" the voice hissed. "Are you trying to get killed?"

I clamped my hand over my mouth, glancing frantically around, but there was no one with me among the shelves. And it wasn't the tree. She had never spoken, and this deep voice was decidedly male.

I had to be hallucinating. Now I was hearing voices instead of seeing muscled men. I clamped my lips shut and continued dragging the chair to the window.

"You need to get back down to the atrium," the voice insisted. "I'll distract the dragon while you make a run for it."

Oh no. I wasn't going to face the dragon head on. Kneeling down, I heaved the chair's seat upward with the legs sticking out away from me.

"You don't seriously think you can break the window with that thing, do you?"

"Go away," I said, despite my resolve to keep quiet. I lumbered closer to the window.

"Even if you could toss that chair, which you obviously can't, you'll hurt yourself jumping that far down."

"You're not real," I tried to reason.

"I'm the only real thing that's going to save you. Here, let me show—"

A series of rapid snaps, like boat sails whipping on the ocean, cut off the voice. A sharp wind blew through the shelves, toppling one honeycomb case completely over and sending scrolls rolling around the floor.

I turned into the wind, finding the dragon hovering midair at the third story railing, only a few aisles away from me. Its yellow eyes pierced mine.

It let out a roar that knocked over another scroll shelf.

Desperate, I flung the chair at the window in a last-ditch effort to save myself. One chair leg did bonk against the glass but bounced off without a scratch.

I was dead. So dead.

"Hey you!" my imaginary voice yelled. "Come get me!"

I whipped back around to find the back of a massive man in front of me. He had his arms held out wide, stretching the red, blue, and green pattern of his plaid shirt.

It was the man at the atrium door. I reached forward to confirm he was real.

Plaid Shirt lunged away before my fingertips could touch the fabric, bolting for the staircase leading up to the fourth floor. To my amazement, the dragon followed him. It spat a fireball, missing the man by inches. Undeterred, Plaid Shirt leaped up the stairs and disappeared onto the floor above me.

The dragon beat its wings, flying after him.

I hesitated for only an instant before I realized the dragon had another target. I was in the clear.

I could escape through the front doors.

I ran faster than I ever had in my life. Bookcases flashed by me in a blur as I pounded down spiral staircases. My bare feet hit the atrium floor, slapping with each strike. The barely open doorway loomed ahead.

I could make it. I was almost there.

Until a fireball exploded between me and the door.

I skidded to a halt, the flames so close that I worried they might singe my clothes. Blood pounded in my ears as I slowly turned around to face the dragon.

It slammed into the ground in front of me, nearly knocking me off my feet. It opened its mouth, exposing teeth, as its head came down. I raised my arms in futility, knowing they could not protect me.

Seconds passed. Nothing happened.

I lowered my arms. The dragon was staring at me, head tilted as if studying me. It sniffed the air.

A rumble reverberated throughout its scales. Like a . . . purr?

"Get away from her!"

Plaid Shirt reappeared next to the dragon. He brandished a fire poker and slashed it on the dragon's rump.

The dragon screeched, skittering away from us.

"Now, Wallace!" Plaid Shirt screamed.

The library doors glowed and burst open as if a giant had pushed them. Standing in the doorway, the elderly man's hands waved like a conductor, a huge metal tub hanging in the air above him. With a flick of his wrist, the tub zipped across the room and overturned above the dragon.

A deluge of water poured onto the dragon as it opened its mouth to spit out more flame.

The dragon sputtered, wings flapping. Plaid Shirt pushed me to the side just in time to avoid getting knocked over by the escaping dragon. The elderly man flung himself to the side as the dragon swooped down the hallway and out into the open sky.

My handsome rescuer approached me, making my heart flutter. "Thank you so—" I tried to tell him.

The sharp end of a fire poker waved at the tip of my nose, cutting me off.

"You've trespassed into the Library of Atlantis," Plaid Shirt said with menace. "You're coming with me."

CHAPTER 6

THE MAN IN THE plaid shirt took me to an office.

I had no idea how I'd gotten to such a mundane building from the magical tree library. Plaid Shirt made me put my wet shoes back on. He also put a cloth bag over my head before we left the tree. We didn't walk far on the paths, although my legs weren't happy about trudging back up the rim of the crater. My "handsome rescuer" refused to respond to my questions or complaints. I was about to sit down on the forest floor and demand answers when suddenly the temperature shifted and indoor heating washed over me.

Plaid Shirt removed the cloth bag and tossed it aside as we navigated the narrow corridors. The place couldn't have screamed 9-to-5 drudgery more if it tried. A few fake potted plants underscored large, mass-produced photographs of mountains and waterfalls. We passed a few empty office rooms with desks and computers, a kitchen with some café furniture, and dual men's and women's restrooms.

Keyboard clacking emitted from one room but abruptly stopped as we passed by the door.

"Henry? Is that you?" a female voice asked.

I tried to peek into the office, but my sullen captor pulled me forward by the wrist. "Yeah."

"Who's that with you?" the voice called after us.

"A problem."

"I'm not a problem!" I protested.

I glanced over my shoulder as a woman about my age left the office and entered the hallway. She had frizzy chestnut hair pulled back into a French braid, a handful of strands shaken loose. Her navy-blue blouse matched the cardigan, slacks, and sensible pumps, completing the business casual outfit. Laugh lines crinkled around her green eyes, although they were currently flashing with concern.

"That's a person, not a problem."

Henry finally stopped in his tracks. "I don't have time for this. I'm supposed to be prepping for the coronation."

"Looks like you're going to have to make time."

Henry let out a long-suffering sigh as he shoved me into a nearby open door. It was a conference room with a large table, swivel chairs, and a projector hanging from the ceiling. Before I could demand what was going on, he slammed the door in my face.

Henry and the woman launched into an argument out in the hall. I ignored their muted conversation, instead rummaging through my messenger bag, still miraculously attached to my side. I snatched my phone and dialed 9-1-1 with shaky fingers.

The call never connected. I wasn't receiving any signal.

Panic rising, I twisted the knob on the conference door. It wouldn't budge.

I banged on the door with my fist. "Let me out of here!"

The argument behind the door stopped. "Did you lock her in?" the woman demanded.

Henry muttered something in response.

I pounded the door again. "If someone doesn't open this door, I swear—"

I nearly fell over as the door swung open, revealing the woman again. She caught me by the shoulders.

"Whoa, there," she said as she gently steadied me to my feet. "Are you okay?"

I stared at her in disbelief. "Okay? I was whisked away to a tropical paradise, found a magical ash tree that I could open with a touch of my hand, and almost got mauled to death by a dragon!"

She made sympathetic noises. "That's a terrible way to get introduced to the fae world."

"Fae?" I squeaked, my wet shoes squelching as I backed up in surprise.

She frowned at my feet. "I'll explain everything, but first, why don't you kick off those shoes. You can place them on that vent over in the corner."

Although I wanted to disobey out of spite, the truth was, my feet were getting rubbed raw. It was heaven peeling off my wet shoes and socks again. Too bad the industrial carpet felt like scratchy rocks under my feet as I spread them over the vent.

"We haven't properly been introduced," the woman said, extending a hand. "I'm Melissa Hartley."

I hesitated, unsure of whether I should give her my name.

She didn't seem to mind either my lack of handshake or my silence. Her hand dropped back to her side. "You know what always helps me in stressful situation? Coffee. I've got a nice expensive roast in the kitchen. Can I get you some?"

"I'm not really a coffee drinker," I admitted.

Melissa's confidence cracked. "You don't like coffee?"

Henry snickered outside the door. "Not everyone's an addict, Mel."

I stiffened, reminded of his presence.

"You're scaring her again," Melissa snapped. "Go away."

"Sorry." He popped out of sight.

I shrieked.

"I said go away, not go invisible," she yelled where he'd been.

"Same difference."

"Get out of here!" She shoved like a mime at the spot, but I could hear footsteps as she knocked something off balance.

"Fine," Henry's disembodied voice said, "but I'm getting Gabriel."

"Go right ahead!" Melissa called after him. Then she turned back to me, a genuine smile on her face. "Not into coffee? No problem. How about tea? Water?"

"Uh, water?"

"Great. Have a seat. I'll be right back."

She left me without a backward glance.

CURSE OF THE FAE LIBRARY

I scanned the room. What was this place? Should I run? I poked my head out the door and saw nothing but bland, bare walls stretching to either side. I doubted I could get very far, and besides, I could hear Melissa rustling around in the kitchen.

I didn't have a lot of good options, but Melissa appeared normal enough. She at least had gotten Henry off my back, and she'd left the conference room door open and unlocked. Besides, I needed answers. All the answers.

What in the world was going on?

Melissa returned with a glass of water as I plopped down in a conference chair. "I see you already met the rougher side of Henry Salish. I'm so sorry if he frightened you. I'm not sure if it's because he's a sasquatch, but he's not exactly great at people skills."

"Henry's a bigfoot?" I asked, an involuntary squeak at the end of my voice.

"Sasquatch. A type of fae that can go invisible, as you've already seen. You can always tell by their excessive body hair. And just an FYI, they hate to be called 'bigfoot.' Their feet are no bigger than a normal person's."

"Of course." A nervous chuckle escaped my throat. I'd been saved by a sasquatch named Henry who wouldn't like to be called 'bigfoot.' That made total sense.

"This is a lot to take in," Melissa said gently. "I went through all the emotions you're feeling now. I used to be a boring, middle-aged single mom who worked as the office manager at a tech firm."

When she paused to take a sip of her own coffee, I asked, "So what happened?"

"A fae cult tried to kidnap my teenage daughter to fulfill an ancient prophecy."

I'm pretty sure my jaw hit the floor trying to make sense of that sentence.

Melissa laughed, cupping her mug. "Yeah, that's how I felt too. But don't worry, my story has a happy ending. Everyone's safe and sound, and now I'm employed here at Stronghold. I'm doing the same type of work I did before but with the added twist of doing some human-fae relationship building on the side."

"So the fae are everywhere? Not just on that weird island?"

Melissa nodded.

"How did I not know about this? This should be all over the social media. You can't keep secrets in this day and age."

"You'd be surprised. Fae magic doesn't mix super well with technology, which prevents a lot of recorded documentation. But honestly, the fae's secrecy lies mostly with their leader, Queen Mab. It's a very complicated situation, but trust me, it's in everyone's interest that the fae remain hidden."

"And it will remain hidden with you," a deep baritone voice announced.

The largest man I'd ever seen in my life entered the conference room. His expensive black suit nearly took up the doorframe. Graying temples framed his dark brown hair, but it clearly denoted experience rather than frailty. As he took a chair at the table opposite us, his movements belied solid muscle underneath his clothes. I tried not to gulp as he sized me up with his steel gray eyes.

Melissa, instead of cowering before the newcomer, scowled at him. "You don't have to be so dramatic."

"We take security here very seriously."

"Thanks for repeating our unofficial motto," she said with heavy sarcasm. Melissa then turned to me. "May I introduce Stronghold's CEO, Gabriel Alston?"

"And you are?" Gabriel asked me.

I felt compelled to answer under his strong scrutiny. "Rosalind Baldwin." I should have lied, but my brain wasn't functioning properly in front of this brute.

"Finally, a name," Henry grumbled as he trailed into the room after Gabriel. He also took a seat across from me at the conference table.

My fear melted into anger at his condescending tone. "I've just been through a lot. My estranged grandmother insisted in her letters that I should replace a stone back in a 'fairy ring.' How was I supposed to know that fairies were real and putting a brick into some creepy archway would take me to a tropical paradise?" I knew I was rambling but couldn't stop myself.

Gabriel thankfully cut me off. "Most fairy rings that lead to the island of Atlantis should have been deactivated."

"There are tons of fairy rings on the island, though," Henry interjected. "Some of them haven't been used for decades or even centuries. She must have stumbled across one of them."

"But there shouldn't have been a rune stone lying around to reactivate one," Gabriel said, glowering at me. My heart pounded in my chest.

Melissa leaned toward me. "Where did you get the brick to put in the archway?" When I hesitated to answer, she patted my hand. "I understand why you don't trust us. This is all scary, but I swear, we're only trying to help."

She was probably playing good cop, but she also didn't seem afraid of the well-dressed barbarian across from us. I decided to trust her.

"Grandma Clio left it for my mother."

Everyone else in the room jerked backward simultaneously in shock.

"Clio's your grandmother?" Henry asked.

"When did this happen?" Gabriel demanded at the same time.

Melissa patted my knee. "I'm so sorry for your loss."

I focused on Melissa's reaction. "What are you talking about?"

Melissa threw a hand over her mouth. "You don't know?"

An awful ball twisted in my gut as I asked, "Know what?"

"There's no easy way to say this," Melissa whispered. "Clio is dead."

CHAPTER 7

I DIDN'T THINK I could feel loss for a woman I'd never met, but when Melissa said my grandmother was dead, I couldn't fight back a string of tears. Now she would never answer all the questions I had about my mother, their relationship, and this whole crazy mess.

Melissa pulled out a package of tissues from her pocket and put it in front of me.

I ignored them, blinking back tears. I refused to break down in front of strangers. "How did Clio die?" I asked, trying to sound calm.

Gabriel's face showed no emotion. "She burned to death."

So much for control. "What?" I yelled.

Henry pounded a light fist on the table, also upset. "It's that damned dragon, the same one that attacked you. Everyone told Clio it was a bad idea to take her in, but she wouldn't listen."

I gasped, fresh, fat tears flowing down my cheeks. I finally grabbed a tissue. I tried to blow my nose discreetly but ended up sounding like a bullhorn.

"This is ridiculous," I said, ripping out another from the package. "I never even met her."

"I realize you are going through a lot," Gabriel said, "but we must know every detail about how you arrived at Atlantis."

Melissa nodded. "We'll answer any questions you have as well."

"Within reason," Gabriel added.

I took a few moments to pat my eyes dry, determined to reign in my emotions. "Okay," I finally said, "let's start with the obvious. Was I really on the mythological island of Atlantis?"

"Yes," Melissa said. "Henry found you inside the Library of Atlantis. But right now, you're in Salem, Oregon."

"Wait, what? How did I get here?"

Melissa looked bewildered. "Didn't you recognize the fairy ring Henry took you through?"

"It's hard to see anything with a bag over your head."

"With a bag over your—" Melissa choked on the words. She flashed a murderous glare at Henry. "You paranoid creep! No wonder she's scared out of her mind."

Henry bristled at the insult. "I didn't know who she was. We still don't. She's a huge security risk."

Gabriel agreed with him. "We have no idea what kind of magic she's capable of."

"*If* she has any magic," Melissa said, "she'll be a muse like Clio. Not exactly someone with dangerous magical gifts."

"But powerful nonetheless," Gabriel said.

I paled. "I don't have magic."

"That remains to be seen," Gabriel said. "Now it's our turn for questions. How did you find a fairy ring that led to Atlantis?"

I hesitated as the trio focused on me. I didn't really want to talk, but none of these people would let me walk out of here without an explanation.

"My family used to hike up in the woods near our house. There was an archway up there we visited often when I was a kid. It turns out that was a fairy ring." I couldn't believe how crazy the words sounded coming out of my mouth, even if they were true.

"And you just now used it to visit Atlantis?" Henry asked skeptically.

"It was missing a brick. I found it among my parents' stuff. My father left a note telling me where it had come from." My voice caught in my throat. "The archway was where my dad met my mother."

"And who's your dad?" Gabriel asked.

"No one you'd know. Just a regular guy. A mechanic."

"And I suppose you were raised as a human and never exposed to the fae?" Gabriel asked.

Before I could answer, Henry snorted. "I can answer you that. She's definitely clueless about the fae."

Even though he was right, I couldn't help but glare at him.

Melissa straightened in excitement. "So that's what happened to Sophia. She must have met a human man, gotten married, and swore off fae life."

I gaped to her. "You knew my mother?"

"Knew of her. I did some research into Clio's family after she died. We uncovered that she had a daughter but couldn't find any record of what happened to her. Most fae believe Sophia died."

"So now we know how you ended up on Atlantis." Henry leaned forward, forearms on the table. "Wallace said he found you in the library. You're lucky he came here to Stronghold through our fairy ring so I could save you."

"Is Wallace the elf I found in the library?" I asked.

"He's a hob," Melissa corrected. "Hobs are homebody fae who magically bond to one place and take care of it. Wallace chose the Library of Atlantis. He's the only one besides Clio who can get in and out of the tree."

"Except for you." Henry pointed a suspicious finger at me. "How'd you get inside?"

I shifted uncomfortably in my seat. "I don't know. I just felt the tree's . . . presence in my head. Then she let me in."

No one seemed weirded out that I'd given the tree a gender. In fact, Gabriel asked, "Did you hear her voice?"

"No, mostly vague impressions and feelings. I felt her happiness, for example. She somehow urged me to touch her bark, and then the tree created an entrance for me. I walked right in."

"I told you Rosalind was a muse," Melissa told the men triumphantly. "Only a muse can communicate directly with Yggdrasil."

"The tree's name is Yggdrasil?" I asked, the word a mouthful. "Isn't that some mythological tree of life?"

"Actually, the myth probably came from the tree, not the other way around," Melissa said. "From what I've gathered, some Norse guy visited the library once, and afterward he told his friends about it back home. It created the modern-day human legend."

Gabriel tried to suppress a smile toward her. "You've been doing your homework, I see."

"Of course," she said. "I needed all the details. I take job fulfillment very seriously, especially in this case."

"What job?" Following this conversation was as confusing as finding a living tree in the middle of a fabled isle.

"Your grandmother Clio was the Librarian of Atlantis," Gabriel explained. "Her death effectively shut off Yggdrasil to the world, since Wallace only maintains the grounds. Without a proper librarian running the place, there's a huge knowledge vacuum in the fae world."

"And because the tree is sentient, she won't accept just anyone for the position," Melissa said. "Clio comes from a long line of muses who've been running the library. It was a shot in the dark to think another muse family could run it in the first place. Now that we've found you, we finally have someone who can become the new librarian."

"What?" Henry and I asked at the same time.

Gabriel merely shook his head. "You can't throw this poor human into the Library of Atlantis. She's completely ignorant about the fae."

"But she's Clio's granddaughter," Melissa said. "And Rosalind has clearly inherited her family's muse magic."

69

"Muse? Magic?" My head began to spin. "What are you talking about? I don't have any special powers."

"Oh, but you do," Melissa said firmly. "I've been tracking down potential muse candidates for weeks to fill this position. Muses are rare as it is, but even among the handful I've located, not a single one has been able to connect to Yggdrasil. You're the only one the tree will bond with."

"But isn't that the tree's magic?" I argued. "How do you know it has anything to do with me?"

"Muses have several layers of magic. They're famous for inspiring others to do extraordinary things, like in the Greek legends." Melissa leaned toward me. "Have you ever influenced an artist to complete a great masterpiece or something similar?"

I was about to object furiously, but then all my past boyfriends and their various accomplishments flashed across my mind.

I slumped in my seat. "No . . ." I whispered.

"See?" Henry said. "She's not a muse."

But Melissa was undeterred. "Finish the sentence. No . . . what?"

"No, I can't believe it," I said. "I can't be the one who talked all my exes into pursuing their dreams. It has to be a coincidence."

Melissa smiled in triumph. "Rosalind's going to be perfect for this job."

Gabriel ran a hand over his face. "She's going to be a nightmare. You more than anyone knows how much work it takes for Stronghold to take on even a low-level human contractor. You want me to ask Queen Mab to put a human in charge of the Library of Atlantis."

"Not a human, a muse," Melissa said. "Muse magic only passes down the female line. There are plenty of muses whose fathers have been pixies, dryads, and yes, even the occasional human. Their mother's magic is what sparks their fae abilities."

Well, that explained why Clio only wrote letters to me and not Jason.

"Yes, but muses are usually raised in the fae world." Gabriel looked Melissa dead in the eye. "Rosalind never even met Clio. She's simply not one of us."

Melissa met him, stare for stare. "Then you'll have to shutter the Library of Atlantis permanently. I'm out of muse candidates to interview, and it's not like we can post a job listing online."

Gabriel didn't look happy, but he also didn't disagree.

Henry peered from Gabriel to Melissa and then back at Gabriel. "You can't be seriously considering this?"

"There's never been a period in history where the Library of Atlantis hasn't been open," Gabriel said. "So many aspects of fae life and culture depend on that place. And I'm not even sure if we can reopen it without a relative of Clio's in charge."

"So you're willing to make any idiot the Librarian of Atlantis, as long as she's related to Clio?" Henry demanded.

My face flushed.

Melissa also took offense. "Don't be such a jerk, Henry. This is an opportunity, not a threat."

"I don't see how." Henry pointed an accusing finger at me. "She bumbled around the library, clearly in over her head. If that

DM FIKE

dragon doesn't fry her in a week, then any number of fae patrons will manipulate her into doing something unimaginable. Being the Librarian of Atlantis is not for the feeble minded."

I jumped to my feet, surprising even myself. But once committed to defending myself, the words spilled out.

"Look, buddy," I snapped at Henry. "I don't know who any of you are, and frankly, I don't care. I went to that island to find my grandmother, and now she's dead. Maybe I don't even want to run your magic little library."

Both men stared at me as if I'd grown two horns out of my head.

Melissa slowly got to her feet so she could view me at my level. "No one's going to force you to do anything," she said slowly, "but aren't you even a little bit curious about your heritage?"

I wanted to say no, but I couldn't. Despite everything that had happened, I yearned to discover more about the fae. I couldn't help myself. I loved learning new things, and this was the granddaddy of new experiences.

Like a shark, Melissa sensed blood in the water and continued. "Maybe you've got something else going on in your life? Someone special back home? Kids? A great career?"

I thought about my recent divorce and tried not to let it show on my face. "No. Nothing like that."

"Then this is the opportunity of a lifetime. You'll learn more about your fae heritage in a fascinating environment. Not only that, but Atlantis has fairy rings connected to tons of different places on Earth. You're more than welcome to explore them all. Imagine being able to hop over to Fiji or Argentina at a moment's notice, just for lunch."

That gave me pause. I'd always loved traveling but hadn't had a lot of money to go many places.

Henry scowled. "Melissa's leaving out the bit where you'd possibly get burnt to a crisp by a dragon, like your predecessor."

"We can mitigate that risk with a bodyguard," Melissa dismissed with an easy wave. "Someone strong and capable who can deal with the dragon."

I couldn't believe I was considering this, but I sat back down, weighing my options. "What kind of duties would I do as the librarian? I don't have any sort of degree or experience."

"You won't need either of those," Melissa said, also retaking her seat. "The Librarian of Atlantis, first and foremost, is Yggdrasil's guardian. She communicates with the tree so the library runs smoothly."

"So that's it?" I asked. "I take care of a tree?"

"Well, there's also the muse part of your duties. Fae will come to the library for all sorts of reasons. Maybe they're researching a certain type of magic, or they want access to some historical document. Although the tree can help, you will be the ultimate guide to the knowledge the library contains."

"How am I, a random human plucked out of thin air, supposed to understand the intricacies of a people I didn't even know existed until now?"

"Great question," Henry said, still frowning at Melissa. "Fae culture is intricate and full of contradictory pitfalls. You think she's going to understand the nuances?"

Melissa glared at him. "Rosalind's a muse. She has an innate talent for sensing what people need in order to reach their goals. She'll be able to steer them in the right direction without even knowing it."

"That sounds great on the surface," I said, "but also terrifying. What if someone shows up at the library wanting me to help them do something awful, like create a magical weapon? How would I live with myself just blithely instructing them how to do it?"

"Muses can choose who receives their magical gifts," Melissa said. "If your gut tells you not to help someone at the library, you can deny them. In fact, that's part of the job. The library has restricted knowledge that can only be accessed by a few authorized people or none at all."

"And you trust me, a stranger, with that kind of power?"

"It's not so much I trust you. Yggdrasil does. That's really the only endorsement that matters."

Henry grunted in disagreement.

But I ignored him. Yggdrasil had seemed so happy to meet me. I had to admit that, as weird as it sounded, I did feel a special connection to her.

Melissa went in for the kill. "And did I mention the fully competitive compensation package? It actually pays even better than my job. I'm a little jealous."

"You're kidding me. A magical job with benefits?"

"No really. The paperwork you'll need to sign will give you carpal tunnel syndrome, but it's a really great deal."

There didn't sound like a lot of downsides, but I had one last reservation, especially given how often I'd cycled through jobs over the years. "What happens if I try it and things don't work out?"

"Being the Librarian of Atlantis is a lifetime position," Gabriel warned. "Once you accept, you can't quit."

"I knew there was a catch," I said. "That's a dealbreaker for sure."

"Maybe we can compromise" Melissa said. "If we could find a way to give you a trial period at the library, say a week, would you at least give it a try?"

"Maybe," I said, hedging. Inside, though, I couldn't deny the extreme pull to explore the library.

Gabriel balked at Melissa's suggestion. "You want me to ask Queen Mab to allow Rosalind to become librarian as a temp?"

Melissa shrugged. "Why not? Mab has material in that library that she likes to access on occasion. She's going to be even less thrilled if we mothball the place permanently."

Gabriel growled, a true animalistic sound in the back of his throat, but he didn't argue further.

"This sounds like a disaster in the making, but I guess it's above my paygrade." Henry stood. "Have fun sorting this out, Mel. I've already wasted enough time as is."

Melissa waited until he'd made it to the door before she called out, "Actually, there is one other thing."

He turned around slowly, looking at her suspiciously. "What?"

"We need to determine who will take care of that dragon on Atlantis."

CHAPTER 8

"MELISSA OWES ME," HENRY said for the third time as we strolled along an island path, this time without a bag over my head.

It had taken an hour, but Gabriel did leave and come back with permission to let me "try out" working as the librarian for a week. The waiting had felt like forever, but I preferred it to the stack of papers he plopped down that took twice as long to fill out. Melissa mentioned I'd have quadruple the paperwork if I took the actual job. Given how much my hand cramped already, I wondered if I made a huge mistake accepting even the temp job.

My regret heightened when I wasn't allowed to gather any of my personal belongings for the week. Gabriel insisted that I had to start immediately and tell absolutely no one. They allowed me to make a phone call to Jason on their official landline to tell him I'd be gone. Jason was too busy to answer his cell, so I'd had to leave a message. I tried to sound cheerful about landing a unique opportunity that I couldn't pass up without giving any details. I ended the call promising to touch base as soon as I could, hoping he wouldn't worry.

But perhaps the thing that almost made me run screaming was when Melissa assigned Henry to be my bodyguard and dragon hunter. Even though he was supposed to be doing security detail on some royal coronation later in the week, she insisted he drop it to take this gig. Henry had been upset, but in the end, when Gabriel ordered him to do it, he obeyed.

That didn't mean Henry didn't complain about it. He barely let up as we left the Stronghold office through their own fairy ring, landing back on the cobblestone courtyard. I should have been scared about running into a fire-breathing dragon, but somehow, I was more irritated hanging out with a grumpy sasquatch. I was also mad at myself because I still found him physically attractive despite his poor attitude. He really did look like he could knock out the dragon if he got in a good punch.

He was also walking way too fast. I almost had to jog to keep up with his strides, making my already sore legs burn.

"You realize I got pulled off guarding a prince this week for you?" he called behind his back. "All for someone who probably won't last here three days. You better be grateful."

"I'd be grateful if you slowed down!" I huffed.

He glared at me but did slow his pace. "We need to get inside the library pronto. That's the best way to protect you."

I almost tripped over a tree root but managed to stay upright. "Sure, because being indoors clearly kept me safe the last time."

"You were a trespasser, but now as librarian, the tree should protect you with her magic."

"That didn't work for Clio."

"She was killed outside library grounds. Yggdrasil's magic doesn't extend beyond the moat."

"So why are you here, if the tree can protect me?"

"Because the tree's magic isn't infallible. The dragon could launch a sneak attack and get you before the tree can retaliate."

"And how are you going to stop a fire-breathing dragon?"

"I have my ways. She won't be able to get past me."

I ignored his arrogance and focused instead on something else he said. "How do you know the dragon's female?"

"Because Clio named her Agatha."

Agatha the dragon. My world was crazy sauce. What had I gotten myself into?

My heavy doubt, though, evaporated like smoke as we crossed the moat bridge toward the library. The tree's joy flooded my mind, clearly excited to have me return. It only amplified when I brushed my fingers against the open doorway leading into the tree.

It felt like my mom and dad standing at the front door, welcoming me home.

I stroked a nearby branch that jutted out from the wall. "Good to see you too, Iggy."

Henry's face scrunched in confusion. "Who's Iggy?"

"The tree."

"Her name is Yggdrasil."

A rush of warmth trickled down from my brain. "She doesn't mind being called Iggy. In fact, she likes it."

"Sure, she does." Henry leaned against the entry doorframe.

"Aren't you coming in with me?"

"Nope. I'm supposed to be on dragon watch."

"I could close the door behind me."

"I want to see if the little beast will show herself." He scanned the skies as if willing the dragon to appear.

I glanced at him dubiously. "And what am I supposed to do while you wait?"

Henry shrugged, the gesture awkward against the wall. "You're the great Librarian of Atlantis. You figure it out."

"But I don't know anything about my magic."

"And you think I do?"

"No, I suppose not," I said, flipping around into the hallway.

Henry waited until I'd almost disappeared out of view before calling, "Wait!"

His voice sounded so warm that it fluttered in my chest.

Henry pulled a slightly crushed envelope from his back jeans' pocket. "Give this to Wallace. It's the official notice that you'll be working as temporary librarian for a week."

Great, more bureaucracy. I snatched it from Henry's hands.

"You're welcome," Henry called after me.

"I didn't say thanks!"

He muttered something under his breath. I'm glad I didn't catch it. The less I talked to that hairy grump, the better.

Crossing the hallway and entering the large library doors, I found Wallace scrubbing the white marble floor as if he had a life grudge against it.

Henry wouldn't help me, but maybe Wallace could. I took a step forward.

"Stay back!" Wallace scolded. "Or you'll rub it in more!"

That's when I noticed the thick black smudges. Wallace was scrubbing right where the dragon had launched a fireball.

"And what are you doing back here?" he demanded, glaring up his bulbous nose at me. "I thought the sasquatch took you away for good."

I bit back a retort, deciding to start firm but polite. "I'm here to be the librarian." I waved Henry's envelope at him.

He sighed. "I was afraid of that."

"You're not surprised?"

"I've got eyes, don't I? You look enough like Clio. Same complexion, same body shape, even the same stubborn tilt of your chin. You must be her granddaughter or something." He threw his rag near a bucket of dirty water. "It figures her ungrateful daughter would have an equally disagreeable brat."

"Who says I'm disagreeable?" I countered.

"You're disagreeing with me right now, aren't you?"

I opened my mouth but words didn't come out. He had me there.

He shook his head. "Give me the notice."

I offered the envelope. He first dried his palms, then tore it open. I waited silently as he read the slip contained within.

"'Temporary' assignment?" he asked, raising a bushy eyebrow. "What in Queen Mab's name does that mean?"

"I'm doing a week trial period to see if I'm cut out for the job."

A wave of sadness hit me. Iggy wasn't happy about that.

Neither was Wallace. "This isn't a part-time summer job. Being librarian isn't something you do halfway. You're either in charge or you're not."

"Well, I'm temporarily in charge," I said. "For a week."

Wallace tossed the notice onto a wet spot in the floor. "Disgraceful!" he declared so loud, it reverberated up in the high ceiling. "You don't get to waltz in here and play pretend in the Library of Atlantis."

I tried to explain. "It's just that I've been raised in the human world and—"

"—and you have no business being here," he finished my sentence. "I don't care what Alston says, I won't follow the directions of some young idiot who wants to mess around with the most powerful collection of knowledge in the world."

And with that, he grabbed his bucket and rag and stormed out the door.

I wanted to shout at him, to tell him that I deserved to be here as much as him, but who was I kidding? I stared up at the rows and rows of shelving towering six stories above the atrium. I had no idea what I was doing. I knew next to nothing about running a library and even less about the fae.

"I can't do this," I whispered.

A trill of comfort shimmered in my mind. Iggy believed in me.

"That's great," I said, feeling a bit foolish talking to the air, "but how can I run a library that I don't know anything about?"

A rustling sound reached my ears. The ropey branches forming a nearby wall twitched, suddenly alive. A strand separated from the others, pointing its single leaf at me. Then it gestured back at the wall, the other strands folding in on themselves like a strange kaleidoscope made of bark.

"Should I touch that?" I hesitated. The living wall both mesmerized and freaked me out a little.

The branch waved up and down.

"A tree that can nod," I mumbled. "I am losing my mind."

The branch waved furiously around, and Iggy herself sent me a wave of determination in my head.

"All right, all right. I'm coming."

The branch beckoned me forward as I approached, but I stopped, not wanting to get too close to the wriggling mass. "What happens when I touch it?"

The branch suddenly whipped around my wrist, pulling me forward. I tugged back instinctively, but it wrapped itself too tight for me to break free.

I tried to slap the branch away. "Hey! Let go!"

Iggy responded with another sharp jerk. I lost my balance, and my free hand slapped palm first onto the wall. The coils flowed over my fingers like little snakes.

I shrieked. "Get them off! Get them off! Get them—"

Something solid bumped into my palm. The branches slid back, revealing a doorknob.

"—off?" I finished, confused. "Is there a door behind there?"

The branch released my wrist to wave around like a flag. Applause for me finally understanding.

"Oh," I said, feeling silly for acting like such a coward. I gave the doorknob a twist and pulled.

A rectangular outline appeared in the wall as if it'd been there the whole time. Wooden panels emerged from behind the branches, creating a door that hadn't been there before. As it swung open, I held my breath. What would be on the other side? More books? A secret passage?

Instead, I got a storage closet.

My shoes slapped onto the concrete floor of the cramped space. Crude wooden shelves mounted on the walls held cleaning detergents, wholesale packages of sponges, and rolls of paper towels. A large bucket on wheels sat in one corner, a mop handle leaning awkwardly to the side.

"Not to be rude," I told Iggy, "but this is the biggest magical letdown ever."

The branch curved over my shoulder, winding to a shelf on my right. It pointed at a black bottle.

I picked it up, the glass cool in my hands. Turning it over, I found a simple white label with letters written with marker.

"'Grimoire Ink?'" I read. Where had I heard that word recently? I glanced back into the library and immediately pinpointed the huge leather-bound book on the pedestal that dominated the atrium.

Wallace had called the book the Grimoire. I'd almost written in its pages with my pen since its ink pot had run dry.

Excited to have made the connection, I left the strange storage closet and trotted up to the book. Removing the quill feather, I poured ink into the pot, careful not to fill it more than two-thirds so I wouldn't create a mess. Then I dipped the feather back inside, watching blobs of blackness drip back into the pot's depths.

I glanced at the untouched pages of the book itself and hesitated. "Am I supposed to write something?"

Iggy beamed with joy inside my head.

I took that as a 'yes.' But what to write? I settled on something short and simple.

Hi.

As I removed the quill from the page, the letters faded into the book, the paper absorbing them into their depths. I watched with excitement, waiting for something to happen.

Several seconds passed. Nothing.

I frowned. I wasn't sure how much anticlimactic magic I could take.

Encouragement flooded my senses. Iggy didn't want me to give up.

Clearly, I was missing something. I leaned over the huge tome. Given its prominent position inside the atrium, it obviously served an important function. A card catalog perhaps? Most people wouldn't know the names of the books they were looking for in a library. They'd input the keywords first and find books related to that topic.

I dipped the feather back into the pot and wrote in neat print. *The Library of Atlantis.*

The words slowly faded away again. I slouched, putting the quill away. At least I'd tried.

Before I turned away, however, new script began to appear, different from my own.

A Trip to the Library of Atlantis. Lydgate, Drummond. 1.1 9.4.

My excitement matched Iggy's dancing around in my head. It looked like a call number!

Still, there were six stories of books in front of me. I didn't understand the library's organizational system. It would take me forever to find this one book.

"Where could this book be?" I asked Iggy.

Movement stirred on the first floor. A ropey branch detached itself from the wall, deep within the rows of shelves, waving at me with three fluttering leaves. The first "1" in the call number must have referenced the floor number. I jogged toward the branch.

As I passed shelves, I glanced at the books. Unlike libraries I had visited, they weren't labeled with call numbers on the spine. However, I noticed the shelves themselves had numbers painted on them in highly visible areas: the top, the sides, even the boards themselves. Each shelf appeared to have only one number, and as I dove farther in, the numbers climbed. 5, 8, 12...

By the time I reached the shelf the branch was pointing at, I knew it would be shelf 19. It was a gargantuan shelf too, almost as tall as I could stretch my fingers upward.

The branch tapped the top shelf and I groaned. I'd probably need a ladder to properly see up there. But then the branch tapped twice on the second shelf. Three times on the third. And finally stopped with four taps right in front of me.

"The last number is the shelf, ordered from top to bottom!" I exclaimed. The branch squiggled to confirm my hunch, then slid back into the wall with its coiled brethren.

The fourth shelf had dozens of books, all so thin that they had no actual spines, almost like thick pamphlets. I began flipping through them, noting some of the other titles: *A Day at the Northern Court, Making Ambrosia on Mount Olympus, Amaterasu's Cave of Sunshine*. Although aging with some wear and tear, they'd been made of thick paper stock and bore bright, colorful pictures of people doing magical things like casting sunbeams or summoning an ice storm.

"Are these children's picture books?" I asked Iggy.

Her embarrassment flooded me, tinged with a hint of apology.

"No, it's fine," I told her. "I'm like a child when it comes to all this. Better to start with the basics."

I found *A Trip to the Library of Atlantis* near the middle of the shelf. The gorgeous full-color illustration of Yggdrasil on the cover drew me in despite the simple text in big letters and pen drawings within.

Regardless of its intended audience, the book presented a nice overview of the Library of Atlantis. Situated in the Bermuda Triangle, the fae had hidden the island from human intervention and planted a sentient tree on it. Over centuries, as the fae hid more and more sacred knowledge on the isle, the tree grew into her role as Library of Atlantis. Fae patrons from all over the world were connected to Atlantis through the various fairy rings, like the one I'd taken from the Oregon Coast. The

Grimoire acted as a card catalog, as I'd guessed, although it referenced not only material on the main six floors, but apparently another restricted section called the Forbidden Tomes.

But what fascinated me the most was the explanation of the librarian. She was described as a "descendant of the original muse Clio," which I presumed was the same from Greek legends. While the tree guarded the knowledge inside the library, the librarian managed the tree. She could purportedly "rearrange" the space to her liking. She also helped patrons find answers to particularly difficult questions. The book also spent four pages talking about some highly anticipated event called "Fable Story Hour" that the library hosted once a month. The example showed the librarian riding a unicorn in front of an excited crowd.

Once I read through that book, I intended to find other books about the library so I could get a better idea of my job duties, but while reshelving the books, I couldn't help but browse through a few. *A Day at the Northern Court*, for example, outlined the royal duties of Queen Mab and how she settled disputes among fae scattered throughout the world. The book mentioned different kinds of fae other than the sasquatch and hob I'd already met, including dwarves, mermaids, and even leprechauns. The fae apparently couldn't tell a lie outright but were really good at misdirection and subtle inference to the point that it almost didn't matter.

Once finished with that book, I read another, and then another. I became lost in the fascinating information at my fingertips. I'd just finished learning that fae who changed into animals were called shifters when a voice broke through my preoccupation.

"Hey, Rosalind! You in there somewhere?"

I leaned over to find Henry entering the atrium, a reusable grocery bag in one hand, a duffel over the other.

"Over here!" I called. My left leg had fallen asleep as I'd sat cross-legged on the floor, so I struggled to stand.

Henry made his way over to me as I winced through the pins and needles. I tried not to notice how wonderfully tousled his dark copper hair looked at the end of the day. It didn't help that an amused smile played on his lips as he surveyed the disarray of colorful books around me.

"Enjoying the kiddie section, I see."

My cheeks flushed, but my voice didn't betray any shame as I said, "Laugh it up all you want, but I've learned a lot in the past hour."

"Try hours. It's well past sundown, or haven't you noticed?"

I glanced up at the atrium's dark windows. "No, I didn't notice."

Henry held up the grocery bag, which smelled divine. "Fortunately for you, Gabriel dropped by with dinner. I hope you like pasta alfredo and salad."

"I do." I leaned for it.

He yanked the food out of my reach. "Where are your manners? We're in a library. No food or drink allowed."

"Oh, right. So where can we eat?"

He flipped back around on his heels. "I'll show you to your grandmother's apartment."

"She had an apartment? Here?" I couldn't keep the surprise out of my voice.

"Of course she did. Did you think the librarian slept among the stacks?"

"I guess I hadn't given it much thought."

"Clearly," he said dryly. "Now c'mon before the food gets cold."

We entered the great hallway that connected the library proper to the front entrance. I thought maybe Henry would lead us outside the tree, but instead, he walked straight toward the wall.

"Here's where it gets tricky," he said. "We can't get to Clio's apartment without your magic."

I tried not to visibly balk. "What do I need to do?"

"You should be able to touch the wall here and have Yggdrasil create a stairway that will lead to your grandmother's apartment."

"Inside the tree itself?"

"That's what Melissa said."

"Okay." I placed my palm onto the wall, the tree's general cheeriness sharpening in my mind as I made contact. I felt foolish as I asked, "Uh, can you make some stairs, Iggy?"

To my relief, the branches parted and twisted like they had to create the storage closet. Instead of creating a doorway in front of me, though, the vines parted upward. Narrow planks sprouted every six inches or so, along with a thin railing made of leafy branches. The conjured staircase led up the high ceiling of the hallway, past the leafy boughs above, aligning perfectly with a set of small windows.

It looked like something out of a dream.

"Whoa," I breathed.

Henry whistled. "I have to admit, that's pretty impressive."

I beamed with pride until I worried that the fragile-looking staircase might not be able to hold our weight. Fortunately, the boards didn't so much as jiggle as we plodded up the stairs. The railing, though skinny, felt solid underneath my grip. Besides my thighs hating me, it was a pleasant climb past the ceiling until thick foliage crowded on either side. We kept going upward without being able to see the hallway below. I was beginning to wonder how high the stairs would go when they finally ended at a plain wooden door.

I swung it open. It was a little disconcerting to go from a leafy walkway into a quaint, if outdated, kitchen. Rough beige tile underscored emerald green cabinets. Floral wallpaper popped with pink roses and yellow daffodils at irregular intervals. I homed in on a black stove mounted on four legs with a range top.

"That's not electric, is it?"

"Nope. There's not a lot of electricity on an island in the middle of the Atlantic Ocean."

"Then how does it work?"

"With fire, of course." He was back to glancing at me as if I were an idiot.

I defended myself. "Fire seems very dangerous inside a tree."

"Not in a living tree that can manipulate her own fire magic. Who do you think lit all the candles in the wall?"

Now that he mentioned it, there were all sorts of glowing lanterns strung about the place. I'd seen them flickering among the library walls, and here in the kitchen, a few hung in strategic places: above the stove, over a cherry red dining table, and a chandelier above us.

"Iggy's incredible," I said in awe.

Henry plopped the bag of food on the table. "From what I understand, the tree can do all sorts of things. Between her magic and Wallace taking care of other maintenance, you'll be able to focus on patrons tomorrow."

I froze as he began removing little boxes of takeout. "Patrons? Tomorrow?"

"Yep," Henry said casually as if he hadn't dropped a bombshell. "The library's opening back up in the morning under Gabriel's orders. He says you won't be able to get a feel for being the librarian without some experience."

"But I just got here," I protested.

"Melissa made the same argument, but Gabriel wouldn't budge. He did make a few concessions with limited hours from 9 a.m. to 3 p.m. local time, and he's limiting access to Northern and Southern Court patrons for now. He declared that a fair compromise for getting your feet wet."

"More like throwing me in the deep end," I groaned. "I have no idea what I'm doing."

"Well, if you're going to flail about tomorrow, you might as well do it on a full stomach." He gestured toward the carton of pasta he'd opened for me.

Even though I felt a little sick to my stomach at the thought of running the entire library tomorrow, I sat down. Henry found silverware in a drawer and gave me a set along with a glass of water from a faucet (apparently Iggy also handled the indoor plumbing). A few bites in and my appetite returned in full force. Stress made me eat as fast as I was creating lists in my head for what to do tomorrow.

"Whoa there," Henry laughed as I shoveled salad into my mouth. "You might want to savor that."

I swallowed hard so I wouldn't talk with my mouth full. "I've got no time. I'm going back downstairs to read more about the library. Maybe something down there will tell me what to do. I should also explore the rest of the tree. I read something about restricted books and—"

"What you really need," Henry cut me off, "is a good night's sleep. You aren't going to do anyone any good rambling on incoherently."

I paused with a huge glob of pasta twisted around my fork. "I am rambling, aren't I?" I looked at him with pleading eyes. "Do you really think I can do this?"

Once the words were out of my mouth, I wished I could take them back. Henry didn't want this assignment, and he couldn't care less about me. Asking him for encouragement was like asking to borrow lunch money from the school bully.

Henry bowed his head, focused on his food. He wasn't going to respond. His silence made me more anxious, but at least it was better than being ridiculed.

Suddenly, he lifted his head with a scowl. "You'll be fine."

"Really?" I asked. His expression sure didn't seem encouraging.

"You don't have to mope around like a teenager. I've dealt with one of those recently, and it doesn't suit you."

"And how do you know what suits me?"

"I've seen you square off against a dragon. You were scared, of course, but kept your cool. That beast could have clawed you to death, but you faced it head on." He pointed his fork at me. "Focus on that part of yourself if you want to succeed here."

His words soothed my rising panic. He had a point. I'd already survived a dragon. I'd learned a lot already about the library in one day. Plus, Iggy had my back. She would help me muddle through.

"You're right," I said. "I need to zero in on what I can control."

"Which isn't much," Henry added, digging back into his food.

His subtle dig should have stung, but it didn't. If this grumpy sasquatch believed I had a chance, then I had a chance. I just had to believe that I could do the job.

CHAPTER 9

I was ready to quit before lunchtime.

Henry left the island after dinner, making me seal the tree's entrance so the dragon couldn't sneak back in. He told me to reopen the door no later than 8:00 a.m. to let him in an hour before the library opened. I'd assured him I would, mentally reminding myself to set an alarm as I walked back upstairs.

But the minute I stepped foot inside the apartment, I felt an overwhelming need to take a shower. I was grimy from the day's adventures. Had I only just been at my childhood home this morning?

I checked out the apartment's only bathroom, taking stock of the blush pink fixtures with teal countertop. Clio sure liked color. The combination tub and shower looked standard if a bit old, but the showerhead sprayed with surprisingly good water pressure when I turned it on. The water came out hot very quickly but the lone knob didn't change the temperature. It took me several minutes to realize I had to ask Iggy directly to change it by placing my hand against the wall.

Finally satisfied, I ditched my clothes in a pile and stood under the stream, letting the water pour over me. I sighed with relief. There was a small bottle of shampoo and body wash in the corner. I scrubbed myself clean, trying to feel normal again.

As I exited the shower soaking wet, I realized I'd made a huge mistake. There wasn't a bath towel hanging on the rack next to the tub. Only a small hand towel hung near the sink.

"Where are the normal-sized towels?" I asked aloud, bracing one hand against the wall to support myself on the slippery floor.

The branches of the wall parted beneath my fingers. I let out a gasp as they formed a narrow bifold door with plantation shutters.

I folded the door open, revealing four rows of plush teal towels, from small washcloths up to bath-size sheets. I grabbed the biggest towel and wrapped it around myself. Once I closed the closet door, the branches absorbed it back into the wall.

"Iggy, you're amazing."

My mind lit up with warm pride.

After thoroughly drying myself off, I shuffled to the room where Henry had left the duffel bag stuffed with clean clothes. Clio and Jason clearly shared the same genes because their spare bedrooms were so similar. Trade the dusty guitar cases for stacks of crates and boxes, and the two rooms could have been twins. Even the navy-blue comforter on the twin bed seemed the same.

I shoved on a slightly too-large black T-shirt and sweats for pajamas. Finding an unopened toothbrush and toothpaste at the bottom of the duffel, I brushed my gunky teeth, completing my bedtime routine.

I couldn't stop yawning. Henry was right. I needed sleep. With eyelids almost too heavy to keep open, I snuggled under the mound of comforter and blankets. Within seconds, my muddled thoughts faded into the empty blackness of dreamless sleep.

Unfortunately, my stupid body decided to jerk itself awake for no apparent reason.

Ugh. The older I got, the more my body hated me. I flipped around for a while, hoping I could still lapse into slumber. No such luck. The adrenaline that had kickstarted my nerves made sleep impossible. To make matters worse, I found myself studying the contents of the open crates, illuminated by soft light streaming through the window. A barn owl statue with wings stretched in mid-flight. A set of Russian stacking dolls tossed willy-nilly ranging from champagne glass to peanut sizes. A purple geode with crystals cast rainbows from the moonlight.

I'd never get to sleep staring at this stuff, but I also couldn't take my eyes off it. I would have drawn the curtains to darken the room from the moonlight, but there were none. Frustrated, I kicked off the covers, wondering if there was another place to sleep in the apartment.

The short cul-de-sac of a hallway held another bedroom, twice as large as the one I'd left. It had to be Clio's room, with floor-to-ceiling shelves packed with books. A fireplace dominated one wall while a mahogany desk pushed underneath an arched window took up the opposite side. A gigantic walk-in closet and bathroom adjoined the room.

By now I admitted to myself that it wasn't the room I was sleeping in. I was just wide awake. I examined the nearest shelf full of books. Many of them had the same old-fashioned leather bindings as those down in the library, but I was surprised to find some mass market paperbacks as well, from memoirs to suspense thrillers to sci-fi. Like me, Clio had eclectic taste.

But one book without a name, shoved into one corner, stood out from the rest. I thought at first it might have been a binder, but it was a photo album. Three metal rings held the pages, each of which had a sticky backing with a plastic covering to hold Polaroid pictures. The first pages of the album contained baby pictures in black and white, the child slowly getting older as she went from newborn to toddler. It wasn't until the pictures shifted to color that I recognized the growing girl.

They were all pictures of my mother as a child.

I gasped. Mom hadn't owned any pictures from her childhood. The earliest pictures I'd seen of my mother were after she'd gotten together with my father.

I stretched out on Clio's bed, propping up on my elbow as I examined each picture more thoroughly. I stifled a yawn as I soaked in the details. Some of the pictures had been taken at famous places. I found one of Mom around six years old, waving up at the Leaning Tower of Pisa. A few years later had her throwing a "V" sign in front of the Taj Mahal. Yet, most of the photos had been shot around the library: climbing around Iggy's roots like a jungle gym, reading a book at the base of the

Grimoire's pedestal, and my favorite, a bored teenager rolling her eyes in the middle of the cobblestone courtyard.

I'd hoped to find a picture of Clio, but this had clearly been an album dedicated to Sophia's childhood.

I must have flipped through the photos a dozen times, well into the night. I didn't realize I'd fallen asleep until something poked me.

Disoriented, I wiped drool from my face and found a branch waving frantically at me.

"What's up, Iggy?" I asked.

The branch pointed to the window above the desk. A stream of morning light enveloped the room, accentuating a bright blue morning sky.

I jumped to my feet. "What time is it?"

The branch slithered along the wall to an analog clock on the fireplace mantle. 9:00 a.m.

"I'm late!" I cried, rushing back to the spare bedroom. Flinging clothes from the duffel, I found a bra and put it on underneath my T-shirt, then shoved on a pair of slimming jogger pants that thankfully passed off as business casual. I couldn't clean my dingy gray sneakers with mud intertwined in the laces. At least they were dry. I slapped a palm on the wall in the kitchen to open the staircase, and then ran down the slats as they formed, further risking a fall by using my fingers to thread through my hair instead of holding the railing.

A voice drifted up to me as I passed under the hallway ceiling. "You're late!" Wallace called as I darted onto the ground floor.

"Why didn't you come get me?" I demanded as I ran toward the entryway.

"It's your job to be on time, or you're not fit to be Librarian of Atlantis."

I didn't have time to argue with him as I placed my palm on the wall to open the doorway. It was only a few minutes after nine. Probably only one or two patrons were waiting at most. I hoped I could smooth things over with my customer service skills.

As the branches pulled back, though, my heart dropped. A crowd of a dozen older men and women, all shorter than me, had gathered right on the other side. They wore thick wool sweaters despite the summer heat. All the men had beards and, surprisingly, so did one of the women. Their glares sharpened as I came into view.

I waved nervously at them. "Hi," I said in a timid voice before clearing my throat. "Welcome to the—"

"Just move aside," a man with a red beard in the front said, pushing me out of the way. "We've got work to do, and no time for idle chitchat."

His cohorts all grunted in agreement, surging forward. I barely skirted out of the way as they marched past me, some throwing me disgusted looks as they stomped into the hallway.

I took a deep breath. I couldn't be intimidated. It was my job to help these folk. I walked after the last short woman who passed me.

I didn't get very far as a rough hand clamped down on my shoulder. "I thought I told you—" a voice said in my ear.

I shrieked because I couldn't see anyone to go along with the voice.

Henry blinked back into visibility, scowling. "—to open the entrance at eight o'clock," he finished with a growl.

"Why were you hiding?" I demanded.

"You clearly have never hung around a bunch of irritable dwarves. They prize punctuality, and they hate being left waiting." He kept his pointed glare at me. "Is this why you never keep a job for long?"

My face burned. "You read my employment history?"

"Stronghold always does a thorough background check on all its employees, temporary or not. I read your file."

"Great, you're a stalker."

"As your bodyguard, I have every right to know who I'm protecting."

"That's right. I'm a middle-aged woman who's never held down a job for very long. Very threatening."

I'd almost made it to the hallway when Henry called after me, "Bit of friendly advice: don't approach the dwarves. Let them come to you."

Should I have listened to the sasquatch who clearly understood the ins and outs of fae culture? Probably. But was I going to follow his advice after he made me mad? Unfortunately not.

I spent the next hour or so trailing after the dwarven patrons, trying to be helpful. Half of them blatantly ignored me, even if I tried to draw them into conversation. The other half outright walked away if I got within conversational distance. There was one young female dwarf with red hair who looked like she might speak to me, but when the red-bearded leader gave her a stern shake of his head, she shied away. I finally gave up and ended up watching them scurry around the various floors of the library, pulling off scrolls and discussing them in hushed tones.

Frustrated with myself, I wandered back into the hallway. I passed Wallace scrubbing the floors with his rags. When I said "hello," he whispered something under his breath that didn't sound friendly.

I considered popping back up to the apartment to properly dress for the day when I realized how gloomy the hallway was for midday. I placed a hand on a nearby wall.

"Iggy, would you mind lighting the hallway for our guests?"

The lanterns lining the hall immediately flared up. There. I did something.

Wallace was less impressed. "You should have Yggdrasil create more windows," he grumbled. "Natural sunlight is better during the day."

Before I could reply to his suggestion, a wave of dread that wasn't mine washed over me. Iggy had become agitated. I didn't understand why until Wallace also glanced up and stiffened, the rag dropping from his hand.

A new pair of patrons had entered the library. An impossibly gaunt man with sallow skin and bushy black hair had eyes that gleamed yellow despite the increased brightness. Small, curved horns like monochrome nautilus shells with a sharp end point were stuck to either side of his face. He wore a navy fur-lined robe, and his feet ended in a pair of hooves that clicked every time he stepped.

The second man was shorter and around my age with a strong chin, thin cheekbones, and tan complexion. Wispy blond hair curled around his brow, matching his barely-there eyebrows. He wore a green tunic with gold trim and walked with a cane with a round golden handle, which supported his slight left-side limp. Despite looking like the more polished of the two, he clearly deferred to the taller man.

Wallace clicked his heels together and took a deep bow. "Lord Krampus!" he proclaimed in a steady voice, even though his knees wobbled.

No wonder he was scared. Krampus was a winter boogey-man from German folklore who would show up in towns and kidnap misbehaving children. Tales said he either ate them or dragged them to the underworld. Definitely not the kind of person I wanted strutting into my library.

Krampus ignored Wallace and instead favored me with a forced smile, I suppose to put me at ease. It only made my own anxiety spike up to match Iggy's.

"You must be the new Librarian of Atlantis," he said.

I nodded, extending my hand. "My name's Rosalind Baldwin."

He raised an eyebrow in disdain. "What do you want me to do with your fingers?"

Wallace inclined his head forward. Oh, right. He had bowed to Krampus. I did the same, not knowing how deep to go and ending up flinging my unbrushed hair all over the place.

Krampus sneered as I rose. "Clearly, you are not accustomed to the ways of the Court."

My face flushed, but I tried to stay polite. "I was raised in the human world, sir."

"Oh?" Krampus asked, amused. "Fresh meat, is it?"

Swallowing saliva that had gathered in my throat, I nevertheless refused to be intimidated. "I'm sure I'm tougher than your normal fare, probably not worth the effort."

Wallace's eyes bulged out of his sockets. The man with the cane also looked taken aback.

But Krampus merely laughed, exposing an entire set of perfect white teeth. "You're a feisty one, like your grandmother."

"You knew Clio?" Despite the situation, I couldn't keep the yearning out of my voice.

"Better than you, I presume, since she never mentioned you."

My heart sank. This was not the person to ask about my grandmother. "It's a long story."

"And a boring one, I'm sure. We didn't come all this way for a chat. Egan"—he gestured at the man with the cane—"and I have critical research to conduct. Hopefully, you're up to the task."

I straightened my spine and projected my voice with confidence. "How can I help you?"

"Egan has a malady in his leg that requires special treatment. The knowledge we seek lies in the Forbidden Tomes."

I didn't know where those were and didn't want to come off as complete idiot. "Let me see what I can . . ." I began to say.

A rush of violent anger from Iggy cascaded over me. She definitely was not on board with me fulfilling this request.

Wallace also nervously cleared his throat. "Not to intrude, Lord Krampus, but only certain fae citizens are allowed access to—"

"Keep your lips shut, hob," Krampus snapped, his eyes flashing bright yellow. Wallace reestablished his gaze on the floor.

Yikes. I wasn't super keen on making an enemy out of someone with so much obvious clout, but given Iggy's emotions roiling in my brain, I couldn't let him access the Forbidden Tomes. And probably for good reason if Wallace had dared to speak up.

I tried to defuse the situation. "I'm sure we can find some solution to Egan's problem. Maybe there's something else in the main library that—"

"Only the Forbidden Tomes will do," Krampus said. "Either you'll lead us there, or you're nothing but some two-bit muse charlatan who's just playing at librarian."

Ouch. That played right into my insecurities. I should have been properly intimidated like Wallace.

Except I'd had a terrible morning. I was sick of being treated like a nobody. I may have been a complete novice to this world, but Iggy chose me.

I pasted on a smile. "Then I suppose I can't help you after all. I'm sorry you came all the way here for nothing."

A splash of angry red blotched Krampus's cheeks. "Are you dismissing me?" he asked, as if the concept was foreign to him.

"Yggdrasil clearly doesn't want to give you access to the Forbidden Tomes," I said.

"Then tell the stubborn tree to change her mind."

Iggy reeled in my mind, shocked at his suggestion.

"I'm terribly sorry," I said sweetly, "but that's not how my relationship with Yggdrasil works."

Krampus looked like he wanted to throttle me. A shiver shot through me, but I held my ground.

Egan took a timid step forward. "Perhaps we got off on the wrong foot. I—"

Krampus cut him off with a swift shake of his hand. "Don't you dare make any suggestions, not after what you've done."

Egan clamped his lips shut.

Sympathy overrode my lingering fear. "Is that how you normally talk to sick people?" I asked.

Krampus regarded me with cold, calculating eyes. Clearly, the wheels were churning in his head, although I couldn't tell for what. I braced myself for a new bullying tactic.

I was surprised when he simply said, "Fine."

Egan also looked taken aback. "My lord?"

"We've wasted our time here." He sneered at me. "Can you at least escort Egan back to the fairy ring? He could use the extra support."

I hesitated at that unexpected request. "I'm supposed to stay inside the tree today."

"Then you are, indeed, completely worthless." Krampus flipped around, the clicks of his terrible hooves echoing in the narrow chamber.

I tried not to seethe. Worthless, indeed. I didn't see "his lordship" offering Egan a hand.

Egan waited until Krampus was out of earshot before giving me a long, courteous bow. "I am dreadfully sorry, librarian. Lord Krampus can be abrupt, but he means well. It was a pleasure to meet you. Good day."

Egan winced as he shifted directions, favoring his bad leg. His cane echoed in a discordant beat as he caught up to Krampus's strides.

My resolve faltered as I watched the man limp away. He was obviously in a lot of pain. The whole reason they had come was to alleviate his suffering.

"Wait!" I called after him. "I'm coming."

Krampus did not turn around, but Egan did. He waited for me to reach him, offering his free arm.

"Shouldn't you be leaning on me, not the other way around?" I asked.

"I've found this works better with the cane. You will actually provide me extra support if you'll hold on. But if you don't want to . . ."

I immediately latched on to his arm. "Of course I will."

Egan did seem more steady as we chased after Krampus, who hadn't bothered to slow his gait for us. Krampus had already made it outside of the library when Egan and I made it to the entryway.

Henry was scowling at Krampus, but his frown deepened when he noticed my hand in the crook of Egan's arm. "Where do you think you're going?"

"I'm escorting these two gentlemen to the fairy ring."

"They can walk themselves," Henry said. "You should stay here."

Krampus acknowledged all of us behind him. "She's fulfilling a basic request from a library patron. It's no concern of yours."

"Her safety is very much a concern of mine," Henry shot back so fiercely, my heart thumped in my chest.

"I recognize you." Krampus sneered. "You're Alston's minion. What authority does Stronghold have here?"

"Queen Mab sent us to guard the librarian," Henry shot back. "Feel free to take it up with her."

"Queen Mab clearly doesn't trust the librarian if she's having Stronghold flunkies guard the library. Either the library's safe, or this whole setup is a charade."

"It's not a charade," I insisted, looking at Henry. "And I can escort you. Alone."

Henry's jaw tightened, but he didn't say a word as Egan and I trailed after Krampus. I glanced back at him several times, and although he kept staring at us, he didn't follow.

We climbed up the hill and over the rim that overlooked Yggdrasil. Egan panted the entire way, alternating leaning against his cane and me. Each step on his left side caused him to grunt. I wanted to soothe him but bit my lip. I'd been the one to deny him access to the Forbidden Tomes. Anything I could have said would only sound insincere.

Once Yggdrasil's boughs were out of sight and we were marching downhill back into the jungle, Krampus finally slowed so he could speak to me. "It's a pity."

I knew he was baiting me, but I responded anyway. "What's a pity?"

"That you will only last for a short time. Clearly, you're not cut out for being the Librarian of Atlantis."

"And how have you come to that brilliant conclusion?" I asked.

He didn't seem offended by my tone. Just the opposite. An amused smile spread across his lips, raising the hairs on the back of my neck.

"The fae are dangerous. We may play nice with humans because Queen Mab has forged her little treaties, but we have long memories. Most of us hate your kind. Having you protect our most precious knowledge source will not stand."

I swallowed a lump in my throat so I wouldn't stammer. "I'm the last muse in Clio's line," I said firmly. "Without me, no one will have access to the Library of Atlantis."

"Maybe that would be a good thing," Krampus said smoothly. "Better to have the knowledge locked away inside Yggdrasil than have it lost or defiled by a filthy human."

The vine-filled trees lining our path parted, exposing the cobblestone courtyard with the six archways. When Henry and I had walked through yesterday, all the archways but one had all been inert, but someone had replaced the stones in half of them, causing their runes to pulse with glowing light. White crystals drifted out of two of them. It wasn't until I caught one in my hand that I realized they were snowflakes.

As Krampus moved toward the glowing fairy ring on the far end of the courtyard, Egan whispered in my ear. "Again, my apologies, Ms. Baldwin. I wish we could have met under more pleasant circumstances."

"It's not your fault," I said, still glaring at Krampus.

"But I do feel responsible, nonetheless. Perhaps I should—"

A roar shook the skies above us, cutting off his sentence.

Egan paled and stumbled backward, almost taking me with him. "Oh no," he whimpered.

As I desperately kept us both balanced on our feet, a shadow slashed overhead, giving us little warning before an iridescent mass of scales slammed into the ground. Agatha the dragon snapped her sharp teeth at Egan.

I pulled Egan back before she could bite a chunk of him. He did fall back then, letting go of me and his cane as he collapsed on the ground.

Agatha screeched, the sound like twisting metal, overpowering Egan's screams of terror. Her neck whipped backward, and I recognized the stance.

She was going to fry Egan.

I couldn't let that happen. I shoved myself between the dragon and Egan, spreading my arms out wide.

"If you want me, here I am!" I yelled at her.

Agatha snarled, the sound deep and menacing. But she hesitated, the fire burning so brightly inside her that it outlined her throat.

"Stay back!" a voice yelled in my ear. Henry appeared out of thin air beside me, fury etched on his face. He flung his hand outward, tossing an object forward. A silvery disc twice the size of a quarter slashed through the air like a frisbee, landing right where Agatha's skin flared with fire. The object shattered against her scales and burst into a cascade of water so vast, waves of it splashed back against Henry and me.

Agatha howled, her wings flapping desperately to get away. She managed to hover for a few beats, shrouded in steamy smoke. With one last grunt, she took off to the air and dashed away.

Seconds passed as I took huge gulping breaths. As heat rolled over me, I realized how close I'd been to becoming barbeque.

Henry reached out a hand as if to touch me but then stalled. "Are you okay?"

Before I could answer, Krampus tramped over to Egan, his face scrunched in anger as he hauled the man roughly to his feet.

"This is an outrage!" he yelled as he scooped up Egan and his cane. "You can't even protect yourself, much less a defenseless library patron. You'd better get rid of that dragon before it destroys the entire island."

And with Egan trembling against him, Krampus disappeared into the snowy landscape of the farthest fairy ring.

CHAPTER 10

Henry's hands clenched into fists in Krampus's wake. "Good riddance."

I fought the shivers that refused to leave my body. "I'm sorry," I whispered.

"You should be," Henry said. "Thinking you could run around the island with that dragon around. You're lucky you aren't toast."

He was right, of course. So was Krampus. I'd become so wrapped up in too many things—my yearning to belong someplace, my secret fae heritage, and now this wonderful library—to see the truth.

Henry guided me back toward the library. I barely noticed the aching in my legs as we trekked down the path. How had I ever believed I could fit into this strange magic world?

Henry noticed me staring off into space as we re-entered the tree and wandered into the main hallway. He waved a hand over my face. "Are you okay?"

I blinked back to the present. "Oh, yeah. Sure."

Henry's face filled with concern. "It's perfectly normal to freak out a little. Krampus is scary enough, but a dragon—"

"I'm fine," I insisted. "I just need lunch. I'm allowed a lunch break, right?"

"Sure, you can take twenty minutes or so back in the apartment. I'll keep watch until you get back. But are you sure you don't want to talk about—"

"Nope," I said firmly. I refused to discuss my inner thoughts. "Be back in twenty."

I placed my hand on the nearest wall and had Iggy create branch stairs for me before Henry could protest further. I could feel his eyes on my back as I wound upstairs. He knew as well as I did.

I just wasn't cut out for this job.

I didn't eat anything during my break. I would have thrown up if I had. Instead, I tidied the apartment, packing all my discarded clothing back into the duffel bag. I decided to leave the place the way I found it.

The tree tried sending soothing vibes in my mind as I scurried about preparing for my departure. "I'm sorry, Iggy, but I can't be the librarian. I'm not good enough."

But as I shoved a wrinkled T-shirt into the bag, I couldn't help but wonder what I would do once I left. I had no job prospects. Moving to yet another city held no appeal. Jason would let me stay with him as long as I wanted, but I needed more than my brother to survive.

What was I going to do?

I swallowed a lump in my throat, wishing I could talk to my dad about what to do. He'd always known what to say. Even after all the years of him gone, I missed him terribly.

I shrugged off all my crushing self-doubt. One thing was certain, my dad would frown upon me leaving a job in the middle of a shift. I had to at least finish out the day. I forced myself to eat a few crackers from the bag of food Henry had left. I ran a wet washcloth over my face. I even did a few yoga stretches to get the blood pumping, then trudged back downstairs.

A trickle of conversation drifted from the library as I padded onto the hallway floor. I identified most as the diligent voices of dwarves going about their business, but one loud man boomed with an exclamation, followed by a crisp bark of laughter.

"You've got a new VIP patron waiting for you," Henry said in my ear.

I shrieked as he blinked into view. "Stop sneaking up on me like that!"

"You didn't complain when I did it to the dragon."

"Yeah, well, I like being alive." I tried flattening the wrinkles out of my shirt and failed. "Who's the new patron?"

"Krampus's brother."

I recoiled. "Maybe I should hang out in Clio's apartment until he's gone."

"He asked to meet you as soon as you were available."

"Of course he did," I groaned.

Henry gestured toward the large double doors of the library with a smirk. "Have fun."

I returned his amusement with my best glare. "Thanks for reveling in my failure."

"Quit stalling and go introduce yourself."

I steeled my shoulders. Just a few more hours, I reminded myself. Then I could leave and never look back.

When I entered the library proper, I found that all the dwarves had gathered around a man roughly twice their height and several times more their mass. The dwarves excitedly showed off parchment designs, many clamoring over each other to be heard.

"One at a time, one at a time," the new visitor told them with a chuckle. "I promise I'll give feedback on all your designs."

He had his back to me, so I strode over for a closer inspection. He certainly didn't resemble the gaunt, cloven-footed Krampus. This man had thick, wavy hair as white as snow falling to his shoulders. Red suspenders over a white shirt held up sturdy pants. He had a round belly, the kind that likely cushioned a decent amount of muscle along with fat. His legs were round and thick, ending in black work boots.

But what really caught my attention was a utility belt wrapped around his waist. It looked almost exactly like my dad's old one, complete with wrench and plier handles sticking out.

My heart slammed in my chest. My dad had been a bit leaner and sported less hair, but other than that, this man had the same height and build as Linus Baldwin.

"Dad?" The words escaped my lips before I could stop them.

I'd wandered to within a few feet of the dwarven crowd. They all stopped chattering to stare at me with variations of surprise and wariness.

The man turned around at the commotion. If I'd seen him from the front, I would have never mistaken him for my dad. He had the largest, curliest beard flowing down to mid-sternum. His round nose held a pair of small round spectacles that accentuated his sky-blue eyes. Rosy red cheeks, as if chapped by the cold, spread out a heartwarming smile.

"Ah, you must be the new librarian," he proclaimed loudly. "I can see your resemblance to Clio."

"How?" I asked. "Same stubborn tilt of my chin?"

I immediately regretted repeating Wallace's earlier words. Antagonizing Krampus's brother was probably not my smartest move.

But the man only burst out into genuine laughter, his voice filling the air with joy. "Ho, that is a good one! Clio did have a delightful stubborn streak but in a good way. She protected this precious library with a fierce heart, as I'm sure you will."

I smiled in spite of myself. "My name's Rosalind." I almost held out my hand but stopped myself for a deep bow.

Because I was half bent over, I didn't realize the man had crossed the distance between us. And I wasn't prepared for the bear hug until my face became pressed within his soft beard. The scent of cinnamon filled my nostrils.

"I am Klaus, my dear librarian," his muffled voice proclaimed above me. "And you needn't be so formal around me."

"Klaus?" I repeated after he let me go. My brain slowly made the connection between his jolly personality and the name. "Like Santa Claus?"

"Or Father Christmas, Papa Noel, Kris Kringle . . . I am named many things around the world and am delighted by each one."

I couldn't contain my confusion. "I thought you were Krampus's brother."

The dwarves recoiled at the name, but Klaus boomed with mirth again. "I am! We are quite the study in opposites, my brother and I."

Of course. Klaus and Krampus were like night and day, both representing winter traditions to children around the world: one who stole children in the middle of the night, and the other giving boundless joy through his endless generosity.

"She was raised human, sir," the red-bearded dwarf said with disdain. "She doesn't know anything about the fae."

The other dwarves murmured in agreement.

I raised my hands in apology. "I-I didn't mean to offend anyone."

"No offense was taken," Klaus said. "You may not have been raised in our ways, but I have every confidence that you have what it takes to run this library. There is no better endorsement in this world than from the tree of Yggdrasil."

Iggy practically blushed with glee inside my head.

I stared up at Klaus. "You're not worried about my background?"

117

"Of course not. I love all the people of this world. Why else would I give them so many wonderful gifts?"

"Then it's true that you give kids gifts?" My eyes widened. "But that doesn't make sense. I know for a fact that my parents 'played' Santa Claus. I discovered my gifts in their closet one year."

"I can't possibly give every good child in the world a present, nor would I want to. I always pick and choose those precious few who are worthy of some magic in their lives. That is why my engineers are at your library today."

"These are your elves?" I asked.

A fierce grumbling rose up from the dwarven ranks. The red-bearded dwarf harrumphed at me, folding his arms across his chest.

"Please, never call them 'elves,'" Klaus admonished gently. "They are most definitely dwarves, some of the best engineers among the fae. They help me create my wonders. Would you like to see one?"

"Yes, please."

"Master Forger Brock." Klaus motioned to the red-bearded dwarf. "Please show Rosalind your initial design."

The dwarf hid the scroll behind his back. "She called me an 'elf,' sir."

"I'm really sorry about my ignorance," I said before Klaus could interject on my behalf. "If you don't want to show me, that's okay."

Klaus stuck his thumbs under his suspenders. "I suppose it's up to you, Master Forger," he said neutrally.

Brock sighed as if extremely put out. He brought the scroll forward and unrolled it. "We're designing a trampoline for a little girl in Brazil."

On the page was a rough sketch of a trampoline. It had notes to the side with material specs. Questions had also been jotted into the margins about dimensions and flourishes. All in all, it looked quite simple.

"Oh," I said, not sure how to respond.

"They've only just begun their research," Klaus explained. "This design is very crude. Brock's team will spend the next few days in the library determining how to make it special."

"Special?" I asked as Brock rolled up the parchment.

Klaus nodded. "Magic. The girl who will receive this has recently lost her father after a long illness. She loved him with all her heart and misses him terribly. The family is too poor to afford much. She deserves a little magic in her life, don't you think?"

"Absolutely," I said. "That is incredibly kind of you."

Klaus rocked on the heels of his boots. "We couldn't do our important work without the library. We rely on the Library of Atlantis to implement the unique aspects of our gifts. Every toy we make is custom made."

"But Christmas is so far away. Won't the little girl have to wait a long time?"

Klaus grinned. "I don't only deliver my gifts during the holidays. That would be silly. Kids need cheer all year round."

"So you don't go down chimneys or fly around with reindeer?"

"I didn't say that," he replied with a twinkle in his eyes. "Although I find walking through walls a mite more convenient than sliding down a dirty old flue."

"Well, I'm glad Iggy—I mean, Yggdrasil can help you," I said.

He clamped a beefy hand on my shoulder. "It's not only the sacred tree that keeps my gifts flowing to children. It's you, librarian."

"But the dwarves found all the information themselves today," I pointed out, not wanting to take credit for their work.

"But the tree requires the librarian in order to function. Your mere presence keeps the Library of Atlantis open. Without you, many fae with important magical work will suffer. My workshop has already fallen behind schedule after Clio's death, may she rest in the stars."

I didn't understand why I was so important, and the look must have shown on my face because Klaus gave me a little squeeze. "Please believe me, Rosalind, when I say you serve a very important function. I'm extremely grateful that Yggdrasil found you and wish you many years of good health."

With that, he turned back to his dwarves. "That's all for today! Let's head back."

"Hear, hear!" the dwarves answered, gathering around the giant old man like bees to the largest flower in the field. They buzzed behind him toward the entrance. It may have been my imagination, but once Klaus had left with his dwarves, the library's lights grew a tad bit dimmer.

Unlike me. A surge of brilliance surged through me. It could not have been a coincidence that Klaus looked like my father wearing his toolbelt.

"Thanks for the advice, Dad," I whispered. "I think I'll stay here a bit longer."

CHAPTER 11

NOBODY ELSE VISITED THE library that day, which suited me just fine. I used the time to explore. I started at the Grimoire, writing *Klaus* on the blank page. I first spelled it with a *C* before realizing his name began with a *K*. The Grimoire came back with a list of results, items scattered throughout the various library floors.

One result in particular caught my attention. The title *Fae Individual Registry* was written in red ink instead of black, and the first call number was a -1. Wondering if it was some sort of typo, I searched the first floor for the resource, but the corresponding bookcase housed leather-bound blacksmithing tomes grouped next to handwritten fae cookbooks.

Curiosity got the better of me as I wandered around the first floor, trying to find a pattern to the library's organization. There didn't appear to be any rhyme or reason to the shelves, groups of books packed willy-nilly in no particular order. I climbed to the second floor, then the third, fourth, fifth, all the way to the top sixth floor and discovered more of the same. Fae history resources were shelved on each level, sometimes as scrolls, sometimes as books. Old car magazines written by humans neighbored hand-illustrated fae autobiographies. I giggled at finding bare-chested Victorian romance novels shoved next to scrolls on the fine art of meat packing.

I eventually got sidetracked on the fifth floor by an enormous leather-bound book on magical creatures. Sitting on a lumpy couch, I flipped through the pages and absorbed facts on unicorns, gryphons, and a bunch of other animals I'd never heard of before. I still couldn't believe some of these creatures existed.

"You gonna sleep there tonight?" Henry interrupted while I perused the dragon section. He called to me from across the floor, head poking from behind a shelf.

"Thanks for not appearing next to me out of nowhere for a change."

"I'm a fast learner."

"What time is it?" I asked as my stomach growled.

He grinned. "Suppertime, obviously."

Startled, I glanced past him to the large windows overlooking the atrium. Streaks of orange and pink tainted what had been a pristine blue sky.

"I didn't realize it was so late. I was reading about dragons. Did you know they have a keen sense of smell? I guess a lot of fae believed fire-breathing would dull their nostrils, but research has proven otherwise."

I strained to shut the book and place it on the floor. The thing had to be as heavy a bowling ball.

"Here. Allow me." Henry snatched it as if it weighed no more than a piece of paper. He crammed it onto the nearest bookshelf.

"That's not where it goes," I protested.

"It doesn't matter. The tree knows where it's at."

"Yeah, but no one else does."

"Sure they do. They can ask for its location in the Grimoire."

"No wonder I found steamy books next to ones about meat."

"What?" Henry asked, confused.

"Never mind." Pins and needles pricked up and down my legs. They'd fallen asleep while I read. I winced as I swiveled my ankles to regain feeling in my feet.

"Do you always do that?" Henry asked as he sauntered over to me.

"Stretch after sitting for a long time?"

"No, I mean lose track of time reading. That's twice you've done it now."

I rubbed my calves to encourage blood flow. "Dad did always call me his 'little sponge,'" I said, unable to keep the hitch from my voice.

Henry broke off eye contact. "I'm sorry for your loss."

I jerked my head up at him. "You know my dad died?"

"I read your file, remember?"

"Yeah, but that's private information." I jumped up on my feet, ignoring the tingling sensation in my legs. "How does that help you protect me?"

Henry at least looked chagrined. "I'm sorry. I didn't mean to upset you."

I took a few calming breaths. "It's fine," I said in a much calmer voice. "You'd think I'd be over it by now, but there's been a lot of reminders of him lately."

He offered me his arm when I threatened to topple off balance. "You don't have to explain or apologize. You'll never get over it."

I ignored his arm. "Why? Because I'm weak?"

"Because you loved him," he said softly. "It's not something you 'get over.'"

Something in his voice told me he spoke from experience, but I didn't dare ask. He was a grumpy sasquatch, after all.

But I did take his arm to steady myself. "Thanks."

"You're welcome."

We stood silently for a few beats, me holding on to Henry's surprisingly soft plaid shirt as feeling came back into my legs. He smiled, letting his guard down. A blush formed on my cheeks. Underneath Henry's grumpy façade, he really was a softie at heart. I wondered what it would feel like to have those big strong arms envelop me.

I abruptly let him go, taking a few timid steps forward. I couldn't let my mind wander in that direction.

"So," I said loudly, breaking the silence intentionally, "how are Krampus and Klaus brothers? They look nothing alike."

Henry's smile faded as we made our way down the library floors.

"Krampus and Klaus are a huge mystery, even to the fae. No one even knows where they came from. They just showed up in the Northern Court hundreds of years ago as shadow walkers."

"Shadow walkers?"

"A very special, very rare kind of fae that can walk through solid material."

I balked. "Are you saying Krampus can barge into the library whenever he wants?"

Henry chuckled. "Krampus only wishes he could. The tree's magic is stronger than his. That's why he was trying to harass you into letting him into the Forbidden Tomes."

"He does seem like a big bully."

"And like most bullies, he knows how to get what he wants. Krampus is notorious for collecting oddball fae who worship him, like that Egan guy. He rarely does his dirty work alone."

"Dirty work? Do you mean Krampus kidnaps children like the legends say?"

Henry's voice took on an edge. "He used to, back before Queen Mab brokered a peace treaty with humanity."

"Why didn't she stop him before?" I insisted.

"You have to realize that humans used to hunt fae. It's not an excuse, of course, but we have our own horror stories of humans massacring fae for sport."

His reasoning was fair, but I still wrinkled my nose. "Maybe I should ban him from the library."

"Unfortunately, you can't. Members of the Court cannot have their library access revoked except under extreme circumstances."

"And murdering children isn't extreme?"

"Past acts that were considered fair and legal don't count."

"That's wrong!"

"That's politics. It happens in your world too."

"Maybe, but our tyrants don't live for hundreds of years. Sounds like he's practically immortal."

"No fae is immortal, and most of us lead comparable human-length lives. It's just a handful of special fae, like the queen and the two shadow walker brothers, who live to see centuries."

I shook my head. "How does Klaus put up with that creep?"

"Klaus is an optimist to a fault. He believes his brother will change. The rest of us aren't so sure. But there is one thing Krampus is right about." Henry's face twisted into a scowl. "Something needs to be done about that dragon."

We'd made it down to the first floor. Wallace scrubbed furiously at the same burnt smudge in the atrium. A bald spot on his head flickered underneath a nearby sconce.

"I thought you took care of that yesterday," I said as we passed by.

Wallace blew frustrated air out of his mouth. "As if it's so easy to get rid of with a simple rag and water."

"You could use your glowy magic," I suggested.

He gasped, scandalized. "How dare you?"

I backed away at his vehemence, confused. "How dare I what?"

"Hobs never use their magic to clean," Henry explained.

"Because it degrades the value of our work!" Wallace declared.

"How?" I asked.

"No one knows but them," Henry said dryly.

Wallace's face mottled red. "Because we take pride in our duty! Would you have us do anything less?"

I raised my hands to placate him. "Of course not. I apologize for my ignorance."

"If you apologized every time for that," Wallace said, "we might be here all day."

I swallowed a biting reply, landing on milder sarcasm. "How about soap? Is that off limits too?"

He lifted his bulbous nose in derision. "And where am I supposed to get soap, exactly?"

Henry rolled his eyes. "You can leave the tree and go shopping whenever you want."

"Can he though?" I asked. "I thought I had to open and close the tree every day."

"Wallace has his own exit to the tree. He can come and go as he pleases."

Wallace's mouth scrunched as if sucking on a lemon. "And I do not please. I belong here, looking after Yggdrasil."

Henry sighed. "This is why hobs are such a pain. Sure, they do fantastic maintenance work, but they live by their own set of delusional rules."

"It's fine." I turned to Wallace. "You don't need to go anywhere. I can get you soap."

"Oh really?" Wallace asked skeptically.

"Really." I walked over to the wall, placing my hand on the coiled branches. They parted, revealing the round doorknob of the storage closet. I pulled it open and poked my head inside, pausing only to pat the wall so that a lantern lit the dark space.

"What do you need?" I called over my shoulder. "There are no less than seven different bottles of all-purpose detergent in here. Plus there's a mop, some bleach wipes, and a big rolling bucket. You can take your pick."

When no one answered, I glanced back over my shoulder, only to find Wallace gaping at me and Henry grinning like an idiot.

Henry held out his palm to Wallace. "I told you she'd find it."

Wallace sputtered and pulled a coin from his pocket, giving it to Henry.

Henry shook a finger at him. "That's not all of it. You owe me twice as much because she found it before the end of her first full day."

"And they say leprechauns are the money-grubbers." But Wallace coughed up another coin from his coat and slapped it into Henry's palm.

"What are you two doing?" I asked.

"Wallace lost a bet," Henry said. "He was sure you wouldn't figure out how to manipulate the tree's magical storage before the week was out. I told him that not only you would, you'd do it within the first day."

"How very mature of you," I said, grimacing.

Wallace grunted. "How did you figure it out?"

"I don't know," I shrugged. "I just did it."

"Figures," Wallace grumbled. "She doesn't even understand her magic."

"I would if someone would tell me what was going on," I retorted.

"I can give you a few pointers," Henry said. "If you haven't already noticed, the space inside Yggdrasil is much larger than it appears on the outside. That's because the tree magically manipulates space. She can store things anywhere and conjure them up wherever you ask."

"But I didn't ask for the storage closet," I admitted. "It just appeared yesterday. I thought it was just always here in the wall."

"See, she didn't summon the closet on purpose," Wallace said to Henry. "I want my wager back."

"Not so fast," Henry brushed him off, then gestured at me. "You can do it again, this time intentionally. Go ahead. Have the tree summon another space."

"I don't know," I said.

Henry focused his intense eyes on me. "You can do this."

Still not convinced but bolstered by Henry's confidence, I closed the closet door. The branches braided themselves so it became uniform with the rest of the wall. Then, I thought of how the towel closet had appeared after my shower and pressed my hand against the wall again.

The branches parted, revealing a familiar bifold plantation door. I flung it open to reveal four rows of teal towels.

Henry slow-clapped while Wallace sputtered to himself.

"Wow," I said, patting their plush surfaces. "I had no idea Iggy was capable of such magic."

Henry grinned. "Not just Yggdrasil, but you, Rose. You control all functioning aspects of the tree."

I flushed at his nickname for me. I'd come to hate "Rosie" after my relationship with Mike, but somehow "Rose" felt right coming from Henry.

"So you found some towels. Big deal," Wallace interrupted. "What I really need is supplies for the scorch marks."

"Oh, right, sorry." I quickly closed the bathroom closet and reformed the cleaning supply closet. I gave Wallace the mop, the wheeled bucket, and three different types of detergent.

"You think that will be enough?" I asked.

"Yeah, yeah," he said, waving me away, already engrossed in reading the fine print on the blue bottle.

"Best leave him to it," Henry said, heading for the doorway. "He might be at it for hours."

I made sure the storage closet disappeared back into the wall. As I turned to leave the atrium, a shimmer of light caught my eye. Glancing down at the floor, I gasped as the image of a sea sunset wavered on top of the white marble. It was a reflection of the stained glass window high above us.

"Whoa," I breathed.

Henry also whistled, glancing down at the reflection then up at its source. "That's incredible."

"You're lucky," Wallace sniffed, not even glancing up from his bottle. "The conditions have to be just right for that to appear: time of day, angle of the sun, day of the year, weather conditions . . . most people never see it."

I shook my head. "And yet you're reading a label like it's no big deal?"

He shrugged. "It's part of the tree's many wonders. You get used to it."

I stared at that beautiful image on the floor for a long while. How many other secrets did the library hold within its branches?

CHAPTER 12

I woke up on time for my second morning as the Librarian of Atlantis. I opened the front entrance and found Henry standing there at eight o'clock sharp.

"I need to explore the island," he said as way of greeting. "Close the library up until nine o'clock."

"And good morning to you too," I said sarcastically. "Why did I even bother to get up early in the first place?"

"I need some time to scout around for the best place to lay a dragon trap. If I can figure out where the beast likes to hang out, it'll increase my odds of catching her."

I raised a skeptical eyebrow. "The island is pretty big. You can't search it all."

"No, but I'm hoping to get lucky and catch a glimpse of her flying around."

I shuddered, remembering my previous encounter with Agatha. "Be careful. No matter how many of those water disks you have stashed in your pocket, I doubt they're foolproof protection against sharp claws and teeth."

Henry flashed me a mischievous grin. "Worried about me, are you?"

"Of course," I said with false sincerity. "If something happened to you, who would bring me dinner?"

"No one. You'll have to eat books."

"Guess I'll starve then."

"Or just trust that I can do my job." He vanished from view on that cocky note.

I rolled my eyes heavenward. "Who knew a bigfoot could be so arrogant?" I muttered under my breath.

"I can still hear you!" Henry snapped. "Don't call me 'bigfoot.'"

I placed my hand against the tree wall, allowing the branches to knit itself closed again. "Whatever you say . . . abominable snowman."

I only caught a snippet of his rant about the yeti being a completely different type of fae before the branches closed.

As amused as I was at getting in the last word, I worried about Henry for the next hour as I prepped for the morning's patrons. I refilled the Grimoire ink pot before finding Wallace scrubbing another section of spotless atrium floor. He'd finally taken care of the scorch mark with the extra supplies and had moved on. I gave him another bottle of cleaner, which he took without thanks but also without his usual complaints. I hoped I was growing on him a little and made a mental note to restock our cleaning supplies soon to keep him happy.

Everything was going smoothly until I found a hefty book on metallurgy left on a table by the dwarves. Memorizing the name, I trotted over to the Grimoire and wrote in the book's title.

"Sixth floor?" I groaned as I read its call number. Staring up the atrium, I imagined lugging the book up six flights of discordant stairs. "That'll take forever."

"You could just take the elevator," a voice grumbled behind me.

I twirled around, finding Wallace wiping his hands on a rag as he stood from scrubbing the floor.

My voice rose in spite of myself. "There's a freaking elevator in here?"

"Of course there is. Just use Yggdrasil's heartwood."

He pointed over my shoulder to a wide circular column placed almost in the exact center of the first floor. It wasn't directly connected to the ropey outer walls, and in fact, was a much smoother surface, having only thin bits of rough texture here and there where one could catch a splinter. It would have taken at least a dozen people holding hands with their arms stretched out wide to encompass the entire perimeter of the oddly placed column.

"That's her heartwood?" I thought back to the botany class I took in college. All the outer layers—like the bark, phloem, cambium, and xylem—carried nutrients throughout the tree. "Isn't that the dead part of the tree?"

Wallace jerked back, aghast. "Of course not! The heartwood is where Yggdrasil's consciousness lives: her mind, her emotions, her very soul. Only a human would call it 'dead.'"

"Sorry, I didn't know." I glanced at the column, frowning. "I don't see an elevator there."

"That's because you have to create it with your magic."

"You mean like the storage closet?" I asked, already assuming an affirmative response.

He made me flinch when he shook his head vehemently. "No, not like the storage closet. When you manipulate Yggdrasil's outer layers, the tree can reroute her cells so she can continue to live. Using your magic on the heartwood rearranges Yggdrasil's very essence. It is very powerful magic and can drain her very quickly."

I shied at his intensity. "Maybe I shouldn't create the elevator at all."

"Clio ran the elevator all the time. She just made sure to always revert the heartwood back to its original form as soon as possible."

"I don't know," I said slowly. "It sounds dangerous."

Wallace grunted. "Suit yourself, *temporary* librarian."

On that gloomy note, he wandered off.

I hesitated as I watched his coattails disappear into the hallway. Then I turned around to face the heartwood. My feet brought me over to the column as I contemplated whether to create the elevator or not. Tentatively, I splayed my fingers on the heartwood's smooth surface.

It was warm to the touch. As I held contact, a hum echoed inside my own brain. Unlike the normal rush of Iggy's muted emotions I felt when touching the outer walls, a more powerful wave of positive energy washed over me.

"I don't want to hurt you, Iggy," I whispered.

The humming in my brain crescendoed, a frequency that made my bones vibrate. You won't hurt me, it seemed to say.

I sucked in a breath. "Well, if you say so, then I guess it would be rude not to try."

I pressed both palms firmly onto the heartwood.

When I'd summoned the storage closet last night, the magic just happened. Touching the heartwood, though, sent pulses up and down my nervous system. The warmth emanating from the wood engulfed me, connecting me to that strange yet comforting hum.

I connected myself, body and soul, to Yggdrasil.

My thoughts flowed into hers. *Make an elevator.*

The magic spun around me, shifting inside the heartwood. I felt the tree, and therefore myself, stretching and bending to form a hollow cavity. Pulleys and weights stretched above and beneath the box. Finally, wooden doors slid open to reveal the interior.

I peeked inside before I let go of the heartwood. There wasn't a light source. I searched within Iggy and found fire thrumming deep within her roots. I tried pulling it upward, but the tree stopped me.

Lantern, she whispered.

Ah, right. I didn't want to set the actual wood on fire. I explored Iggy's willowy network until I found another empty space—another storage closet, maybe?—that had candles inside metal cages. I lifted one forward into the elevator, affixing it to the ceiling. Only then did Iggy allow me to draw on her fire magic and light the wick.

I let go of the heartwood, losing that deep connection to Yggdrasil. I was surprised to find sweat covering my brow. I hadn't thought I'd been exerting myself, but now that I'd returned to normal, I felt like I'd run a mile.

And my elevator was pretty crude too, just a wooden box large enough for maybe two people to stand in. A dungeon-like lantern cast a single, flickering flame into the gloom.

I gulped. It certainly didn't look very stable.

But I could still feel tendrils of Iggy tugging at my mind, encouraging me to test my work.

"Well," I gulped. "You only live once." I grabbed the heavy metallurgy book off a nearby table and stepped inside. "And maybe not for very long."

The doors shut slowly behind me, as if giving me time to escape. I was crammed on all sides under the dim light. There were no buttons to push.

"Sixth floor?" I asked, unsure of myself.

The elevator creaked upward. There was no indication of how far or how fast we were going. The box wobbled from side to side. I held my free hand to the wall for balance, even though there wasn't really room to fall.

After what seemed like an eternity, the elevator slammed to a halt. The wooden doors made a squeaky noise as they opened.

I stepped onto the solid ground of the sixth floor.

"Whoa," I breathed, glancing through the colorful rays of the stained glass sunset window, now at eye level beyond the railing.

There was definitely room for comfort improvements, but we'd made it to the top floor.

"What do you think, Iggy?" I asked. "Was that a success?"

A branch pulled off the outer wall and waved at me. I considered that a "yes."

After dropping the metallurgy book on a nearby table, I placed shaky hands back on the heartwood. I knew I had to disassemble the elevator quickly. As Iggy's internal hum overwhelmed my senses, I slowly moved all the materials I'd used to make the elevator back throughout the tree. It took a lot less effort than pulling it all together, as if the tree knew where everything should go.

When I finally finished dismantling the elevator, I collapsed onto a plush chair. I was tired, true, but also in awe. I'd just unlocked another piece of my magic.

CHAPTER 13

H ENRY WAS WAITING OUTSIDE a little before 9 a.m. when I reopened the front door for library patrons.

"Done with dragon hunting already?" I asked.

"There's no sign of the varmint anywhere nearby."

"Did you try near the courtyard with the fairy rings? I've seen her there twice now: yesterday and the first day I found Atlantis."

"Those fairy rings all connect to the Northern and Southern Court. I'd rather not put anyone at risk by laying a trap there."

"Maybe you need some bait then." I hesitated before stating the obvious. "Agatha clearly seems attracted to me. Perhaps I could—"

"Don't you dare finish that sentence," Henry said, his muscles tensing. "It's not going to happen."

"But if it will help capture the dragon—"

"No," Henry snapped.

I grew angry at his stubbornness. "Fine. Don't listen to my ideas. I'm sorry I even worried about you this morning."

Henry broke out into a grin. "Did you now?"

A group of people were coming down the path toward the moat, so I ignored his question. They were all Klaus's dwarves, about the same number as yesterday and still wearing wool sweaters that made me feel hot just looking at them. They chattered amongst themselves as they marched toward us. Words floated over to us in a foreign language. I didn't think anything of it until they crossed the moat and suddenly, I caught snippets of English conversations.

The confusion must have shown on my face because Henry asked, "Is something wrong?"

"Is it common for the fae to speak two different languages simultaneously?"

The tension left his shoulders. "No, they're only speaking one language, Dwarvish. You're only understanding them because Yggdrasil is translating."

My eyes widened. "She does that for me?"

"She does that for everyone. It's part of her magic and one of the reasons the Library of Atlantis is so beloved. It's one of the few places outside of the Courts where all fae can gather and be universally understood, no matter what language barriers lie between them."

I shook my head in awe. "Is there anything Iggy can't do?"

Henry scanned the crowd and scowled. "She can't keep out the riffraff."

A fae in a gold-trimmed green tunic straggled behind Klaus's dwarves. Egan. He tried to stand on his tiptoes and peer above the heads of the crowd but couldn't see much at roughly the

141

same height. He was clearly searching for someone, probably me.

I wanted to run back into the library and hide behind a shelf, but I chastised myself for my cowardice. Straightening my shoulders, I called out to him.

"Good morning, Egan!"

He immediately turned in my direction and made a beeline toward us, breaking away from the dwarves.

Henry folded his arms across his chest. "Why'd you have to summon him?"

"It's my job to help patrons."

"At your discretion. You might not be able to ban Krampus's stooge from the library, but you certainly don't have to encourage him either."

Just to provoke Henry, I gave Egan a deep bow as he approached. "It's good to see you, Egan."

Henry snorted in derision.

Egan didn't even act like he was there. "Ms. Baldwin." Egan inclined his head forward, leaning on his cane. "Forgive me for not greeting you properly, but my leg's acting up today."

"No apologies needed. Can I help you with anything?"

"Perhaps." He shuffled from side to side. It was hard to tell if it was physical or emotional discomfort. "I came here at Lord Krampus's request."

"Always a good lap dog, eh?" Henry asked.

Egan finally noticed him, frowning.

"Ignore him," I told Egan. "He's always grouchy. It's a sasquatch thing."

"What do you know about different types of fae?" Henry argued in exasperation. "You've known the fae existed for three whole days."

"And yet it feels like a lifetime." I offered my arm to Egan. "May I escort you inside?"

He eagerly accepted my arm. "Thank you for your generosity."

Henry looked irritated, but he didn't follow as I guided Egan inside the hallway.

The dwarves had already scurried ahead into the stacks, leaving the two of us alone as we made leisurely progress behind them. "What brings you to the Library of Atlantis?"

"You mentioned there might be resources within the main library that could help with my condition. Lord Krampus is convinced I'm wasting my time, but I'm willing to try anything to help ease my pain."

"I'm happy to do what I can, although I warn you, this isn't a hospital."

"I've already tried every healer imaginable. They cannot help. I have a scirrhous that cannot be cured, either by magical or technological means."

A cold rush went through me. "Scirrhous" was an old-fashioned term that represented a very real modern threat: Cancer.

I'd inadvertently stopped in my tracks. Egan peered at me in concern. "Are you all right, Ms. Baldwin?"

"Yes," I said, resuming our steps. "It's just someone dear to me had the same ailment."

"I'm sorry to hear that. This disease is very slowly and painfully killing me."

I patted his hand. "I'm so sorry."

He laid his fingers over my own. "You are a kind person. I can sense it."

I gave him a forced smile. I didn't feel so kind, especially given how I'd treated Krampus yesterday. I had to remind myself that he'd deserved it with his disdainful attitude.

But nobody deserved cancer. Not even my worst enemy.

Once inside the main library, I pointed at the Grimoire. "Perhaps we can start there?"

It was a challenge making it up the Grimoire stairs, even with Egan supported by his cane and my arm. He winced and rubbed his thigh but otherwise kept on a stoic face. He reminded me so much of my dad during his chemotherapy treatments that my heart literally ached.

Egan didn't need my support once he could lean on the Grimoire's pedestal. I held his cane as he wrote *magical scirrhous of the leg* in scrawling cursive. The page absorbed his words and came back with two entries written in black ink, although a third returned in that curious red ink with a -1 call number.

"I can fetch these first two for you," I said, "but I'm afraid I'm not sure what to do about the last one."

Egan lifted a brow. "The red ink indicates the Forbidden Tomes down in the library's catacombs, Ms. Baldwin."

"Oh," I said lamely, feeling incompetent for not knowing that. I read the words in red ink. *The Taboo Magic of Disease Management.* "Given the title, I can understand why."

"That particular tome has been restricted for those who seek immortality through illicit magical means," Egan said, "but it is also rumored to have cures for ailments such as mine. That's why Krampus wants access to the Forbidden Tomes: to see for himself if there is a way to save me."

Egan's explanation made sense, but I also didn't trust Krampus farther than I could throw him. "We have two other resources to try first. Why don't you wait somewhere comfortable while I go retrieve them?"

"Okay." Before I could stop him, he reached forward and ripped the paper with the call numbers free.

I gasped. "What are you doing?"

He frowned in confusion. "Giving you the call numbers."

"But you just tore this from the Grimoire!"

"Ah," he said, understanding lighting his eyes. "You're not used to this kind of magic. The Grimoire is a self-repairing book. It doesn't matter how many times you write in it or how many pages you rip out, it will always produce more blank pages."

"Oh. I didn't know."

He sniffed. "Yes, I know."

Embarrassment flushed across my face. I shouldn't have been expecting comfort from someone in pain. I escorted Egan down the pedestal stairs to a comfortable armchair on the first floor. Then I ascended all the way up to the fourth floor to retrieve the two books from the ripped Grimoire page. I considered creating the elevator again, but knew it would take as much out of me as climbing the stairs, so I spared Iggy the effort. By the time I made it back to Egan with his materials, he was in slightly better spirits.

"Thank you," he said as I handed him the two handwritten journals on fae medicine. "If you have a bit more time, I wouldn't mind your help riffling through—"

"Librarian," a dwarf called out, startling us both. He waved me toward a group of dwarves huddled around a nearby table. "Got a minute?"

I hesitated between both requests. "I, uh . . ."

Egan waved me away. "It's all right. Go help the other patrons first. I'll tackle this research on my own."

I intended to fulfill the dwarves' request quickly and return to Egan but became too swamped. Klaus's endorsement yesterday must have made an impact on his engineers because they had all sorts of tasks for me. I ended up scouring for books, scrolls, and pamphlets throughout all six floors of the library and bringing them back to various clumps of dwarves. They were scattered all throughout the library, and their projects were fascinating. One group held a rowdy debate on how to make the best rocking horse for a boy with only one arm while another sketched out designs for phonetic baby blocks in Korean. It was a delight to watch them work.

The only group of dwarves that remained standoffish was the group led by the red-bearded dwarf. Most of them were older and sterner, and whenever I approached their table, they'd huddle in and pretend I wasn't there. Only the younger female dwarf with the same color of red hair would occasionally look my way.

At one point, I managed to corner her as she retrieved some scrolls from a shelf. "Can I help you find anything else?"

She hadn't seen me coming, so she jumped. Then she twirled around, clutching the rolled paper to her chest. She whispered something so unintelligible.

I leaned my ear toward her. "Come again?"

"No," she said, this time loud enough so I could hear but just barely.

I didn't want to scare her further, so I gave a deep bow. "Well, if you change your mind, my name's Rosalind."

I'd turned to leave her be, so her next statement startled me.

"I'm Cindy," she said, bowing in respect. "Daughter of Master Forger Brock."

Now their similar hair color made sense. I opened my mouth to attempt some light conversation.

"Cindy!" the red-bearded dwarf had glanced up from his discussion with the other dwarves and did not look happy to see me. "Stop wasting time and get back over here!"

"Yes, Father," she called. She gave me a sympathetic shrug then scurried off to give the group the scroll.

I didn't have a lot of time for disappointment. The dwarves began packing up for the day not long after that.

I remembered Egan and went to check on him. "I'm sorry that took so long. Can I help you with anything else?"

"No," he said, thin-lipped and irritated. "I best be off too."

"I take it the books didn't help."

"They only offered treatments I've tried before. Perhaps, if I tried something new . . ."

"You can try another search in the Grimoire," I said, hope-fully. "Maybe with a different keyword."

"Perhaps tomorrow." He appeared eager to leave with the dwarves, so I lent him my arm so he could keep up.

Henry wouldn't allow me to escort Egan past the entrance. I considered arguing with him but then remembered how the dragon had attacked me. Still, I felt horrible for Egan as he struggled back up the hill.

"Poor guy," I said.

Henry shook his head at me. "You can't trust anyone under Krampus's thumb."

I glared at him. "He's got a terminal illness, unless you think he's faking it."

"That doesn't mean he's above suspicion."

"What made you so jaded?"

"Being put on way too many assignments just like this. The fae are good at hiding their true intentions."

"Oh yeah," I retorted. "And what are you hiding?"

"Nothing. I'm a simple creature. I'm doing my job."

"Then butt out and let me do mine," I flung back at him. He didn't bother to answer as I stalked back into the building. I couldn't decide who irritated me more: Henry for being so suspicious, or me for allowing him to get under my skin.

CHAPTER 14

Aᶠᵀᴇᴿ ᴀ ǫᴜɪᴄᴋ ʟᴜɴᴄʜ, I hoped to have a quiet afternoon to myself, much like I had the day before. Unfortunately, fate had other plans in the form of a new batch of patrons.

I should have known things would get difficult given Wallace's reaction to their arrival. I had just settled down at the Grimoire, inked quill in hand, while the hob polished the pedestal with a rag, attacking some blemish in the fluting only he could see.

Tittered laughter caught our attention. A trio of fae waltzed into the atrium, their gorgeous butterfly wings sprouting in splashes of brights colors: one golden, one cerulean, and one emerald. Although they were human-sized, their proportions were off: their bright eyes too big, the dainty slippers on their tiny feet too small. Those feet barely touched the ground as they seemed to half-float, despite their wings only beating at a languid pace. They each wore extravagant ballgowns with multiple layers of skirts and sleeves. Sparkling dots like fireflies danced around their cascading locks of varying shades of rich brown.

I had never seen anything both so simultaneously gorgeous and gaudy in my entire life.

Wallace gasped and jumped to his feet. He threw his rag into the rolling bucket, which he'd taken to carting around like a security blanket.

"What's gotten into you?" I asked.

"Fairy courtesans." His hands glowed as he attempted to maneuver the bucket in a wide path around the newcomers while simultaneously heading for the door.

I glanced over at the trio, who were laughing like children on a playground. "Are they going to be a problem?"

"Not my problem." By then Wallace was so far out of earshot that I'd have to raise my voice to continue the conversation.

Despite his best efforts, the fairies finally noticed the hob and zipped alarmingly fast toward him, wings beating like hummingbirds to make speed. Wallace threw up his hands and cried out as they swarmed him.

I jogged down the pedestal steps, afraid the hob was in trouble, but the fairies only covered him with kisses. They patted his shiny bald spot, hugged him, and cooed as if they'd snagged a baby kitten.

"Cute little hob!" one cried.

"Love your coat."

"Aren't you adorable?"

I hid my mouth behind my hand as Wallace drowned under their affection.

"Ladies, please." Wallace squirmed. "I have work to do."

"Ah, no fair!"

"You're always too busy."

"You should stay with us!"

Wallace finally managed to break free. "I really must be going, but you can talk to *her* if you need anything."

I froze as three sets of doting eyes pinned on me.

"Is that the new librarian?"

"She's so pretty!"

"I can't wait to say 'Hi!'"

They launched themselves at me. I barely had time to brace myself as the trio hit me full force with their pats, pets, and praise.

"She *is* human, just like we heard."

"How delightfully foreign!"

"Like a miniature version of Clio."

"That's right," I said, trying to get a word in edgewise. "I'm Clio's granddaughter."

"Then you're a muse!"

"A fae like us."

"But with a tantalizing human past!"

I pulled out of their grasp and watched Wallace's coattails vanish through the door. Coward. I would get him for this.

"My name's Rosalind Baldwin," I said, using the very narrow space between us to bow.

My gesture seemed to switch a button inside the fairies. They all backed away and lined up in a neat row, each one bowing in turn as they introduced themselves.

"I'm Twinkle," the golden one said.

"Twitter," said the one with emerald wings.

"And Twilight," the cerulean one added.

They all took a deep bow and then cocked their heads at me, expectantly.

"Nice to meet you," I said, praying that they would never ask me to match their names with the individual fairy.

Iggy sensed my panic and sent a soothing calm over me. It was the tree-equivalent of "Don't worry. You've got this."

I slapped on my most polite smile. "What brings the three of you to the library?"

"Jack Frost's coronation, of course."

"It's the event of the decade."

"No, the century."

And then they yelled in unison, "And we have nothing to wear!"

I stared at their attire. "But the gowns you're wearing are so wonderful."

Moisture gathered at the rims of their enormous eyes.

"This old thing?"

"It will never do!"

"We need something new!"

They burst into tears.

I held up my hands in what I hoped was a placating gesture. Or surrender. Whichever one would get them to quit crying.

"Ladies, it's okay. This is the Library of Atlantis. I'm sure it can help you."

Their waterworks dried up instantly. "Thank you, librarian!" they said simultaneously.

They attached themselves to me: one on my right arm, one on my left, and the last one hovering between my shoulder blades. It made navigating the steps up to the Grimoire difficult.

I spent the next two hours in a crazy blur of search requests, cries of adoration, and flapping butterfly wings. The three fairies had specific ideas about designs and how they wanted their new dresses embellished with magic. I fetched scrolls and books, then had to relocate them several times because the trio always stayed together but never in one spot. They oohed and aahed over certain tomes, wrinkled their nose at others, and once even threw a particularly "offensive" book over the fifth-floor guard rail. Iggy caught it via branch before it got damaged. I almost tossed the whole lot of them out, but Iggy's gentle encouragement convinced me it was okay.

By the time the fairies had jotted down ideas and declared themselves satisfied, I wanted to weep myself. Instead, I trailed dutifully between them, enduring their exclamations of thanks and goodwill as I led them firmly toward the front entrance. Once outside, they flew ahead and did a gorgeous dance in the air, proclaiming me the best librarian in the world before zipping off like birds into the forest.

I didn't even notice Henry standing guard at the entrance until he asked, "So what do you think of fairies?"

All my pent-up emotions came out in a rush. "They're outrageous! Loud! Obnoxious! I've never met such a ridiculous bunch in my entire life!"

Henry grinned. "And you only met a fourth of their family. They're part of the Twelfth fairies, one of several fairy clans with high rank in Court."

I nearly fell to my knees. "There are *twelve* of them?"

Henry dissolved into full laughter then.

I tried to pat my hair down where one of the fairies had frizzed it up while petting me. That only made Henry bend over with harder laughter.

"Yuck it up, Chuckles," I spat at him. I tried to storm past him back into the library.

He caught me by the arm, his grip strong. "Sorry," he said, wiping away tears. "It's . . . whew . . ."

"Yeah, I know," I yanked my arm out of his hold. "It's hilarious watching the idiot human flail in the presence of flighty fairies. What's the big deal about this coronation anyway, that they feel the need to have extra special clothes?"

"Queen Mab's son, Jack Frost, is officially taking over ruling duties in the Southern Court."

"He's replacing Queen Mab?"

"Not exactly. She's still in charge. He'll just handle the lesser Court issues, which he's already been doing for a while anyway."

I harrumphed. "It doesn't sound like a big deal to me."

Henry's expression turned deadly serious. "It definitely is. Jack's sister, and Queen Mab's other child, Carabosse, used to rule the Southern Court. It had been that way for decades until Carabosse betrayed Queen Mab and tried to have her overthrown."

"That sounds bad."

"Catastrophically so. Morale among the fae has been low and fractured at best. Most of us are hoping that officially putting Jack Frost in charge of the Southern Court will squash some rifts that Carabosse's betrayal created, but there will always be loyalists that will see him as an interloper."

"More fae politics, huh?"

"You'll have to get used to it, if you're going to become the librarian."

"Like I'll have to get used to fairies with no sense of personal boundaries?"

Henry's lips twitched. "No one has an easy time dealing with fairies, not even Queen Mab. They're incredibly powerful magical beings but also extremely emotional. You actually did a fantastic job keeping them in check."

"Yeah, well," I said, not sure how to deal with his praise. "It didn't feel so fantastic, not when I almost smacked Twinkle or Twerp or whatever-her-name-was for throwing a book off the fifth floor."

"Tw-twerp?" Henry sputtered.

"Or Twat, if you prefer."

Henry started snickering again. "Please . . . stop."

I couldn't help it. A giggle escaped me. "You should have seen Wallace run."

"Fast?"

"Like Krampus might catch him and eat him."

This triggered Henry again, and soon we were both laughing so hard, we could barely breathe.

CHAPTER 15

H ENRY LEFT NOT LONG after that, running back to the
Stronghold office to grab food. He instructed me to
close the library behind him and reopen it again at 5. Since I was
hungry, I made a mental note not to be late.

I returned to the library, finding Wallace's butt sticking out
of the first-floor fireplace as he cleaned the hearth inside.

"Thanks for having my back there with the fairies," I said
with heavy sarcasm.

He scooted out to sniffle at me. "You're the one who's supposed to deal with patrons, not me."

"You could have at least warned me what they'd be like."

"I believe that experience is the best teacher."

"Do you also believe in scrubbing places that are already
clean?" I asked, pointing to the already spotless stones of the
fireplace. "That thing doesn't look like it's been lit in ages."

Wallace's face suddenly twisted in anger. "That's because it
hasn't, thanks to you." He slammed his rag into the bucket.

"Whoa." I'd clearly touched a nerve. "Are you saying I'm
supposed to be lighting a fire in there?"

He pointed a long fingernail at me. "You're in charge of lighting all the fixtures inside the library every day."

"And I do," I argued. "I switch on the hallway lights as soon as the patrons start coming in. I also light key areas when the sun goes down."

"But you *don't* light this fireplace when the dwarves are here," he said with a "gotcha" voice. "Haven't you noticed they never take off their sweaters?"

"I thought they just liked wearing them."

"They're cold," he snapped. "Dwarves need a lot of heat to keep them warm. Clio always lit the fireplace so they'd be comfortable in the library."

I threw my hands up. "Well, I'll start doing that too, now that you've told me. I'm not a mind reader."

"Clearly." He gathered his bucket and rags and began shuffling off.

"Is there anything else I should be doing?" I asked his back.

He paused, grumbling something I couldn't hear since he wouldn't turn around.

I folded my arms over my chest. "You can complain all you want, but I can't fix things that I don't know need fixing."

He flipped around. "There's also the issue of my burrow."

I frowned. "Your burrow?"

"Yes," he said as if explaining to a child. "My burrow. Where I live inside the tree."

I wracked my brain, but for the life of me, I couldn't think of where Wallace's burrow was inside Yggdrasil. "Okay then, lead me to your burrow, and I'll help you."

He stared at me in shock. "You can't go down there. That's my home."

"Then how am I supposed to fix it?"

Wallace huffed. "I knew this was a waste of time." He began storming off again.

"Wallace," I called after him. "Please don't go. I want to help."

I thought he would ignore me, but he finally slowed in his tracks.

I didn't waste my opportunity. "I'm new at all this. I'm sorry if I'm not getting everything right. Help me understand better so I can help you."

Wallace let out a long-suffering sigh as he faced me once again. "You're like a newborn babe, aren't you?"

"The good thing about babies is they can grow and learn. They just need the right people to guide them."

Wallace tilted his head. "That's true."

He didn't say anything for a long while. I simply stood there, waiting for him to make up his mind.

He finally did. "My burrow is a lot like Clio's apartment. She set it up so only I can create the tunnel that leads down into it. She even insisted on making an exit outside of the tree, although why I would leave Yggdrasil is beyond me." He shuddered.

"I take it that hobs only leave their homes under extreme conditions."

He glared at me. "Like when a stranger brings a fire-breathing dragon inside."

"And I'm very grateful you did leave and got Henry," I said smoothly. "Thank you."

"Yes, well." Wallace actually preened a little. "I suppose it was a nice thing to do."

I held back a smile. "Let me return the favor. What's the problem with your burrow?"

"You haven't been lighting the fixtures or the fireplace. I've been having to borrow a lantern and take it down with me every night. It's very dark down there. And don't even get me started on the plumbing."

"The plumbing?" I asked, growing more bewildered by the second.

"My water tank is running dangerously low," he growled. "I've been rationing drinking water for almost a week now, but soon even that will be gone. You should replenish it."

"I didn't even know the water inside the tree needed to be replenished. It always just arrives in Clio's apartment."

"Of course, it does there," he snapped. "All you have to do is think about fire or water, and it appears for you. That's what the librarian does."

"But how am I supposed to light your fireplace or fill your water tank if I can't enter your burrow?"

"You can change things without seeing them, you silly chit. How else did you open your linen closet inside the library?"

He had me there. I did have knack for making things happen inside Iggy. "So I just touch the tree and ask for it to happen?"

"How should I know?" Wallace countered. "I don't have muse magic. You have to figure that out on your own."

I bit back a retort. Being sarcastic would only put us back at square one. "Okay, I'll see what I can do."

I marched over to the nearest wall, acting more confident than I felt. Wallace watched with skepticism as I thrust my palm over a bunch of ropey branches. They immediately shifted at my touch.

"Iggy," I whispered. "Can you light the lanterns and fireplace in Wallace's burrow and refill his water tank?"

A wave of assurance washed over me. Then my fingertips tingled. I don't know how, but somewhere far below me, within the roots of the tree, things began to shift. A sizzle of fire flashed in my mind, followed by a surge of water running through the tree's trunk, pooling in the same area. I waited until the last trickle died down and I couldn't feel anything else.

"There," I said to Wallace. "I think that did it."

"I'll believe it when I see it," he said. "And now, if you excuse me, I'm retiring for the evening." He left me with the slightest tilt of his head.

I thought about saying something about his "gratitude," but it hit me that Wallace had never bowed to me before. That head tilt had to be a sign that things between us were improving, if only a little. I had to take any victories I could get, no matter how small.

⇒⟫⟩ ⟨⟪⇐

Henry came back right on time, but he didn't only bring back pizza for dinner. He also had Melissa in tow, wearing an oversized purse and carrying the cardboard delivery box.

"Hi," I said in surprise. "Is something wrong?"

"Only if you don't like pepperoni," Melissa replied. "Henry never bothered to ask what toppings you preferred."

"Everybody likes pepperoni," Henry stated.

"Not everyone does," I said, just to be contradictory.

Melissa's brow furrowed. "Will you eat cheese pizza? We can pick the pepperoni bits off and—"

"No," I said. "Pepperoni's fine."

"See?" Henry said, a smug smile on his face.

"Where can I take these?" she asked. "I'd love to have a chat in private, just you and me."

I ushered her toward the hallway where I could generate the stairs leading up to the apartment. Henry made Melissa give him two slices before he took his position back at the entrance of the library. I tried to take the awkward-sized pizza box, but Melissa refused, so she had to navigate it upward. I noticed she didn't breathe as heavy as I did during our climb, even though we were the same age.

Ugh. Maybe I needed to start an exercise routine or something. Why couldn't reading be a form of cardio?

When we breached the boughs and became surrounded in a maze of greenery, Melissa let out a gasp. "It's beautiful up here."

"But cramped," I said, noting how she had to angle the box so it would fit through the door. "We're almost through."

We entered the apartment's kitchen, the west-facing window bathing the room in soft orange light as the sun set behind the rim. Melissa chuckled at the floral wallpaper.

"The place needs an update," I said.

"Actually, I think it has a lot of charm." She opened the box, and the smell of melted cheese filled the room.

"Would you like a drink?" I asked. "I've got tap water, some milk if you can believe it, or I could boil water for tea."

"I'll pass. I brought my own beverage for the occasion." She reached into her purse and withdrew a travel mug with the lid tightly shut.

"You brought coffee with you? To dinner?"

"It's actually early afternoon in Oregon right now. And besides, there's always time for coffee, especially when you're busting to meet a work deadline."

I noticed how tired her eyes looked. "More magical job positions to fill?"

"Sort of. You've probably been hearing people talking about Jack Frost's coronation."

"Henry filled me in on a few details about how Queen Mab's daughter betrayed her, and now her son Jack Frost is taking her place. It sounds pretty stressful."

"That's an understatement. Jack's been dodging assassination attempts over the last few weeks."

"Oh wow! That's terrible."

"It is, but Gabriel believes it will stop once he's coronated. He's already quite popular with the Southern Court for being fair and just, but there are some who don't want him to assume power."

"What does that have to do with you?"

"Stronghold is providing Jack Frost a security detail 24-7. We've put our top people on it. In fact, if you hadn't shown up when you did, that's where Henry would be right now."

"No wonder he's so grumpy. He's watching over a helpless little librarian instead of guarding a fae prince."

Melissa laughed. "Henry's always grumpy. You shouldn't take him so seriously." She plopped down at the dining table, gesturing for me to do the same.

I hesitated. "If everyone at Stronghold is so busy, I'm not sure why you're here."

"To check up on you, of course." She took a quick swig of her coffee. "How are things going?"

"They're going," I hedged, taking a seat across from her.

"Having any issues with your patrons?"

"Some."

"Care to expound?"

"Not really."

She cocked her head at me. "This would go a lot better if you'd open up a little."

"I appreciate you were also introduced to the fae in a weird way, but you don't understand. You don't have magical powers like I do."

She grinned at me over her travel mug. "You might be surprised."

I balked. "You have powers?"

"I'll show you." She leaned forward, opening her palm out to me. "Light my hand on fire."

"What?" I demanded.

163

"Light my hand on fire. You control all the lanterns around the library. Pretend that I'm a candle and light me up."

"I don't want to hurt you . . ."

"You won't. I promise."

"Okay." I leaned over to touch the wall, connecting directly with Iggy. I cautioned myself, thinking that if I started to burn Melissa, I could put her out quickly. Then I concentrated on lighting a fire in her hand.

Nothing happened.

I pushed a little harder. Still nothing. Melissa merely sat there, stoic. I attempted again, imagining lighting up her hand the way I could a fireplace, setting everything ablaze in a burst of flame.

I might as well have been wishing for the sky to fall.

Melissa stood and walked toward the stove. "My magic has two facets. One is that I'm not normally affected by direct magic, not unless I allow it to affect me. It's called void magic."

"And the second?" I asked as she bent over the burners.

"I can also absorb magic and redirect it."

The burner next to her hand sparked to life. Iggy sent me a wave of alarm at having fire not under her control inside the apartment.

"Iggy doesn't like that."

"Sorry," Melissa said, dousing the flames.

I stared at her, mind still reeling. "I thought you were human."

She sat in her seat. "I am, but like you, I have fae ancestry in my blood. Magic runs in my family. My daughter can control other people with her mind, and my mother used to be able to teleport short distances. The point is, some humans do have magical powers."

I lifted my hands up in defeat. "Okay, you win. I get it. Between your magical gifts and what you told me about the whole ancient prophecy thing with your daughter, you might be able to relate to my magical librarian destiny."

I gave Melissa a summary of my last few days: the frightening encounter with Krampus and Agatha's attack, followed by the more inspirational Klaus. I told her how I'd learned to access Iggy's heartwood, and how I could move closets around at will. I even gave an exasperated recount of the Court fairies, which made Melissa laugh.

"Sounds like you're really getting into the swing of things here," she said.

"Maybe, but I also feel really out of my depth."

"You're not going to master your muse magic all in one day. I'd say things are progressing quite well."

"But I only have a few more days to decide whether to stay or not, right?"

"Well, yeah," Melissa admitted, "but I'm sure it's enough time."

"What if I can't? What if I decide to leave, but then change my mind later?"

Melissa shifted uncomfortably. "You won't be allowed to come back. Gabriel already had to pull some strings to secure this unusual trial period. There's no way Queen Mab would let you return if you quit."

165

I groaned. "But you've seen my employment history. I tend to bounce around from job to job."

"I have a hunch you won't quit this one."

"Why?" I demanded as she took another sip of coffee.

"Because of how you described your first couple of days. You're getting into the swing of things."

"Did you not hear about my run-in with Krampus?"

"There will be challenges, but you're rising to them. I can hear in your voice how much you're enjoying helping others, even the fairies. As corny as it sounds, being the librarian almost seems like your calling in life. What would you do if you quit?"

I didn't dare tell her I'd asked myself that same question multiple times. "It's too much to decide in a week."

"Unfortunately, it's the best we can give you." Melissa stood, adjusting her now unburdened purse over her shoulder. "You're welcome to drop by Stronghold if you'd like to talk to me again. Sometimes it's nice to chat with someone who understands what you're going through."

"Thanks," I said, still sounding forlorn.

She flashed me a sympathetic look. "I'm sure everything will work out just the way it should."

"I wish I had your faith."

"All you have to do is believe in yourself." Then she saw herself down the stairs.

CHAPTER 16

I STARTLED MYSELF AWAKE again in the middle of the night.

"Why?" I asked my stupid body. "I'm so tired, I can barely keep my eyes open."

But no, my mind disagreed. I still had to make a decision on whether to stay as the librarian or not. I couldn't stop thinking about it. Even in my dreams, I ran through all the pros and cons. I wasn't good enough. I had nothing better to do. I enjoyed the work. But would I enjoy it forever? I didn't understand the fae at all. I was fascinated by them, though. I craved to learn more.

I kicked off the covers. I definitely wouldn't be falling asleep anytime soon.

I made myself a cup of tea in the kitchen, using the next-to-last bag in the box. I took a quiet moment to appreciate how surreal this whole experience was. Growing up in rural Oregon, I'd imagined what the big, wide world could offer me. I left as soon as I graduated from high school and searched for my passion with earnest. Over countless cities and just as many jobs, I yearned to discover my true calling.

Of course, adulthood has a way of jading us into eventually coming to the conclusion that such pursuits are foolish. Despite dating so many men who unlocked their own dreams, I never could find mine.

Yet here, surrounded by the comforting presence of this ash tree, my heart stirred like a kid again. Not only was there a lifetime's worth of knowledge to master, a prospect that made my heart dance, but only I had the power to keep the Library of Atlantis open. I was important for a change, someone others depended on, and in a capacity that made me irreplaceable.

It still didn't feel real. At any moment, I expected the shimmer of novelty to fade away and pop this intriguing little bubble. But being the Librarian of Atlantis was forever.

"How will I ever know for sure?" I asked as I finished the last swallow of tepid tea.

I wished I could talk to someone about this all, like my dad. Or maybe my mom. She'd grown up in this crazy place. But then again, she'd also rejected this life. That alone should have given me pause.

Except, my mom and I had been different in so many ways. I'd always been much more outgoing, where she'd been like my dad, introverted and quiet. I remembered being envious of the girls whose parents let them get involved in a bunch of activities: Girl Scouts, soccer, and all the after-school clubs. My mom had refused to let me join, saying our family didn't have time with both parents working. But I knew, deep down, she'd rather I explored the nearby woods than hang out too much with the other kids. She'd been much more upset than Dad when I decided to go to a public university in California straight out of high school, rather than sticking around at the local community college.

Then she'd died not long afterward, and it had taken me years of therapy to get over the guilt.

Talking to my parents was out of the question, but I had Jason. Maybe I could reach him before making this momentous decision. I even tried booting up my cell phone again to call him, but it could never find a signal.

I had to figure this out on my own.

Stir crazy, I crept back to the master bedroom. It still felt strange to be in Clio's room, this grandmother I never met but who clearly had tastes similar to mine. I imagined her grabbing a book on her shelf for some light reading before bedtime, either learning something new or perusing familiar paragraphs.

But the only book I wanted tonight was the photo album of my mother's childhood. The pages would never answer all my questions about what had happened between Clio and my mother, but it gave me that small peek to their past.

I cracked it open, arbitrarily landing on a page where my mother wore diapers and nothing else, toddling around the library. She had one hand on the wall to support her chubby, wobbling legs. I smiled at the dimples around her knees. Babies, even ones in old black-and-white photos, were so stinking cute.

I was about to flip the page when something written above my mother caught my eye. In the smooth wooden surface, a faint "-1" glowed above her.

I thought at first that maybe the radiance was a blemish of the picture itself. But unlike the older color photographs—which displayed more blurry, muted edges—this monochrome photo was crisp. The glow didn't appear to be a random artifact of film development.

I stared at the picture, trying to place it within the library itself. It offered few clues other than the wall, my mother, and a shelf of nearby books too far away to discern any specifics. But examining the wall did give away one important detail.

Baby Sophia was leaning against Iggy's heartwood.

I brought up the album close to my nose to get a better view. I had to squint, but there, etched into the wall, I could barely make out the outline of what appeared to be a door inlaid into the wood.

The heartwood had been converted into an elevator.

Giving the photograph one last long glance, I noticed one final odd detail. The floor was obviously some kind of rougher cobblestone, the surface bumpy and uneven in places. It was probably the reason why little Sophia had to hold onto the wall for support. I'd never seen anything like it within the main library.

My mind raced. If that number represented what floor the elevator was on, and the Grimoire had accurate listings, that meant the elevator was probably in the catacombs with the For-bidden Tomes. Clio had likely used Iggy's heartwood to create an elevator to get there.

I couldn't contain my excitement. I shoved the photo al-bum back on the shelf and ran out of the apartment. I made it halfway down the stairs before I realized I was only wearing a T-shirt and underwear, my normal bedtime attire. Even though Wallace was the only other person inside the tree, I dashed back upstairs to throw on some pants and a bra.

As I hit the main hallway, I lit up a row of lights to illuminate my way. The tall windows of the atrium let in streams of pale moonlight, but I lit more sconces to illuminate the path toward the heartwood, located among the stacks.

I pressed both hands into the smooth column, Iggy's warmth flowing directly into me. It was like putting your ear to a conch shell, that spine-tingling sensation of hearing the ocean come roaring back, although not in my ears but throughout my entire nervous system.

Iggy, I thought. *Let's make an elevator.*

The tree stretched itself, causing me to gasp with physical exertion. Like before, a humming vibrated through me as Yggdrasil and I formed the hollow box that would take me down to the catacombs. As the wires and coils stretched taut above the enclosure, I remembered to grab a lantern. I also pulled in some thin discs of metal I found somewhere inside the tree and inserted them near the doors.

When the elevator opened, a comforting flame beckoned me forward. Wiping my brow, I stepped inside and saw the floor numbers I'd created.

I pressed the circular -1 button.

The door creaked closed, and instead of going up from the first floor, the box sunk downward as if being swallowed by quicksand. Although the last ride hadn't been exactly smooth, this hitch felt even jankier, the box itself shivering as if it didn't want to go where I'd asked it to.

The first stab of real fear went through me. I'd been so wrapped up in discovering the library's catacombs, I'd never considered whether I should even go down there or not.

My concern only grew when the elevator finally stopped and the doors whined as they reopened. The entire place was thrown into pitch darkness, only a swatch of uneven cobblestones visible from the elevator's lantern. I had the unsettling thought that it could swallow me whole and leave no trace of me behind.

"Maybe this isn't such a good idea," I whispered.

But Iggy sent a blast of comfort through me. She seemed weak after creating the elevator, but she also couldn't contain her excitement.

She wanted me to explore.

I exited the elevator, keeping my hand on the heartwood so I could turn on some lights. It took me a bit to find the fixtures—more wall sconces and round candle-laden chandeliers hanging from chains above—but they flickered to life, revealing a vast maze of metal shelves and open cubbies built straight into the stone walls. A few of Iggy's roots cropped up here and there, popping in from a corner only to disappear back into the floor. Otherwise, the space was draped in shades of gray with the only color coming from the books themselves.

"I'm not sure I love the whole underground crypt style." I replaced both palms on the heartwood, thinking to dissolve the elevator back into Yggdrasil.

The tree stopped me. I could sense that she wanted me to save my energy so I wouldn't have to recreate the elevator again and tire myself out.

"Okay, if you insist," I said, letting my hands drop to my sides. The tree's presence remained muted with the elevator in place, completing the foreboding atmosphere of the catacombs.

I wandered forward into the stacks. The room was huge, at least twice as large as the floors above. Little alcoves with desks and chairs were tucked here and there, with hard, unforgiving surfaces that didn't invite anyone to stay long. Also unlike upstairs, the materials here were meticulously shelved, not a spine out of alignment, with matching books grouped together.

As I approached the farthest corner away from the elevator, the temperature dropped so suddenly that I instinctively rubbed my shoulders for warmth. My breath came out in visible puffs in the dim candlelight. Ice crystals formed on the floor and ceiling tiles. They became more regular, creating a solid sheet of ice thick enough for skating. I almost slipped and had to hold onto a nearby shelf, peering ahead to where a solid block of ice shielded an open doorway. Embedded into the ice wall, almost like a keyhole, was a smooth stone with a round hole.

Without warning, terror washed over me. I ran backward as if I'd seen a ghost, sliding dangerously on the icy floor. It wasn't until the room temperature rose back to normal that my racing heartbeat slowed down and I could think straight again.

"That was weird," I said. "What was I running from?"

The catacombs weren't going to answer me, so I stayed away from that creepy ice corner, opting instead to retreat back toward the elevator. Wary now, I decided it would be best to leave. No one knew I was down here, and therefore, no one would come rescue me.

One thing became clear on my return journey: the Forbidden Tomes were organized in increasingly dangerous order. Back near the ice, the books had a menacing, decrepit quality to them, but the books' conditions improved to more normal fare as the elevator came in sight.

A few shelves away from the heartwood, a familiar title caught my eye. *Fae Individual Registry.* The Grimoire had given me that listing when I'd been searching for more information on Klaus and Krampus.

I scanned the entire large bookcase, all consisting of the same binder-like spines. It wasn't just one book but an entire collection, like an encyclopedia. Each book held the title along with a set of letters along the bottom. I scanned the nearest ones to me. *Hj-Hn. Ho. Hp-Hz.* They were alphabetized, presumably by name of the individual fae.

I found volume *Kl-Kr.* Bingo.

Despite my resolve to leave, my fingers itched to grab the book. This part of the catacombs seemed safe, and the elevator was close by.

I snatched it off the shelf before I could talk myself out of it.

The book was heavier than it looked. I had to hold it with both hands. I waited a few beats. My hands didn't melt off. The room didn't spin. I felt completely normal, except for a twinge of excitement as I hauled my new treasure off to a small side table, which I discovered had a convenient stand, just the right size for this book. It tilted the pages upward so I could read it without leaning too far over.

I read the very brief foreword section. As I'd guessed, the *Fae Individual Registry* held historical records of significant fae throughout history. The author warned the reader not to use the information contained inside for "ill-conceived purposes," predicting such a pursuit would only end in "the inevitable curse of a death slowly taken."

"Blah, blah, blah fine print." I flipped past the warnings. "Where's the good stuff?"

The entry for *Klaus* came first alphabetically, showcasing a gorgeously-painted, full-bodied portrait of the jolly man. He wore ceremonial red robes with white trim, more like a fantasy wizard's attire than the Christmas legend. Still, the picture captured his genuine joy, so realistic that I half expected him to wink at me.

I devoured the next twenty pages. A lot of the info I already knew, such as the bit about Klaus's unknown birth parents. Other bits offered further insight, such as the fact that he lived with his dwarves near the Northern Court in a gorgeous cottage that served as his workshop. Apparently, before Klaus had come onto the scene, the dwarves had been a bit standoffish from the rest of the fae, but his influence had led them to become more integrated into the rest of Court society.

And that was only the beginning of Klaus's honored achievements. He'd stopped a war in eastern Europe several hundred years ago. He had an affinity for animals and had advocated for their rights and territories. His gifts to children worldwide were regarded as diplomatic aid and held in high esteem. Queen Mab held him in such high regard, he was one of the few members of the Court that she would occasionally ask for advice.

"The man really is a legend." I flipped through the pages for his brother.

Krampus. If Klaus's portrait could have laughed with me, Krampus's would have spit into my face. He wore the same robes as his brother, only navy blue, as if they concealed something sinister underneath. His lip curled in a sneer, and his horns thrust outward, the tips sharp like blades.

Krampus also had a twenty-page entry, and none of it was good. He despised humans from the onset, terrorizing whole villages and kidnapping children until Queen Mab finally forced him to stop with a treaty she made with the humans. He apparently didn't eat his victims, which was a relief, but he made sure they never returned home. He talked a lot of angry fae into committing various criminal acts, then usually persuaded them to take the fall for his actions.

Krampus didn't just dabble in crimes against humanity. He had allegedly staged several Court uprisings to dethrone Queen Mab. None of them had been successful, and Krampus had so many friends supporting him, the queen could not punish him without sufficient evidence. Needless to say, the queen didn't ever ask him for advice.

My hands shook as I closed the book. Krampus clearly hated ordinary people and those who served under Queen Mab. I represented both of those things as the Librarian of Atlantis. I'd have to be very careful around him.

A faint tug of tiredness washed over me. I replaced the volume back on the shelf, then took the elevator upstairs, knowing I would pay the price tomorrow for being up so late.

CHAPTER 17

A s usual, Henry was waiting for me at eight o'clock sharp at the front entryway. I blearily put my palm into the wall to open the library for him, stifling a yawn as the plaid-shirted sasquatch slowly appeared through the cracks of the branches.

"You look like death warmed over," he said cheerfully.

I glowered at him. "I stayed up way too late reading last night."

"You really shouldn't linger in the library near bedtime."

"I wasn't in the normal stacks," I said in my defense. "I figured out how to get to the Forbidden Tomes."

He straightened in surprise. "You were down in the catacombs?"

"You can thank an old photo album and Wallace for that. He's the one who helped me figure out how to create the elevator to get down there."

Henry raised an eyebrow. "Really? The hob?"

"Don't worry. He was very rude about it. Even called me 'temporary' librarian and everything."

Henry chuckled, but then his face turned serious. "You should know that some of those books down in the catacombs are dangerous, even for the librarian."

"Yeah, tell me about it. I found this really freaky ice door with a weird stone embedded in it. It gave me the heebie jeebies."

"That's probably where Queen Mab keeps some of her very personal, very private magical tomes. The doorway probably had an adder stone, which makes people who are not attuned to it run away in terror."

"How does that work?".

"The stone is attuned to specific people's blood. If you imbue it with yours, it won't freak you out anymore."

"Ew! My blood? No, thank you."

Henry shrugged. "That's magic. Anyway, go ahead and close back up after me. I'm off for the next hour to scout out more spots to lay the dragon trap."

"I'm telling you, if the dragon wants me, just give her what she wants. Lay the trap near the library."

"And I'm telling you, Rose, I'm in charge of security. It will be better for everyone if I can find out a place away from the library and put the trap there."

"Good luck with that!" I called after him. He ignored my jab as he stalked away.

The library needed some work before patrons arrived. First, I lit the fireplace on the first floor. It was bizarre seeing the stones flicker with flames without any sort of log underneath. I guessed burning wood wouldn't be very kosher, what with Iggy being a tree herself and all. Then I worked on tidying up a few shelves the fairies had left wrecked the day before,

I was on the sixth floor when I realized I only had a minute before the library opened. I bolted down the various staircases as fast as I could.

"You better hurry," Wallace called after me while he scrubbed around the Grimoire.

"What . . . do you think . . . I'm doing?" I managed, not bothering to slow my pace as I raced down the hallway.

When I opened the entryway, the normal crowd of dwarves had gathered close around the tree. Brock, the red-bearded master forger, greeted me with a frown.

"You're late," he accused.

"Only . . . a few minutes," I panted.

"Late is late," he announced in a loud voice. A few older dwarves around him nodded in agreement.

I backed away as they surged forward. Brock's crew, besides his daughter Cindy, all sneered at me while they passed. The rest of the bunch didn't acknowledge me as they passed. My face flushed even further when Henry, at the back of the crowd, gave me a sympathetic shrug.

I trailed the dwarves into the library. I really thought I'd made progress with them. Had I just undone all the work I'd achieved by being late?

But when the dwarves reached the first floor of the library, a general murmuring rose from the crowd. Many pointed toward the lit fireplace, while others tugged their wool sweaters over their heads, sighing in relief in more comfortable looking embroidered tunics.

Egan arrived behind me, his cane knocking against marble as he approached. "Good morning," he greeted. "I . . ."

"Librarian!" a dwarf who had thrown his sweater over a chair waved at me. "I have a request, if you don't mind."

"Me too!" another dwarf said. "We'll be on the second floor."

"We'll be on the fourth," another called.

I walked toward the dwarves but paused, turning back to Egan. "I'm so sorry. Did you also need something?"

"It can wait," he said in a patient, if somewhat strained, tone. "I'll do some research on my own first."

"I won't forget to cycle back to you," I promised, then headed for the first-floor dwarves. I happened to pass Wallace near the Grimoire.

"Thank you for letting me know about the fireplaces," I said fervently.

He sniffed. "Like a newborn babe." But I swore I caught him smile.

I ran around most of the morning fulfilling twice as many reference requests as the day before. The dwarves apparently had a tight deadline for designs coming up soon, and they wanted all their various presentations to be flawless for Klaus. The rocking horse group even drew me into their debate on how to paint it. Half of them wanted it colored natural shades like a real horse, while the other half favored brighter rainbow hues for a more playful appeal.

"Rosalind," their lead engineer Mikhail, a dwarf with perpetually ruddy cheeks and a pencil stuck behind his ear, called as I brought them over an armful of scrolls. "We can't decide on colors."

"Can't you take a vote?" I asked.

"We're even numbered and at an impasse. We need you to be the tiebreaker."

"I can see an argument for both cases," I said, trying to remain neutral.

"We'll never make a decision. We're too entrenched," Mikhail said.

"You're the librarian," the dwarf next to him added. "You're supposed to inspire us."

All the dwarves stopped writing notes in the margin of their large piece of shared parchment to stare at me with eager anticipation.

I hesitated. If I voted for either natural or rainbow colors, I would please half of them but make the other half upset. It didn't seem like a winning proposition either way.

In the end, my opinion didn't matter. "Do you have a picture of the boy you're building this for?"

"Sure," Mikhail said, shuffling around the various papers at his fingertips. He withdrew a photo that had gotten stuck between his notes and handed it to me. "But I'm not sure how it will help. We took the picture of him shopping with his mother. It doesn't give us any clue what color he might want his horse."

The rest of the dwarves grumbled in agreement as I studied the picture. It was, indeed, a pretty bland picture. A small dark-haired boy of early elementary school age had his sole hand's fingers threaded through the metal cage of the shopping cart as a taller lady, presumably his mother, pushed forward. Food staples layered the bottom of the basket: fruits, vegetables, whole wheat bread, milk, and one box of unsweetened oat cereal. Both the boy and his mother wore sensible clothing in varying shades of gray and black.

"Look at how practical the family is," Mikhail said. "They obviously try to eat healthy and don't wear brand clothing with logos. I think a natural-colored rocking horse would match them better."

"But the boy doesn't get to pick what he eats or wears," another dwarf argued. "He might prefer something more fanciful."

"You see, Rosalind," Mikhail concluded. "We're stuck. You have to make this decision for us."

I shook my head. "You missed one important detail."

"What?"

I placed the photo in the exact center of the table, right on top of their design, where everyone could view it. "Follow the kid's line of sight. He's giving you his answer."

The dwarves all crowded around, trying to get a better look. It was hard to see at first, given how much the boy and mother took up the center of the frame, but if you made a line from his eyes to the shelf, you could see clearly what he was examining.

Hanging in between the shelves of canned applesauce, the grocery store offered small plastic dinosaurs. All of them came in a variety of neon colors.

"He's interested in the bright toys!" one of the dwarves exclaimed in triumph.

Mikhail scoffed. "It could just be a fluke. The colors could have caught his attention."

"No," his companion argued, pointing back to the dinosaurs. "He couldn't be. Look closer. There are actually a few brown and gray dinosaurs up at his eye level. He's peering down closer to the floor where the bright pink and purple ones are."

Mikhail paused for only one more moment before nodding. "So he is. The boy prefers bright colors. His mom is going to have a conniption fit when she views this rocking horse."

"I doubt it," another dwarf predicted. "She's been hoping to buy him a rocking horse since his last surgery. She was heart-broken that they didn't have the money. And when she sees the look on his face when it shows up in their living room, I bet she'll forget all about the color scheme."

The dwarves then began a healthy argument on exactly what rainbow shades to choose from. I tried to slip away quietly, but the lead engineer cut through them by shouting, "Thank you, librarian."

"Hear, hear!" the rest of the group shouted their additional gratitude.

I bowed before leaving, extremely pleased with myself.

I might have let that small victory inflate my ego too much though. After doing a few Grimoire searches for Egan—pointedly ignoring the references to *The Taboo Magic of Disease Management* for a second time—I ran into Cindy in a secluded corner, tucked away from her father's group. She bit her lip as she closed the book and stared off into space.

I tried to ease into her direct vision. "Do you need help?"

She still jumped, the book falling from her lap onto the floor.

I grabbed it for her. "Sorry. I always keep startling you like that."

"It's okay," she said so softly that I could barely hear her. "It's not your fault. It's mine."

"Why would it be your fault?"

"You wouldn't understand." She stood to bypass me.

I moved to allow her to pass. "If you don't want to talk about it, that's fine, but I helped the group with the rocking horse. I'm available to listen if you change your mind."

She didn't say anything as she walked past, so I thought that was the end of it. Glancing at the book title, *A Guide to Alloys in the Fabrication of Complex Structures*, I searched for a place to reshelve it.

"It's about the metal alloy," she suddenly said behind me.

I whirled around to find Cindy studying her boots as she rushed through her explanation. "My father's dead set on using the same materials he used the last time he constructed a trampoline, but that child lived in a climate with average rainfall. Our girl lives on the outskirts of a rainforest. The material will rust too quickly."

"Have you told him this?" I asked.

She finally looked up at me with large doe eyes. "He said it will last five years, but I'm not convinced. I'm trying to find evidence to prove my case. He may be a master forger, but that doesn't mean he can't improve, right?"

I nodded. "Let's see if we can find sources that can back up your claim. Maybe if we go downstairs—"

"Cindy," a booming voice cut me off. "There you are."

Brock rounded the corner and frowned when he saw us together. Cindy backed away from me as if I'd caught a nasty disease.

"What are you two talking about?" he demanded.

"N-nothing," Cindy stammered.

I pulled the book close to my chest so he couldn't read the title. "I'm just reshelving this," I said honestly.

He glanced at us suspiciously. "Are you sure?"

Cindy nodded. "Yes, Father."

He let a pregnant pause fill the air before he finally said, "Well, we're getting ready for a vote on dimensions. You're needed."

"Yes, Father."

As she shuffled past him, he made her stop by holding out his large palm. "Are you sure you don't want to tell me something?"

She shook her head furiously.

He dropped his arm. She streaked past him as if chased by ghosts.

Brock spared me one last glare. "She needs to learn her place," he said with finality. "Just as you should learn yours." He left me on that gloomy note.

I guess inspiring people with my muse magic was more complicated than I thought.

CHAPTER 18

I F I BELIEVED THAT dealing with surly dwarves would be the most memorable part of my day, I was wrong.

While searching the shelves for some pamphlets to fetch for the dwarf on the fourth floor, I heard a commotion down in the atrium.

"It's our pleasure to serve you, my liege," Wallace announced in a voice so grand, I almost didn't recognize it.

Peering over the railing down below, I found the hob giving a deep bow to a very handsome man in a snug-fitting vest and breeches. Honey blond hair swept over his brow in a stylized arch, not a strand out of place. His sapphire blue eyes were so sharp that they almost looked like a CGI enhancement rather than real.

The man smiled pleasantly at the hob. "No need for theatrics, Wallace. I'm not officially in charge of the Southern Court yet."

"But you will be soon after the coronation, my liege."

Butterflies fluttered in my stomach. This couldn't be who I thought it was.

But Wallace confirmed it when he yelled, "Rosalind, come down here. Prince Jack Frost demands an audience."

Murmurs arose around me as I scurried down the branchy staircase to the atrium. I'd already botched my initial encounter with Krampus, and he'd only been a member of the Court. I had no idea how to greet an actual fae prince. I passed by Egan on my way, who hobbled in the opposite direction deeper into the library, probably in search of some book.

By the time I hit the ground floor, I was a little out of breath. I tried to smooth my hair as I approached Jack Frost. He was even more gorgeous up close. With a strong chin, perfect nose, and oh, those eyes, he could have easily been a runway model. He was probably my age but could pass for a decade younger.

I executed my lowest bow, bending over so far that my back protested. "Welcome to the Library of Atlantis, my liege," I said, repeating the phrase Wallace had used.

"Not you too," Jack Frost shook his head as I straightened. "There's no need to be so formal."

"Don't listen to him," Wallace said. "He's one of the most powerful fae alive. He could conjure a storm that could turn our island into Antarctica. His blades of ice are so sharp, they slice through metal. If he decided to control the water in your body—"

"Yes, yes, Wallace, I am a legend in your own mind," Jack Frost cut in. "So legendary, in fact, that when I've visited the library before, you barely spared me a second glance."

"That was before you took over the Southern Court, my liege. There is protocol to be followed, appearances to maintain. Your sister Carabosse would have demanded no less."

"And that's the perfect reason not to make a big deal out of my presence. I'm happy to do the opposite of whatever decision Carabosse made." Jack kept his tone lighthearted, but his expression hardened. He clearly didn't have any lost love for his sibling.

I decided to change the subject. "What brings you here today, my . . . uh, I mean, Mr. uh . . ."

"Jack will do fine," he said, extending a hand. "And you are . . .?"

I took his hand in mine. "Rosalind Baldwin."

"Nice to meet you, Rosalind." He gave me a proper, firm handshake. "I'm sorry to hear what happened to your grandmother. She was a fantastic librarian."

"We never met. My mom was estranged from her." I blurted out the words without thinking. The prince didn't need to know any of that.

Jack didn't seem bothered by my awkwardness. "It's a pity, but I understand such things happen. Just know that Clio was held in high regard as the Librarian of Atlantis for many years."

I straightened my shoulders, determined to come across as capable. "What brings you to the library today?"

"I must take a sacred vow written explicitly for my coronation. The words should be stored in Queen Mab's personal vault."

I thought of that icy door inside the Forbidden Tomes. "Down in the catacombs?"

He nodded. "I'm glad you are familiar with them, since you are the only person who can escort me there. Would you mind?"

"Of course." I silently thanked Wallace for showing me how to create the library's elevator from the heartwood the other day. Otherwise, I would have looked like a complete moron in front of the fae prince. "Right this way."

Wallace's jaw went slack as I motioned for Jack Frost into the first-floor shelves. That's right, hob. I actually know what I'm doing once in a while.

My confidence nearly left me as I stood in front of the heartwood. "This will take a minute," I explained. "And the elevator may not be up to Clio's standards. I'm still getting used to running this place."

"No rush." Jack relaxed against a bookshelf, as if he had all the time in the world.

Although I did have to strain myself to create the elevator, it went faster than before. I didn't feel nearly as taxed when I finished. Out of breath, sure, but not sweating profusely. And I'd managed to place two lights inside and even a string of buttons for each floor of the library. The ride down inside was smoother than ever, despite a small jerk at the end.

"Sorry about that." I motioned for him to exit first, making sure to light up the gloomy underdark.

He waited so we could walk side-by-side through the stone shelves. "I heard a rumor that you were raised in the human world. Is that true?"

My pulse quickened. "Yes. I hope that's not a problem."

"Of course not. I understand the biases some fae have against humans, but I assure you that I hold none of them."

A snort of disbelief escaped my mouth before I could stop it. My face flushed as Jack raised an eyebrow at me.

"I apologize for being so rude," I said in a rush. "But you're a fae prince. You can't possibly avoid bias."

To my relief, he agreed. "You're not wrong. Anti-human sentiment is strong in the Court. I meant to say that I try not to let it rule my decisions. It would be hypocritical anyhow, since I have a half-human daughter."

"Really?" I couldn't keep the surprise out of my voice.

"I thought you already knew since Melissa convinced you personally to take this position."

I frowned. "What does Melissa have to do with your daughter?"

"Well, everything. She's my daughter's mother."

I nearly tripped over my feet as the words sunk in. "Are you the reason Melissa's daughter was involved in some ancient fae prophecy?"

Jack laughed. "You could say that. Fortunately, it's all resolved now."

"That means you and Melissa are . . ." I couldn't bring myself to say "together." I couldn't reconcile this otherworldly charming prince attached to the practical HR manager I'd met. Besides, I could have sworn I saw sparks fly between Melissa and Gabriel Alston.

"We were never together as a couple," Jack said. "It's a long story, but I didn't even have a hand in raising our daughter until very recently. Melissa did it all on her own."

I shook my head as I let it all sink through. "The fae are complicated."

"That we are," he said. We'd just reached the back of the catacombs, where the temperature had dropped to winter degrees. I shivered, partly from the cold but also from the bad vibes emanating from the adder stone ahead.

Jack patted my shoulder. "You can stay here and wait for me. This will only take a moment."

He strode forward on the thickening ice floor. Unlike me, Jack had no problem approaching the block of ice, not so much as slowing his gait. He held up a hand, and out of thin air, created a key made of pure ice.

Neat trick.

He clicked the key into the lock and opened the vault, slipping inside quietly. Even though I couldn't enter the room with him, he left the doors open, giving me a narrow view of his movements. He retrieved some book from the corner of the room, mumbling under his breath as he read a string of words I couldn't quite hear, although it sounded like a chant. Then he put the book down and, still chanting, danced. His legs swept in a circle, and his arms flowed around him almost like a mixture between ballet and martial arts. He went through the short dance several times, chanting the whole while.

After ten minutes, I thought about finding a chair to sit down and wait when Jack finally exited the vault, replacing the icy blockade through a series of wind blasts.

"That looked a lot more complicated than a simple speech," I said as I escorted him back to the elevator.

"That's because the vow is a ritual as much as it is words. I'm making a sacred promise to every fae who lives and breathes. Every gesture, every syllable must be executed correctly once I begin."

"And if you screw it up?"

He shrugged. "The magic of the vow will consume me, and I will die."

"You sound pretty casual for someone who might keel over if you forget to wave your hands around in the right way."

He chuckled. "I'm sure I'll be fine. Nevertheless, I'll probably return the day of the coronation and review the ritual again, with your permission, of course."

"Sure, but wouldn't it be easier if you take the ritual book with you?"

"No. Everything in that vault should always be held under lock and key. Better if I come to it than vice versa and risk having it fall in the wrong hands."

"Oh," I said, feeling ignorant. "I'm sorry. I didn't understand."

We'd cycled back to the elevator. I pushed the button to go upward, happy that it didn't jerk about like before.

Jack scrutinized me from head to shoulders. "May I offer you a bit of advice?"

I stiffened, wondering where this was going. "Okay."

"Never apologize. You are a muse, and not just any muse, but the Librarian of Atlantis. Even if you weren't raised as such, you are a powerful fae."

The elevator stopped on the first floor, bouncing so hard that we nearly fell over each other. Jack Frost caught me before our foreheads smacked together.

I pushed myself upright and exited first. "It sure doesn't feel that way," I mumbled.

"Give yourself a chance. I'm sure your instincts will guide you." Jack gave me a deep bow, a clear show of his respect for me.

I mimicked the bow, trying to absorb his words. I'd already made a lot of progress with the dwarves, Brock's team notwithstanding. And the fairies had gushed all over me. Maybe Jack was right. I needed to focus on my progress, not on the mistakes.

As I watched Jack leave the library, something moved out of the corner of my eye. Egan was tucked away in a little nook, staring after Jack Frost. His face bloomed red, and the set of his jaw could have been chiseled in stone.

He must have felt my gaze because he turned my way. As our eyes met, his scowl deepened into something like pure rage. I took a step back at the intensity of his emotions. Before I could react further, he tucked his chin into his collar, away from me.

I considered ignoring the entire exchange, but sooner or later, I'd have to face him again. Taking a breath, I went toward him, summoning my best smile.

"Egan? Is everything all right?"

"No." He kept his face hidden in response.

I maintained a healthy distance. "Can I help you in any way?"

He finally lifted his head toward mine, eyes blazing with anger. "You can, but you won't."

I glanced at the stack of discarded books and parchment on the table in front of him. "Did these resources not pan out? Because I can do another search—"

"You know what I need," he interrupted, standing. "And it isn't another useless scroll written by some ignorant hack." His eyes wandered over to the heartwood, where the elevator still stood open.

I tried to keep my voice as neutral as possible. "You want to access the Forbidden Tomes."

"Not all of them. Just one. *The Taboo Magic of Disease Management*. It has the answers I seek to alleviate my pain."

"I realize it keeps coming up in our searches, but that book's stored in the catacombs for a reason. I can't let just any patron access it."

Yggdrasil bloomed in affirmation across my mind. She definitely agreed.

By the shade of maroon that splashed across Egan's cheeks, he vehemently disagreed. "You let that prince"—he spat out the word—"down there without hesitation."

"It's not the same situation."

"You're right, it's not. Jack Frost is not dying. He—"

Egan couldn't finish his tirade as his brow scrunched up in pain. He clutched his leg, cane clattering to the floor, and let out a yelp. I barely caught him before he pitched over onto the marble floor.

A group of dwarves on the floor above, who had begun to gather their materials to finish for the day, peered down over the railing. "Rosalind?" Mikhail called. "Is everything all right?"

"Yeah, it's okay," I responded, willing my words to be true. I gently guided Egan back into his seat.

He groaned as I retrieved his cane for him. "I'm sorry, Rosalind," he said, his anger gone as he massaged his leg. "Sometimes I let my malady get the better of me."

My mouth went dry. Flashbacks of finding my dad cursing as he struggled to walk during the last weeks of his life overwhelmed me. I'd never heard him swear until then, no matter how bad things got, even after Mom's death. I would have offered my dad a hand, but he would have refused. Instead, I ignored the swearing as he hobbled to his walker, a litany of four-letter words falling from his lips like prayer.

Egan pulled me out of the painful memory by patting me on the arm. "The dwarves are heading out. I better go too."

"Are you sure?" I asked. "Maybe I could—"

"I'm good for today," Egan said firmly. He leaned more heavily than normal on his good side, grunting with every other step.

"I could help you—"

"No, I'll find my own way out."

I had to clamp my lips shut as he staggered away.

Henry walked in just as everyone was leaving, a bag with lunch tucked in his arms. He warily watched Egan storm past him.

"What's his problem?" Henry asked before Egan was completely out of earshot.

Egan turned his head in profile to glare at him.

I rounded on Henry. "Do you always have to be such a jerk?"

"Only when dealing with people I don't like, and I don't like that guy."

I waited until Egan had left the room before raising my voice. "What did Egan ever do to you?"

"It's not what he's done to me, it's what he's done to others." Henry shot back. "Haven't you ever wondered what kind of fae he is?"

"No," I admitted, "but I have a feeling you know and you're going to lord it over me."

"Of course I know. It's my job to keep you safe. I went through all Stronghold's records on Egan. He's some sort of elemental, probably a sylph with air manipulation since he's been associated with not one, but two tornado attacks against human towns neighboring fae territory. The second tornado took down a bunch of power lines and started a forest fire that killed twenty people."

My hand went to my mouth. "Then why is he walking around free?"

"As usual, Krampus threw two of his other minions under the bus so the majority of his network could remain scot-free. His two patsies swore they were the only ones involved in the tornados."

"Is it possible they were telling the truth?"

Henry shifted from one foot to the next. "There's a slim chance they were the only ones involved, which is why no one else was ever charged. There wasn't enough evidence on Egan or anyone else. And it was definitely too far removed from Krampus to do anything to him."

I mulled over this new information. "I do believe you . . ." I said slowly.

Henry folded his hairy arms across his chest. "Gee, thanks."

"Let me finish," I said curtly. "Let's say Egan was involved in those attacks. Should he be punished? Of course. But even with all that in mind, he's clearly suffering."

"He should be suffering in the Southern Court dungeon," Henry snapped.

"But he's not a threat either way. He's in too much pain."

"Egan is clearly Krampus's stooge. There's always another angle."

I gave up trying to argue with the stubborn sasquatch. No matter what he said, it wouldn't alleviate the guilt I felt at letting Egan suffer when a remedy might be found in the catacombs beneath my feet.

CHAPTER 19

T HAT NIGHT, I TRIED to get some well-deserved rest. It had been a long day, and I hadn't slept much the night before. My feet hurt. I couldn't stop yawning. But as I dove into the covers, I couldn't shut out the image of Egan hobbling away from the library.

I had to find out what was in that book.

Throwing on a robe, I wandered back downstairs into the gloom of the library. I paused in the main hallway to make sure Wallace's rooms had a big enough flame in his fireplace. I'd already lit up his room, but it didn't hurt to check and ensure everything was running smoothly. Otherwise, I'd never hear the end of it.

After finding the call number in the Grimoire, I traveled down into the catacombs. *The Taboo Magic of Disease Management* was located near the heartwood. It was a simple olive-colored hardbound book, the words so faintly etched into its spine that I could barely read it. It looked like the kind of book that people might pass over in a used bookstore for decades before realizing it was even there. Cracking it open, I expected to uncover illicit methods to increase one's lifespan or health.

Instead, I found just the opposite. The book referenced all sorts of ways, not to heal a patient, but to weaponize diseases. Spells and incantations offered things such as spreading a common cold to an entire room of people, creating a poison from an infected wound, and even turning whooping cough into a banshee wail that could shatter glass.

I flipped to the section on Egan's specific problem: magical scirrhous of the leg. Apparently with a little blood-letting and writing a specific rune on the infected leg (in blood no less, ew!), a fae could augment their own magical powers for a few precious seconds. The book outlined a handy list of how different fae would be affected. Leprechaun luck magic would surge to make impossible things a reality. The sasquatch, normally only invisible to the eye, would also be mute to the other senses such as smell and hearing. Wind elementals like Egan would be able to conjure a violent tornado, although it wouldn't last long.

And after each magic power boost, the fae would keel over dead from a heart attack.

Horrified, I shoved the book back on the shelf. My instincts had been right. This book was not only best kept from public consumption, but it wouldn't help Egan at all.

I wandered back upstairs, an all-too-familiar defeat wracking my nerves. I drank a cup of tea to settle my nerves. It didn't work. I couldn't shake the powerlessness that accompanied fighting a terminal illness.

I had no idea how to help Egan.

I returned to the master bedroom, bone-tired and defeated. I was about to climb into bed when a loud thud outside the window shook the boughs. I stared out of the glass. The moon cast silver beams directly at my feet. It couldn't have been lightning. And it had felt too localized to be an earthquake.

The tree rocked again, branches scratching at the glass. I braced myself with a bedpost as an ebony shadow blocked out the moonlight. Whiplashes cut through the air, and when the blob shifted, I could make out glowing yellow cat eyes.

The dragon Agatha craned her slender neck as she peered in through the window, directly at me.

I froze, still as a statue, wondering for an illogical second if she was like the tyrannosaurus rex in that movie that had given me nightmares as a kid. Maybe dragons could only sense movement.

But Agatha spotted me and let out a heart-pounding squeal. She definitely knew where I was.

I hugged the bedpost. What could I do? Only a thin pane of glass separated me from a deadly dragon.

No, that wasn't right. Agatha was perched directly on Iggy's branches. The tree should have protected me, but Iggy did nothing as Agatha screeched at me.

"What's the holdup, Iggy?" I asked the tree. "Why aren't you getting rid of that thing?"

Iggy sent me a strange wave of comfort.

I pushed it aside. "Those claws can tear me to shreds. Please do something!"

Iggy responded with an apologetic warmth and another wave of comfort. The tree didn't find the dragon threatening.

"You realize that dragon killed Clio, right?" I asked, my voice rising in panic as Agatha opened her mouth to reveal two rows of unfathomably sharp teeth.

Iggy surprised me by flooding me with something like skepticism or denial. Worse, instead of batting the dragon away with her magic, she made the glass panes disappear.

I screamed, running for the bedroom door, but when I tried to turn the knob, it was locked.

"Are you trying to kill me?" I demanded as Agatha thrust her serpentine head into the room.

Yggdrasil didn't reply as the dragon entered the room up to her shoulders. She was too big to climb all the way through the window, although she tried, scraping the sill with her talons. I splayed myself on the opposite wall, waiting for her to open her jaw and fry me.

Instead, she cocked her head and blinked at me.

The analog clock ticked, one for every two of my racing heartbeats. Agatha made no other move to harm me. No snapping teeth. No fireballs. Instead, she mewled, almost like a kitten.

Was Agatha . . . tame?

No. I shied away physically at the thought. My grandmother Clio had been torched to death. Agatha was the only one who could have done it. There wasn't any other explanation.

But as Agatha continued to whine at me, her neck muscles stretched taut to close the distance, I found myself wanting to pet her snout. My hand twitched upward, inching toward her. She grunted as I took a step forward.

Before I knew it, my fingertips connected with her nose. Bumpy and rough, it also exuded warmth, like a mug of steaming hot tea.

Excited by the contact, Agatha lurched forward, leaning her jaw into the palm of my hand. I nearly let go but fought the urge, even stroking as I worked my way up past the bony ridge extruding outward from her forehead. Little flappy ears, miniature versions of her wings, flung out, tickling my arm hair. She rested her face against the crook of my arm as I rubbed a surprisingly soft spot behind the bone.

She rumbled, deep in her belly, the vibrating purr so powerful that it created goosebumps all over my arms.

We clung to each other. Her scales scored the branches when she leaned in for more, and her talons squeezed the windowsill so tight that a piece snapped off. Even the thick branches that held her weight protested in loud creaks.

Agatha may have been an affectionate dragon, but there was no doubt that she could rip me to shreds if she wanted to.

It was clear she didn't want to.

I'd assumed in our previous encounters that she'd been coming after me. Now, viewing Agatha in this light, I could also imagine that she recognized my smell as being similar to Clio's. Maybe she just wanted to check me out.

Eventually, a branch broke off beneath the dragon. Iggy winced inside my head, slapping Agatha with leafy boughs to keep her from doing more damage. The dragon pulled back, biting at the branches, but the tree won out. With one final huff of farewell, Agatha took off into the night sky. I leaned out the window and watched her get smaller until her shimmering form faded behind the trail rim.

"You let the dragon do *what* last night?"

Henry's angry shout made me jump back from him. I'd just opened the library doors to let him in when I mentioned my encounter with Agatha. I expected him to be concerned, but he looked like he wanted to kill something with his bare hands.

"Agatha showed up outside my window. I petted her. She obviously didn't hurt me because I'm standing right here telling you about it."

"Only because Yggdrasil would have torn her to shreds if she tried anything. And even then, the dragon could have roasted you before the tree could protect you." His entire body visibly shook.

I laid a comforting hand on his shoulder. "I'm fine. You don't have to worry about me."

He shrugged me off. "The hell I don't. Why didn't the tree squash that dragon flat?"

"Iggy isn't scared of Agatha. She made that very clear." I was about to explain how she removed the glass panes so I could interact with the dragon when Henry kept ranting.

"Then the tree isn't doing her job to keep you safe," Henry growled. "And that means I'll have to take drastic measures."

"Like what?"

"Like setting up the dragon trap on the other side of the moat. I really wish I had more time to find a location farther away from the library, but unfortunately, that's our best option at this point."

"You aren't going to kill the dragon, are you?" I asked in alarm.

"No. There aren't a whole lot of dragons left in the world, especially young ones. Even though this one killed a fae in cold blood, it's been decided she should be captured and transported to a remote wildlife sanctuary far away from Atlantis."

"Good because I don't think Agatha is as dangerous as you believe she is. If Iggy trusts her—"

"Yggdrasil doesn't understand. Clio's murder happened outside her sensory range. All the tree knows is that Clio loved the dragon enough to keep it around. She's just extending it the same warm welcome."

"But I told you, the dragon didn't harm me last night, even when it had the chance."

"It doesn't matter. It also lulled Clio into a false sense of security before killing her. Dragons are wild beasts. They can attack you at any time."

I glared at him. "I'm surprised you haven't hurt your back reaching so far to make all these assumptions."

"Better hurt my back than have anything happen to you," he said, almost under his breath.

It would have been endearing if it wasn't so frustrating. "Henry, I'm trying to tell you the dragon isn't a threat."

He pointed a finger right at my face. "And I'm telling you it's my job to keep you alive. Now, if you'll excuse me, I have cage materials to bring back."

And with that, he stalked back off toward the rim.

CHAPTER 20

T HE NEXT FEW DAYS went by in a blur. The dwarves visited the library from opening hour to closing time to finish their projects by the deadline, the day before the coronation. They ran me ragged asking for suggestions and resources. I tried to help Cindy with her metal alloy problem, but she avoided me at every turn. With Brock always glancing over her shoulder, I finally gave that up as a lost cause.

Egan was a more difficult problem. Although I didn't have a lot of bandwidth to help him due to the dwarf's requests, he did corner me several times to namedrop *The Taboo Magic of Disease Management.* Even after I explained the terrible contents of the book, he insisted I must have read it wrong. He claimed it was his only hope. He was in so much pain, I doubted he could think clearly. My heart hurt that I had to deny him his request, but it wouldn't have helped him anyway. He took to sulking in a first-floor alcove, looking despondent.

While I scurried about the library, Henry erected the cage for catching Agatha on the other side of the moat. He spent hours burying a metal sheet with a pressure-sensitive trigger into the ground, alongside a set of three iron-barred walls that would snap shut into a prison pyramid when activated. I tried to tell him he didn't need to build the trap at all, but Henry ignored me. He made me so mad, we rarely spoke anymore, even when he gave me lunch or dinner. He also started spending the nights in the library, sleeping on a first-floor couch, declaring he would be here the next time the dragon returned.

Agatha never did come back to the tree after our last encounter, although I caught glimpses of her soaring over the canopy late at night in the far distance. The more I watched her dip and fall, almost like a dog running in a field, the more I became convinced that she was harmless. It made me uneasy to wonder who else might have hurt Clio, but I didn't even know how to begin solving that mystery, especially since everyone assumed that Agatha had.

But my real problem was whether I should keep my job as librarian or not. I loved Yggdrasil and all her secrets. I spent every waking moment pulling books off shelves and learning about the fae, even if I only had a five-minute break between material requests. I made a dozen mental lists of how to improve the library's haphazard organizational structure. I loved interacting with the friendlier dwarves. I even created a few more windows in the hallway so Wallace had more light when he swept every morning, although he didn't thank me for it.

As I leaned into my responsibilities, though, I was reminded of my inadequacies. A pair of pointy-eared fae visited one afternoon to inquire about gardening tips. They were less than impressed with the materials I found. I also avoided the Forbidden Tomes, scared of what else I might find down there.

The day before the coronation ceremony, with one day left of my temporary assignment, I couldn't imagine how to decide whether to stay or not. I kept wishing I could call Jason and get his opinion on the whole mess. After the dwarves and Egan had gone home, I even pulled out my phone and waved it around the sixth floor, hoping to snag a signal. I might as well have been waving a stick in the air for all the good it did me.

When I went back to the atrium, defeated, I bumped into Wallace. He asked me for more cleaning supplies, but when I opened the storage closet, I found that we'd run out.

"Useless," Wallace said as he stalked away.

His grumbling planted a seed in my mind. It bloomed into a full-fledged scheme, and I ran back upstairs to grab the messenger bag I'd been wearing when I first arrived at Atlantis. I then went to find Henry standing guard at the front entrance.

"Hey," I said as way of greeting. "I'm off on an errand for the library. You're welcome to escort me."

Henry recoiled as if I asked him to cut off his arm. "You're not going anywhere."

"Yes, I am."

"There's a dragon out there with your name on it."

"A dragon, yes, but she won't hurt me."

"Yeah, that sure worked out well for Clio," he retorted. "And what kind of errand could you possibly need to run?"

"Wallace is out of cleaning supplies."

Henry put his forehead in his hand. "You'd risk your life for some soap?"

"Okay, not just soap," I admitted. "I want to go back home and visit my brother before I make up my mind tomorrow whether to become the librarian permanently."

"You're not allowed to tell outsiders about the fae."

"I'm not going to tell him anything about the fae. I'll simply discuss the ups and downs of this position in vague terms. You know, get advice from someone I care about, like a normal person."

"Well, too bad." Henry folded his arms over his chest. "I'm not letting you leave."

I straightened and mimicked his pose. "That's funny because I don't remember asking permission. I remember telling you that I'm going on some errands, and you can either come with me or not."

He sized me up, from the bottom of my feet to the top of my head. "I've got more than twice your mass. You can't get past me."

I patted the wall of the tree beside me. "Iggy begs to differ."

The tree responded to my boast by pulling a branch out of the wall and wrapping it around my shoulders in a show of support. I really did love her.

Henry narrowed his dark copper eyes. "You wouldn't dare."

I smiled sweetly. "You may be double my mass, but to this tree, you're a teeny little bug. One way or the other, I'm going to talk to my brother. You're either coming or not. Your choice."

Henry considered it for a few moments, craning his head up at Yggdrasil's bark to her branches above. She shook them for good measure.

"Fine," Henry growled. "Just don't blame me when you're burnt to a crisp."

I didn't reply as I closed the front entrance of the library, leaving Henry and me on the outside.

Henry led me to the fairy ring courtyard first, gesturing me toward the sole archway without a snowscape on the other side. "You want to take the Stronghold exit?"

"It'll be faster to take the original fairy ring that I used to get here. My brother's house is within walking distance of it."

"But it might not be secure."

I rolled my eyes. "If it was such a problem, why haven't you gone and dismantled it like you have the others?"

Henry at least looked chagrined as he muttered, "I didn't know where to find it."

"You could have asked me where it was."

"Would you have told me?"

"Probably not, especially if you were going to shutter it."

He threw his hands up. "What would be the point of me asking you then?"

"I would have gotten a kick out of it," I said, failing to stifle a giggle as I marched forward.

"I'm not here for your amusement," he yelled as he caught up to me.

"Yeah, you're here to protect me from dragons that won't ever hurt me."

That set Henry off on a long tirade about the instability of dragons. I mentally blocked him out, concentrating on retracing the steps of my initial hike on the island. It had been almost a week, but fortunately, I remembered the landmarks that would take me back thanks to all those years hiking with my dad.

". . . sharp talons that can tear into flesh," Henry was saying when he noticed the forest change to swampland. He did a double take. "How far is this fairy ring anyway?"

"On the beach past this swamp."

"I didn't know there were any fairy rings that far out."

"I have a feeling Atlantis has a lot of secrets you don't know about." The path took us close to a pool of murky water.

Henry suddenly yanked me back. I yelped in surprise.

I rounded on him. "What was that for?"

"You almost ran into that snake!" He pointed to my right. A cream-colored boa was coiled over a long, spindly branch.

"Hey," I called to the reptile. "Are you the same fellow I saw coming in?"

He tilted his head at me curiously, tongue flicking out of his mouth.

"You talk to venomous snakes now?" Henry asked incredulously.

"He's an inhabitant of the island just like me, and besides, he's not venomous."

"How do you know that?"

"Boas kill their prey by squeezing them to death, not by biting them." I confidently strode past the snake. "And he's not long enough to harm either one of us."

Henry grumbled something, giving the snake a much wider berth, but he kept up with me as we hiked through the swamp.

The path finally ended at a familiar beach, the white stones of the archway still glowing with their magical runes. Between the columns, the field of purple and red wildflowers swayed in a gentle breeze.

I was about to step through when Henry pushed past me. "I'll go first."

"After you," I said sarcastically as he butted his way in. I followed him without waiting for him to give the all-clear.

The temperature dropped significantly on the other side, causing a shiver to run through my body. Even though it was summer at the Oregon Coast too, I was no longer in a tropical paradise. And while it had been afternoon at the library, it appeared to be closer to noon here. At least the sun was shining overhead.

Henry glanced back at me, rubbing my bare arms. "What's wrong?"

"It's cold."

"No, it's not."

"Says the guy wearing a full-length plaid T-shirt with fur underneath."

"It's not fur! It's thick body hair."

"Whatever." I swept past him.

He trailed after me down the hill. At least going down the mountain was relatively easy. I was already dreading the climb afterwards.

"How'd you find this place?" Henry asked as we trampled through the forest. It must have seemed aimless to him since there wasn't a path.

"My dad brought us here a lot as kids."

"So we're not far from Otis?"

"How do you know the name of my hometown?" I asked before shaking my head. I already knew the answer. "You read it in my file."

He shrugged in agreement.

"What's my brother's name?" I asked.

"Jason."

"My parents?"

"Linus and Sophia."

"My pet goldfish when I was a kid?"

He huffed. "What kind of question is that?"

"I'm just trying to figure out how much is in that stupid file of yours."

"It's all publicly available information. I know the names of every school you attended. Some of your former mailing addresses. You sure have a lot of them."

"I moved around a lot."

"Why?"

"Because I liked the change of scenery."

Maybe that used to be true, especially in my 20s, but now, it felt so hollow. I yearned for a place to stay.

A reason to belong.

Henry shook his head in disbelief. "That's a lot of scenery changes. Maybe if you'd—"

A sharp ringing interrupted our conversation, coming from my phone in the messenger bag. We must have wandered back into cell tower range.

I clicked on the phone screen, hoping it wasn't spam, but it was worse. Mike's name flashed on the screen.

Henry peered over my shoulder. "Isn't that your ex-husband?"

"Why bother asking questions to which you already know the answer?"

The call went straight to voicemail after just two rings. That meant I had other messages. I tapped on the voicemail app.

Mike's name dominated the screen from top to bottom. He must have been calling me since the moment I took the job at the library. Most days had at least a dozen calls from him, some spaced apart by only a few minutes.

Henry watched me scroll through the missed calls, his expression growing dark. "What is that loser's problem?"

"We're newly divorced. He calls about stuff."

"Every hour?" Henry demanded.

He had a point. I'd started taking Mike's calls after the whole lost diploma thing, but this was ludicrous. Mike was the one who dumped me. Why did he need to talk to me so much?

The most recent voicemail popped up. I tapped on it.

"What are you doing?" Henry demanded, drowning out Mike's voice.

"Seeing what he wants."

"He wants to keep tabs on you. Don't let him do it."

"Shush," I snapped, restarting the message.

215

Henry pursed his lips shut as Mike's nasal tones drifted out from the phone. "Why aren't you answering my calls? Is it because you destroyed the receipts my accountant needs? Are you trying to deliberately sabotage me, Rosalind? Because if you are, mark my words, I'll sue. It'll make shredding your college diploma look like child's play."

I sucked in a breath as the line went dead. Before, Mike had said he had "accidentally tossed" my college diploma, not that he'd destroyed it on purpose. I hadn't realized it was some sort of retaliation play after a perceived slight.

Henry shook with fury, cursing under his breath. "Let me talk to him. He won't be making threats after—"

I held up a hand, trying my best to stem the heat rising up my core. My emotions must have shown on my face because Henry went silent, nodding in satisfaction.

Taking a deep breath, I returned Mike's call.

He answered on the first ring. "Finally, you've come to your senses and called me back. Where did you put all those receipts that—"

"I'll tell you one thing I didn't do to them," I interrupted. "I didn't shred them."

"'Shred' them? Who said anything about shredding?"

"You did in your voicemail. To my diploma. The one that you supposedly 'lost.'"

"D-did I say that?" he asked, trying to sound confused. "It must have been a slip of the tongue."

"A slip of the tongue on Bella is how you ended our marriage," I shot back.

Henry slapped a hand over his mouth to hide his amusement. He flashed me a thumbs up with his free hand.

"That's nasty and crude, Rosalind!" Mike replied in shock.

"It's more crude to cheat on your spouse."

"Oh, is that what this is about?" Mike said, his voice dropping low. "You're a woman scorned, and now you're going to take it out on me?"

"I would have to care that you slept around to be scorned, Mike. At this point, I don't care where you stick your tiny penis."

Henry doubled over in silent laughter.

"Well, I . . . it's not little . . . the receipts . . .?" Mike couldn't hold on to a thought.

"I didn't do anything to your precious receipts. Unlike you, I'm not a vindictive toad. They're probably right in the file cabinet where I left everything else."

"I don't believe you!" Mike screamed so loud I had to move the phone away from my ear.

"Mikey?" Bella's whiny voice interrupted. "Is that you on the phone with your ex again? You said you'd stop calling her."

"Stay out of this!" Mike yelped.

"Actually, I'm with Bella on this one," I said, cutting through his tirade. "Stop calling me, Mike. It's over. You finished it. I'm blocking your number from here on out."

"But you still haven't told me where the receipts are!" he screamed. "I'll call my lawyer! I'll—"

I hung up. He tried calling back almost immediately, but I ended that call too. In the time it took him to go through voicemail, I made sure his number would never pop up on my screen again.

As I stuffed the phone back in my bag, Henry gave me a loud slow-clap. "Bravo, Rose. Bravo."

"I should have done that a long time ago," I admitted with a sigh.

"But you did it now. And you certainly didn't need my help. You put that cheating jerk right in his place."

"Thanks," I said, unable to stop a beaming smile from breaking out across my face.

CHAPTER 21

E MBOLDENED BY MY POWER move against Mike, I strode down the mountain feeling like I could tackle anything.

Henry put the kibosh on that as we rounded the corner and my childhood home came into view. "Remember, you can't tell your brother anything about the Library of Atlantis."

"Trust me, I don't want to. Jason's a levelheaded guy. He's not the kind to believe in fairies and stuff."

"What's your cover story, then?"

"I'll say I was offered a unique position at 'a library.' That sounds vague enough."

"And what about me?"

I frowned. "What about you?"

"How are you going to explain the reason I'm with you?"

"You're not going to be with me when I have this conversation."

"Wanna bet?"

I halted in the middle of the road. "That wasn't part of the deal!"

"There wasn't a deal!" Henry shot back. "You informed me you were going to see your brother. I had to tag along to keep you safe."

"Are you trying to tell me I'm not safe around my own brother?"

"It's my job to monitor you while under temporary contract. I'm also supposed to make sure you don't go blabbing fae secrets."

"I promise I won't."

"Pardon me if I'm skeptical of the person who threatened to beat me up with a tree, a tree which, by the way, won't stop me from hauling you out of here."

I gritted my teeth in frustration. "Fine, you wanna be there while I talk to my brother? Just do your invisibility thing."

"You don't want to introduce me?"

My cheeks flushed red. "You heard my conversation with Mike. The last thing I want is to give Jason the impression that I've found my rebound guy."

Henry's jaw went slack. "I meant as a coworker or something, not as a . . ." He trailed off, waving his hands as if he could make the next word appear instead of saying it out loud.

"And why would I bring home a 'coworker' instead of a . . ." I also trailed off, mimicking his hand waving.

Henry cleared his throat. "Right. Invisibility it is."

"Thank you for coming with me on this." I stalked toward the house.

Henry jogged to catch up with me. "You'll have to keep the door open a few seconds to let me slip in behind you, otherwise you'll shut me out."

"And if I did slam the door in your face, you'll make a huge scene that I'll never live down. Got it." I rummaged around in the messenger bag for my keys. "But first, we're going for a drive."

"I thought you wanted to talk to your brother."

"Jason's at the garage. He won't be home until lunch. We might as well get our errands done first." I unlocked my cheap sedan, still sitting in the driveway. "You coming or not?"

Henry mumbled in response, but he did get into the passenger seat.

I considered driving out of Otis and toward the larger coastal towns for supplies, but I didn't have enough time to make the drive and be back during Jason's break. So instead, I drove to the town's sole marketplace, more of a convenience store really. There were no other cars in the seven spots out front, so I took the farthest one to the left.

When Henry made a move to get out, I put a hand on his shoulder. "You better stay here."

He yanked away as if I'd seared him with fire. "Why?"

"Because this is a small town, and if anyone sees you, word will get back to Jason that I was hanging out with a strange man."

"I could go invisible and follow you."

I flicked my eyes skyward for patience. "Are you really worried I'm going to tell a random person at the store about the fae?"

221

"No, but—"

"And do you anticipate any fire-breathing dragons in there?"

He threw himself back against the seat. "Okay, you got me. You can go in by yourself." He then disappeared out of sight.

"Thank you, oh great magnanimous one." I opened the driver's side door.

"Don't take too long," his disembodied voice warned, "or I will come in to get you."

"I wouldn't dream of disobeying you." I got out of the car but paused before shutting the door as I viewed an advertisement taped to the window. "Which do you prefer: blue or red?"

"Why does it matter?"

"I'm just trying to buy you a . . . you know what, never mind." I pulled away from the car.

"Blue," he said before the metal door slammed shut.

I pushed aside my anger as I entered the marketplace, a familiar hangout that reminded me of my high school days. I glanced over at the counter, half expecting the elderly store owner, but instead, a bored-looking teenager leaned against the counter. She didn't so much as glance up from her phone as I grabbed a plastic red basket from the door.

The cleaning supplies were stored in a back corner, far back on the bottom shelf. My knees protested as I squatted to view the limited selection. To avoid injury, I sat on the tile, despite the various dark stains all around me. The teenage clerk couldn't see me, but I wished she'd channel some hob-energy and pick up a mop once in a while.

Surveying my choices, I winced at the prices. The markups here were worse than I remembered. Maybe I should have driven to a big box retailer. I placed a pack of sponges in the basket and reached for liquid detergent.

"Ms. Rosalind Baldwin," a voice boomed overhead. "We meet again."

I nearly dropped the plastic bottle in surprise but managed to keep my grip as I stared at the sneakers, up the track pants, and straight to the baseball cap of Mr. Dalton. Of course he would be here. The storage place was right next door.

"Hello, Mr. Dalton," I said with as much dignity as I could muster lounging on the dirty floor. "How are you?"

"Not so great, actually." He narrowed his eyes at me.

Worried he might order me to do push-ups with that stern expression, I got back to my feet. "I'm sorry to hear that."

"You should be. You're the one who caused it."

"Oh?" I asked, confused. Clenching the basket in my hands, I retrieved the packet of sponges. "Did you need these because they're the last batch?"

He waved them away. "I don't need that. I'm talking about Aydin and those ideas you put in his head."

It took a second to jolt my memory. Aydin was his grandson who worked at the storage unit, the one who'd rather spend his summer at the Oregon Shakespeare Festival. I'd told him he should go for it.

"Did he get the internship?" Once the words left my mouth, I realized how enthusiastic I sounded.

Mr. Dalton's scowl intensified. "'Course he did. He just had to call that uppity drama teacher of his."

I tried to sound more neutral. "But that's a good thing, right? He's getting a chance to try out his passion."

"You sound just like her. She was hired right before I retired, and I knew she was trouble." He wagged a finger at me. "Your family was more sensible. At least, your dad certainly was, and your brother followed in his footsteps. Dependable, work-a-day folk."

"It's just a summer internship," I said. "What's the harm?"

"He could be working for me, saving up for college to get a useful degree, like teaching. Now my son and I are worried he'll be thinking about majoring in theater."

I should have tried to placate Mr. Dalton, but I couldn't help myself. "What's wrong with that? If he doesn't make it on stage, he could teach drama instead."

Mr. Dalton's frown intensified. "I should have known you would act so cavalier, given your own life choices."

I stiffened. "What's that supposed to mean?"

"Are you trying to pretend you're not in town recovering from a failed marriage?"

I'm sure I'd only told Jason and Lindsey about the divorce, and yet somehow, news had traveled across town. Someone probably saw my car at the house, looked up Mike's social media accounts, and discovered the news. I'd forgotten how desperate small towns were for gossip.

"Who cares?" I asked. "Lots of people get divorced."

"Do lots of people also flit about from job to job like a butterfly on the wind?" Mr. Dalton shook his head. "You have no sense of responsibility."

"That's not true," I said, arguing as much at myself as with him. "I just haven't found my passion, that's all."

"And what has your passion bought you? No spouse, no kids, no career. You're back living at home, two decades out of high school with nothing to show for it."

My jaw dropped, both out of a sense of shame but also because it hit right at my self-doubt. As much of a jerk as Mr. Dalton was being, he wasn't wrong.

With my silence, Mr. Dalton recognized that he'd crossed a line. "I'm sorry, Ms. Baldwin. I'm just worried about my grandson."

Mr. Dalton tried to walk away, but I felt a stirring in my gut. "Aydin's going to be fine studying drama," I called to his back.

"I hope you're right," he said, not sounding at all convinced as he wandered over to the counter with the bored teenager.

Flustered, I shoved a few more cleaning supplies in the basket, wanting to leave the market as soon as possible. I would have bolted out the door if Mr. Dalton hadn't been standing right there making his purchase. To kill time and put distance between us, I wandered back to the slushy machine and got two of the advertised specials: one red and one blue.

As soon as Mr. Dalton left, I paid for everything as quickly as possible, then ran out to the car, ready to hide away from the prying eyes of Otis, Oregon.

CHAPTER 22

"THIS IS AMAZINGLY GOOD," Henry said, slurping on the last of his blue slushy as we drove back to the house.

"Glad you like it," I said tersely, the first four words I'd uttered since getting into the car.

"You realize 'blue' isn't a flavor, though?"

I shrugged. I wasn't in the mood to argue.

Henry leaned forward, forcing me to view him in my periphery. "Did something happen inside the store?"

I refused to tell him how much Mr. Dalton's words had struck right to my core. He was right. I did flit around from place to place, never satisfied. Even though I loved the library, how could I stay?

But then again, what would I do with myself if I left?

"I just need to talk to my brother," I said.

Given how surly Henry had been all day, I anticipated pushback or at least more grumbling. When he reached over and put a hand on my shoulder, I blinked in surprise.

"You're gonna be fine," he said, echoing the very words I'd just told Mr. Dalton about his grandson.

My body warmed despite his hand, cold from the slushy. "Thanks."

"If your brother gives you any guff, I'll beat him up for you."

So much for the warm fuzzies. "Don't you dare lay a finger on Jason. If you do, I'll make sure Iggy folds you like a pretzel. And when she's done with that . . ."

I trailed off when Henry began chuckling. "You're fun to rile up."

I pulled into the driveway next to Jason's pickup. "Whatever. Just go invisible and try not to interfere during our chat. It's weird enough that I know you're going to be listening in."

Henry blipped out of sight. I exited the vehicle and tried to close the driver's side door when it pushed back against me.

"I told you before that you'll have to leave doors open a little longer to let me through," he growled.

"I thought you were going out the passenger side."

"And make everyone think your car's possessed by ghosts?"

"Nobody's watching."

"Except your brother at the window."

I lifted my head and sure enough, my brother's face peered out, brow wrinkled. Fortunately, his pickup was blocking the view of us.

I waved at him, saying to Henry out of the corner of my mouth, "You better behave."

"That's what I'm supposed to say to you."

I tried my best to ignore him as Jason opened the front door. My brother still had his work clothes on, but he'd scrubbed his hands.

"The prodigal sister returns," he said, standing at the threshold. "You staying longer than two days this time?"

I smiled, relaxing at seeing him in what felt like forever, even though it had been less than a week. "Actually, that's why I dropped by. I wanted to tell you what's been going on."

"I hope it's more detailed than that mysterious message you left on my phone. I tried calling you back a few times and was really starting to get worried about you."

"As you can see, I'm great." I tried to infuse as much cheeriness into my tone as possible.

He craned his neck to look past me. "Are you alone?"

"Of course," I said, maybe a little too quickly. "Why would you ask?"

"Because I swear I saw someone else with you in the car."

"It must have been shadows playing tricks on you." I gestured him to go inside. "Let's have lunch and talk."

He hesitated. I worried he might insist I go in first, but he finally trudged inside. "Maybe my optometrist is right, and I really do need glasses."

I stepped discreetly to the side, keeping the door open a few extra seconds. A whoosh of air told me Henry snuck in past me. Then I shut the door behind me and followed Jason into the kitchen.

"I wasn't expecting you so I grabbed a burger for myself on the way home. You'll have to make your own lunch."

"No problem." I rummaged through the refrigerator for bread, ham, and cheese. My stomach rumbled in anticipation. Henry would have to watch us eat in front of him. Served him right for insisting on monitoring me with my brother.

Jason sat at the dining table, unwrapping his meal as I slapped together a sandwich and poured a glass of iced tea. He waited until I sat down across from him before asking, "Is everything all right with you?"

"You're the second person to ask me that today," I said without thinking.

"Who else asked you that?"

I scrambled for a benign answer. "A coworker at my new job."

"Ah, yes. Your mysterious new job." Jason leaned forward with his arms on the table. "After you didn't answer your phone, I looked up the number you called from. It led back to a military contractor. Fortress, Incorporated or something like that."

"Stronghold," I corrected him. Was it me, or did I hear someone shuffle beside me? Well, if Henry was upset I'd mentioned his employer, too bad. Jason had already found that out on his own anyway.

Jason's face scrunched in concern. "It doesn't seem like your kind of company."

"And just what is my kind of company?"

"I don't know," he admitted. "You do tend to bounce around a lot, I guess."

"Yeah, I know," I grumbled. "I have no sense of responsibility."

"I didn't say that," Jason said defensively.

"You didn't have to. Others have told me so." I pushed my sandwich away, suddenly not as hungry. "I envy you."

"Me?" Jason asked with raised eyebrows. "Why?"

"Because you've always known your purpose in life. You were fixing cars with Dad before graduating high school. You folded into the business like it was a part of you."

He shrugged. "I guess it suits me."

"Well, I'm trying to find what suits me, and I could never find it. That is, not until I stumbled upon this current job. But it comes with a lot of strings." I hesitated, wondering how to explain without having Henry pop into view and give my brother a heart attack.

"Such as?" Jason prodded.

"It's an archivist position," I finally said. "Call it a librarian if that makes it easier. I'm maintaining . . . records and data for the company. Some of it very classified."

"That sounds lonely," Jason pointed out. "You're a people person."

"But that's it, I actually do mingle with a lot of people. They're coming for information all the time. I help them. I'm learning a lot about their culture."

"Military culture?" Jason asked.

I internally cringed. "Not exactly. People come to me from all walks of life. I'm learning more about the world than I thought possible."

Jason looked skeptical. "Where did you even hear about this job?"

"Through a friend," I hedged. Even with permission, I didn't think Jason was ready to hear about his lost-long magical grandmother. "But here's the kicker: I really do love this job. My boss Iggy is an absolute dream. She chose me personally from a pool of possible candidates. She and I instantly gelled together as a team. With her, I can make a real difference."

"I sense there is a 'but' coming on," Jason said wryly.

"But it's not perfect," I conceded. "Because it is such a different . . . culture, I don't necessarily get along with all the patrons who come searching for records. Some think I can't handle it."

Jason dismissed that concern with a wave. "That's customer service for you. You can't please everyone. You have to deal with self-righteous pricks."

"That's not the worst of it, though." I paused for a breath. "It's a lifetime appointment."

Jason looked taken aback. "Like a judge?"

I nodded. "If I accept, I'm supposed to stay until I retire. Leaving will be . . . difficult."

"That doesn't make any sense," Jason said. "That kind of thing can't be legal."

"Trust me, it's legit. It's complicated, but let's just say I'll learn a lot of secrets at this job. They won't let me quit on a whim."

"Freaking military control issues," Jason groaned.

I flexed my hands underneath the table to stem off nerves. "They let me try the job on a trial basis, but that's ending soon. I have to make up my mind whether or not to stay."

"It sounds like a hard 'no' to me," Jason said.

"But you don't understand," I protested. "The job is tailor-made for me. I do love the work and most of the people. I know I'll learn and grow. It's fantastic."

"But it's just a job."

Was it though? I mulled it over in my mind before answering. "It's more than that. It's like a calling."

Jason regarded me. "Then maybe you should go for it."

"But what if I change my mind later? Argh!" I slumped forward and smacked my forehead against the table. "Tell me what to do."

"If I did that, you'd blame any outcome on me."

"I thought you loved me."

"That's exactly why I'm not telling you what to do."

"So how do I decide?" I lifted my head from the table to stare at him imploringly. "How did you know you'd be content running Dad's garage for the rest of your life?"

"I dunno. It always felt right, even from the beginning."

"You never had any doubts?"

"Well yeah, I had doubts. Still do. There are months where money is tight and I wonder why I don't join a bigger shop with a guaranteed salary and benefits. Sometimes I daydream about getting a desk job where I don't have so many aches and pains, especially as I get older. But at the end of the day, I love helping people with their cars. It's fulfilling. I wouldn't want to do anything else."

Did I feel the same way about the Library of Atlantis? My heart said "yes" but my brain said I was crazy. Wonderful.

I sighed. "I guess I'll have to think on it some more."

Jason patted my hand. "No matter what happens, I'm sure you'll make the right decision."

"You're just saying that."

"I'm saying that because it's true. I trust you, Rosalind. You're a smart woman with good instincts."

"Despite my recent divorce?" I asked wryly.

"Everyone makes mistakes once in a while, but you, more than anyone I know, can roll with the punches. You're flexible, adaptable. I'm sure you'll thrive wherever you go."

Even though I wasn't any closer to making a decision than before, my heart swelled. "Thanks, Jason. You make me feel better."

"Of course I do," he said. "Now eat that sandwich before you get hangry and figure out I'm not as wise as I sound."

We finished our meal without any more discussion of my employment problems. I told him I had to travel back to work, and he gave me a quick hug on his way out the door.

Henry didn't pop back into sight until Jason's pickup had long disappeared down the road. "Was coming here really necessary?"

"We got supplies for Wallace, didn't we?" I asked as I unlocked my car to grab the plastic bag.

"Yeah, but the real point was to talk to your brother. He didn't help you make a decision at all."

"I honestly didn't expect him to. I just wanted to see what he would say."

Henry shook his head in exasperation. "I'll never understand you, Rose."

233

"The feeling is quite mutual."

We didn't talk as we hiked back up the hill, but Henry did take the plastic bag of supplies from me when I began to fall behind.

CHAPTER 23

A GATHA GOT CAUGHT IN the trap the next day.

It happened after dawn lit up the library apartment. I finally left the spare bedroom, unable to sleep with the looming decision hanging over my head. Was it as simple as Jason had said? Could I really make the right decision by the end of the day? My answer swayed back and forth, like a rocking boat. I had a bit of morning tea to steady myself.

While sipping my cup, I heard the sharp crack of metal on metal, followed by a ferocious cry that set my teeth on edge.

"What on earth?" I almost spilled tea on myself as I put it down. I ran over to the nearby window. Iggy, also alarmed, expanded the glass panes wider so if I stood on my tiptoes and peered down, I could view across the moat bridge.

Agatha shoved herself against the steel bars, but fat lot of good it did her. She barely had enough room to turn around, her tail slashing hammer blows against her pyramid prison. Even from this distance, I could see runes on the metal light up with each strike, magically enhancing its strength. Enraged, the shimmering black dragon drew in a deep breath and blew out a wave of fire. It singed all the grass in front of her, almost scorching the edge of the wooden bridge. Even the cage's metal bars glowed with faint orange light as they superheated, but they did not lose their form.

Letting out a cry of despair, Agatha curled up into a tight ball on the cage floor and wept.

Concerned, I flew down the stairs, Iggy forming each step a split second before my bare feet hit the surface. I ignored the stab of pain as I ran flatfooted down the hallway, the front entrance forming well before I arrived. Agatha lifted her head as she noticed me rush toward her, doleful eyes forlorn.

She choked on a squawk, her request obvious. Please, get me out of here.

"I'm coming," I called, ignoring a splinter as I dashed across the moat bridge. Once on the other side, where the dirt still felt hot from Agatha's fire, I lost contact with Iggy, although her last emotion echoed in my brain: a plea for her dragon friend.

But I had no idea how to open the cage. It had no discernible door, no lock, only those runes written across the bars, way up top.

I strained my fingernails toward them, hoping to scratch them off.

"What in Queen Mab's name do you think you're doing?" a voice shouted in my ear.

I gasped in surprise just as Henry appeared next to me from out of nowhere. I'd forgotten he'd been spending nights in the library in case the dragon showed up.

"I thought I told you to stop doing that!" I yelled at him.

"And I thought you had more common sense than a toddler." He grabbed my arm and forced me back from the cage. "Are you trying to release this bloodthirsty animal?"

I pushed his hands away. "She wasn't hurting me or anyone else. She deserves to be free."

"She killed your grandmother!"

"You don't have any proof!"

"Neither do you! We only have facts and sheer logic to go on. This dragon came to live on Atlantis, and not long after, Clio got burned to death. Who else could have murdered her?"

At the mention of Clio's name, Agatha's head whipped up, and she growled low in her throat.

Henry pointed at Agatha. "You see?"

As my eyes met Agatha's, she drooped her head as if in shame.

My heart sank. "I guess you have a point."

My sudden gloominess made Henry's brows furrow. "Look, I know this is tough, but it's not so bad. We'll move her to another remote area where she can live out her life without hurting anybody else."

Agatha whimpered in the back of her throat, her head sinking back to the floor.

"She'll be so lonely," I said.

"Better lonely than dead, which is what almost any other creature would get if they killed the Librarian of Atlantis."

Henry nudged me back toward the moat bridge. I reluctantly followed. "How long will she stay in that cage?"

"Just until tomorrow, after the coronation. Stronghold's got every last available body doing security detail at the Southern

Court this afternoon. We'll have enough people to transport her tomorrow."

I threw one last glance at Agatha. She sniffled, burying her head under her front talons. I tried not to let it bother me as we entered the library.

The dwarves and Egan arrived at their usual time right at opening, despite the auspicious day. Henry worried Agatha might try to torch them as they walked past, but the cage had been placed far enough away from the path that even she couldn't spit fire that far. She did get upset when they appeared, snarling and screeching as they marched past, which made Egan almost trip on his cane. Henry pointed this out as a sign of Agatha's guilt, which I pointedly ignored.

Once inside, Egan went about his normal Grimoire searches, but the rest of the dwarves requested a large, open conference space. I led them to the third floor, which boasted a modest stage with a podium in front of a half dozen round tables and chairs. The dwarves clustered in their previous groups, only Brock breaking away to stand in front of the crowd for an announcement.

"The engineering phase for this round has now concluded. All committees will now present their final designs for further scrutiny before we give them to Klaus."

"Hear, hear!" the dwarves shouted in unison.

As I turned to leave, Mikhail called out, "You must stay, Rosalind."

I flushed at all those dwarven eyes staring at me. "I don't want to intrude on your meeting."

"It's not an intrusion. This final debate allows each committee the chance to hear criticism from everyone, which will improve the overall design. Clio always sat in to offer her sound advice."

The rest of his team nodded in approval.

"Okay," I said, taking a seat behind their group at the back of the room. Brock frowned but didn't say anything as he left the stage to let the Korean block group present their design.

If I thought the dwarves argued vigorously before in small groups, it was nothing compared to the rigorous debate of the entire bunch. As the first group of dwarves showcased their parchments, questions flew through the air, all of them delivered in sharp staccato. Would the wood base stand up to the handling of the child in question? Had they considered other paint schemes? Was the number of blocks considered lucky in Korean culture? The presenters sometimes could barely answer one question before the second one flew. It felt like a verbal firing squad with the presenters volleying back, answering as quickly as possible to get to the next.

In the end, after the issues had been addressed and a few modifications made, someone called out, "On to the bit o' magic!"

"Hear, hear! Bit o' magic!" the dwarves said, much like a ritualistic chant.

I leaned forward so I could whisper to Mikhail. "What's the 'bit o' magic?'"

He bent his ruddy cheeks my way. "We always etch a rune into every toy as a little extra surprise."

I blinked in shock. "You give human kids magic toys?"

"Of course. If we didn't, we might as well just go buy something cheap and plastic at the store."

With all the planning the dwarves put into each toy, I didn't think the comparison to retail merchandise was fair, but I didn't argue as another rousing discussion began. Dwarves shouted ideas from all sides of the room.

"A rune so the child can stack the blocks even if they're lopsided!"

"Make the paint so the characters will shimmer of their own accord!"

"Strengthen the blocks so they can't be destroyed!"

But the winning idea came from Brock. "Have the blocks whisper their sounds so the child can learn to read faster."

Murmurs of agreement rose from the ranks, although one dwarf shook his head. "You don't want the parents to get suspicious. They're supposed to be ordinary wooden blocks."

Brock nodded in agreement. "Make it so only a very young child can hear the sound. No one pays any mind if a child says they 'hear things,' and the child will naturally age out of hearing the blocks before it becomes a problem."

"It will take some extra work to get those specific runes right," the lead engineer of the Korean blocks said, "but it's a brilliant idea. All in favor?"

"Aye!" the room roared.

"And opposed?"

Silence.

"Then it's settled. Our project design is approved. The next team can come up to present."

As the rocking horse team stood to take their place, I noticed movement in my periphery. Cindy hid between the shelves at the back of the room, a book clutched to her chest as if holding on for dear life.

I slipped quietly toward her as the questions began getting tossed to the second group. Cindy didn't notice me until I was almost next to her, despite the fact that I approached her head-on. She was too busy concentrating on the debate.

"Hello," I whispered.

"Oh!" she let out a gasp when she finally saw me. Her face flushed as she lowered her voice. "I didn't see you coming."

I almost apologized but stopped myself. "Why aren't you with the others?"

"I'm just listening."

"I thought this was supposed to be an open debate. Even I'm supposed to ask questions."

She sighed. "You're right." She ducked down the aisle, away from the cacophony of dwarven shouting.

I trailed her until we were well out of earshot, tucked amongst some wooden shelves. "Is something wrong?"

"No. I mean, yes. I mean . . . argh!" She tossed the book she'd been holding onto a nearby table. It landed with a loud thud, although the dwarves couldn't have heard it over their vigorous arguing.

It was *A Guide to Alloys in the Fabrication of Complex Structures.*

"I take it you're still studying the trampoline's metal alloy," I said.

"Yes! It won't last, and I have all the proof I need in this book. I just need my father to listen."

I gestured toward the sound of rising and falling voices. "He has to listen if you mention it there."

"You don't understand. Everyone views me as daddy's little girl, that I don't belong on the engineering team. He's the brilliant Master Forger. No one would take me seriously over him."

"They will if you present good evidence. I'm confident of it. Even as an outsider, the dwarves have listened to my ideas."

"But you're the Librarian of Atlantis," she said. "Everyone thinks you're brilliant."

I couldn't help it. I laughed out loud.

She winced in surprise. "Did I say something funny?"

"I'm brand new at this job. A lot of fae have been looking down their nose at me. Most don't like that I was raised in the human world."

"Really?"

I nodded. "It's been incredibly demoralizing. I've wanted to quit several times."

"Why haven't you?"

The question should have given me pause. I'd asked it myself a million times. And yet, standing here in front of this vulnerable girl, who so desperately wished to prove herself, I found myself relating to her experience.

"Because I love being here," I said, my voice growing firmer with each word. "Before discovering this library, I drifted through life. I could never find something that held my interest, and worse, I let other people's dreams dictate my own. But here"—I pressed a hand against a nearby wall, feeling Iggy's happiness flow through me—"I have a sense of purpose. I can't wait to get up every morning and learn something new, whether that be in a book or with the people I meet. It's exciting. It's wonderful. And despite the naysayers, I really don't want to leave."

Cindy hung on my every word, eyes growing almost comically wide. "That's exactly it. I'm not here because I'm my father's daughter. I'm here because I love designing toys. I'm a solid engineer."

"And you can prove it." I pointed at the discarded book.

The sparkle in Cindy's eyes dimmed. "I don't know."

A rousing "Hear, hear!" followed by a vote rose from behind the shelves. The rocking horse team had finished its presentation. Brock's trampoline team was up next.

"Ready or not, it's your turn," I said.

Cindy didn't reply as we headed back to the conference area. Brock stood at the lead podium, the others on his team forming a straight line behind him. Cindy joined them, but held half a step back, barely visible behind the older dwarves.

Brock may not have been my favorite dwarf, but I had to admit, he gave a great presentation. His team had more visuals than the rest, and he had a booming voice that commanded everyone's attention. It didn't hurt that their trampoline was almost a work of art, with supporting bars that held the nets spreading outward like a flower opening itself to the sun. Brock even joked that they might have to enchant the thing to make sure bees wouldn't swarm it, making everyone laugh.

But when he discussed the materials they would use to make the trampoline, including the metal alloys, Cindy slunk even farther back behind her teammates. She wasn't going to say anything.

By the time Brock opened the floor up for questions, I had to hide my disappointment. As the other dwarves debated the design, I almost raised my hand to ask about the metal alloys but thought better of it. I didn't have the knowledge to give intelligent advice and besides, only Cindy could prove herself.

After Brock reassured Mikhail that the flower design would be as safe as a standard trampoline, he gave one last glance over the crowd. Everyone appeared satisfied with the presentation.

"If there are no other questions," he announced, "on to the bit o'—"

"I have a suggestion."

The interruption was so abrupt, the dwarves all looked around to see who had spoken. Even Brock was confused as he surveyed the room. "Who said that?"

"Me," Cindy said, stepping out from behind her teammates to face her father on stage. She clutched *A Guide to Alloys in the Fabrication of Complex Structures* to her chest. I grinned. I hadn't noticed her retrieve it when we joined the others.

Brock's eyebrows lifted in surprise. "You have a question? But you're on our team. You should have said something during our discussions."

"You're right," she said softly. "I should have."

Mikhail leaned forward, his ear craning toward the stage. "What's she saying?"

"She needs to speak up!" another dwarf across the room yelled.

Cindy's face burned as bright red as her hair. She glanced discreetly over at me.

I shot her my most confident smile. I mouthed the words: You got this.

She trembled, but when she turned back to her father, she did raise her voice. "I-I have a suggestion for the metal alloys we should use."

Brock frowned at her. "We're going to use the same materials we used last time we built a trampoline. It's a proven method."

"Yes," murmured the dwarves on stage around Brock.

"But that trampoline was built for a much drier climate. It won't last the 5-year lifespan we hope to achieve." She opened the book to a page she had marked by a blue ribbon. "I can prove it with these charts. Note the durability column where it references humidity damage for our specs."

She passed the open book to the nearest dwarf, who glanced at the page. He read it for a few seconds before glancing back at her. "So?"

"So that damage rate is equivalent to someone living in a moderate to dry climate," Cindy's voice gained confidence and volume the more she spoke. "Our child lives in an area with twice that daily humidity, not to mention a much higher average rainfall. The metal will wear out before five years."

The first dwarf appeared uncertain, but when he passed the book to the female dwarf next to him, she read the page and nodded in agreement. "The young engineer has a point."

Murmurs went through the rest of the team on stage.

Brock silenced them with a wave of his hand. "Maybe it's true, but we can't build a trampoline without metal components."

Mikhail nodded beside me. "You should suggest an alternate solution," he said to Cindy.

The room rumbled in agreement.

My heart sank. Cindy may have been able to prove her point, but in the end, it wouldn't do her any good.

To my surprise, Cindy straightened and told the dwarf holding her book. "Flip the page."

The female dwarf did. "What is this?"

"A similar mixture of metallic elements, although with different proportions," Cindy said. "You'll notice that the damage factor for humidity is reduced almost by a third."

Brock stomped over to the female dwarf and held out his hand. "Let me see that," he demanded.

The female dwarf gave him the book, and he read over the charts. He flipped the pages back and forth, examining both charts.

"You may have found a more durable material," he admitted slowly, "but this new alloy also has a weaker stress point. This might work for a more traditional trampoline, but the flower structure we created would break at these rates."

"I realized that too," Cindy said, reaching into a pouch that hung on her belt and pulled out a folded bit of scrap paper. "Which is why I added two more petals to our original 8-petal design. These extra supports should provide sufficient distribution of force to compensate for the difference."

Brock scrutinized the paper. The other dwarves on his team crowded around him.

"It appears quite sound," one of them said.

"A clear improvement," said another.

Ripples of approval rose throughout the group. But in the end, they all looked up at Brock, who remained stoic as he stared down at the design.

Cindy wrung her hands, the words tumbling out of her. "If there's a flaw, I'm happy to rework the design. There has to be a way to compensate for the rain. I want our child to enjoy this trampoline for years to come and I—"

"It's brilliant," Brock cut her off.

The room went silent.

"Really?" Cindy whispered.

Brock nodded, smiling for the first time. "It's an ingenious bit of engineering and with very little extra material cost to boot. I couldn't have come up with a better design myself."

While Cindy gaped at him, Brock passed the book and the design down to the other dwarves. As the entire room had a chance to scrutinize Cindy's specs, everyone appeared satisfied with the results. A few even pumped their fists toward a stunned Cindy in a show of support.

"Unless there are objections," Brock boomed once the last dwarf had a chance to see the new design, "we will incorporate two new petals and change our metal alloy composition."

"Hear, hear!" the room cheered.

Brock walked over and smacked Cindy hard between the shoulder blades. "Our newest engineer has finally found her place in Klaus's workshop!"

A roar of applause went up through the crowd. I joined in wholeheartedly as happy tears leaked out of Cindy's eyes.

It took a while for the dwarves to settle back down. Cindy's team congratulated her, giving her whacks on the back for approval. Some of the older dwarves on the floor, like Mikhail, went up to congratulate her.

When Mikhail came back to sit down, I pulled him aside to ask, "Why's everyone so excited?"

Mikhail beamed. "By contributing a substantial component to a project, young Cindy has become a full-fledged engineer."

"She wasn't before?"

He shook his head. "She was on trial assignment. Brock knew she had the brains to be a permanent member, but she had to prove herself."

This bit of information confused me. "Cindy realized the metal alloy wasn't ideal for the trampoline. Why didn't she tell her team sooner?"

"Because this was trial by fire. Klaus has found that the best engineers will speak their minds without being asked. No one on temp assignment knows what they have to do to become permanent engineers, and we're sworn not to tell them."

Suddenly, Brock's words about his daughter made a lot more sense. "Cindy had to find her place," I repeated.

Mikhail nodded enthusiastically. "Indeed, and she did just in the nick of time. There was no guarantee she would have been allowed to come back for a second project. The demand to become a workshop engineer is high among dwarves, and we have limited openings. This is the first new member who's joined our ranks in three years."

I glanced over at Brock, who had his arm wrapped around his radiant daughter. Brock hadn't wanted Cindy to fail. He'd been hoping she would speak up and earn her spot on his team.

Eventually, Brock returned to the podium and called out, "All right, settle down. We'll celebrate the admittance of a new engineer later. Right now, we have a project to finish. On to the bit o' magic!"

"Hear, hear!" the dwarves cried, Cindy's voice one of the loudest as she stood proudly in line with her fellow teammates.

Brock flashed a picture of a smiling young girl of about six or seven, her frizzy black hair full of leaves as she lay on a yellowing field of grass. "Before we begin suggestions, keep in mind that this girl recently lost her father. No toy can ever replace such a profound loss, but we always try to make Klaus's gifts extra special for this very reason."

A hitch caught in my throat as the dwarves grunted their agreement. It had been hard enough losing my father as an adult. I couldn't imagine the kind of pain that girl was going through.

A dwarf from the rocking horse team called out immediately. "Make the trampoline springier, so she can jump higher than normal."

A dwarf next to him shook his head. "That might be a little much for the poor child's mum, who's suffered a loss too."

"How about extra safety runes so she'll never fall off?" someone else called out.

"We've already incorporated that into our design," Brock said. "We want to go above and beyond that. For the child."

The dwarves murmured as they pondered other ideas.

My mind went back to my own childhood. At that age, Dad would pick me up and toss me into the air. "You're an eagle!" he would yell as I hung midair. "Spread your wings!" And for a split second, as I neared the apex of the climb before falling again, I really believed I could fly.

I had wished I could stay in that moment forever.

"What if," I called out without thinking, "you could do something to suspend her in midair?"

All eyes swiveled to me at the back of the room.

Brock contemplated me. "What do you mean 'suspend' her?"

"Sorry," I said. "I shouldn't have interrupted your meeting."

Cindy took a step forward. "We want to hear your idea."

A few other dwarves nodded, including Mikhail, although most of Brock's group remained stoic.

I cleared my throat. "I don't know what's possible with your magic, of course, but what if you could make the trampoline suspend her in midair at the top of the jump. It doesn't have to be for long"—I added in a rush before Brock could interrupt—"just an extra split second, a smidge longer than it should last. But in that moment, if she closes her eyes, she might feel like she's actually flying."

Titters of approval rippled through the crowd. Mikhail gave me a thumbs up. Several dwarves around Brock lost their indifferent expressions, warming to the concept. A large smile spread across Cindy's face, indicating her endorsement.

Only Brock remained silent, his expression unreadable. "Are there any objections to this proposal?"

I stiffened, waiting to hear the arguments.

None came.

Brock grinned at me. "Then we have our bit o' magic. Thank you."

"Hear, hear!" the dwarves chanted in unison.

With the three toy designs now complete for Klaus's approval, the dwarves mingled amongst themselves, congratulating each other on a work session completed. Mikhail drew me into his group first for some sound whacks on the back, but soon all the dwarves were including me in their wrap-up session. I found myself returning their thumps, although they laughed at how weak mine were in comparison. It wasn't until Brock tilted his head in my direction, the slightest of bows, that I knew I'd been truly accepted.

As Iggy sent me a flood of congratulation, I realized I couldn't give this job up. For the first time, I felt like I could make a real difference. I could help others with their work. I could learn and grow in a way that I'd only dreamed about before.

I chose in that moment to become the Librarian of Atlantis.

CHAPTER 24

J ACK FROST ARRIVED AS the dwarves were leaving. I caught him talking to Henry as I escorted Klaus's engineers to the door. Henry did not look happy as he argued with the fae prince, who casually shrugged at his concerns. The pair stepped aside as the shorter dwarves excitedly chatted to each other about their designs.

Henry watched me waving to each and every one of them as he passed, a grin growing on his face. He waited until they'd marched out of earshot before asking, "Guess you made some new friends, huh?"

"Definitely." I couldn't hide my own smile as I bowed low to the prince.

As I straightened, Henry addressed Jack Frost by gesturing toward me as evidence. "See, the librarian's doing great. The library's running smoothly. We've got the dragon caught over there." He pointed to a miserable Agatha stuck in her cage, ignoring the departing dwarves. "The Library of Atlantis is more than safe now. I should accompany you back to the coronation."

"And I assure you just as strongly that I'm fine," Jack said. "Gabriel has thrown every last resource he has at the Southern Court."

"Which is clearly not enough because you came here on your own."

"I'm perfectly capable of walking through a fairy ring."

"Not when you can't predict what's on the other side!" Henry said with a frown.

I interjected before one of them lost their cool. "Is there a problem?"

"No," Jack said.

"Yes," Henry said at the same time. "I'm trying to convince this idiot to let me guard him for the ceremony today."

I snorted. "You might have better luck if you didn't call the prince an 'idiot.'"

Jack laughed.

Henry folded his arms across his chest. "I'm not joking. There are too many fae who aren't happy about Jack officially taking over the Southern Court."

"I've made a lot of strides in the last few months," Jack argued.

Henry grimaced. "Are you trying to tell me that no one wants to see you dead?"

"Well, no," Jack admitted, "but they aren't nearly as vocal as they once were."

"That's probably because they're plotting to kill you."

"It's only a rumor," Jack corrected.

"What rumor?" I asked.

Henry turned to me. "Gabriel's security team stopped a group of fae without proper invitations trying to wrangle into the pre-celebrations this morning. They were all Princess Carabosse loyalists. Apparently, they're under the impression that someone is going to set off a bomb and kill the prince."

"Which isn't going to happen," Jack said, "because every single guard in that place has a scrying wand. No one will be able to slip in with a magical device."

"But no one will be guarding you personally?" I asked Jack.

Henry interjected before Jack could answer. "Gabriel needs the rest of the Stronghold team surveying the floor for suspicious activity. He doesn't have the manpower to protect you."

"Then Henry's right," I announced. "He should go back with you to the coronation ceremony."

Jack balked. "But what about you?"

"As Henry said, there's no threat to me here." I decided not to mention that I no longer considered Agatha dangerous even if she hadn't been caught in that dreadful cage. "And it's just for a few hours. I can lock up the library during that time if it makes you feel any better."

"You're both being overprotective," Jack said.

"Better safe than sorry," Henry countered.

Jack held up his hands in surrender. "I can tell when I've lost. If I continue to argue with both of you, I'll miss the entire ceremony."

I motioned Jack forward. "Let me take you down to the catacombs."

With Jack's back to him, Henry winked at me. My face flushed as a tingle went through me, but I squashed it as I escorted the fae prince back into the library proper. Henry stayed behind to guard the front entrance.

It took considerable effort to create the heartwood elevator as always, but I completed it in record time. I ushered Jack Frost inside first and was about to follow when an elderly fae with thick glasses shuffled up to me.

"Excuse me, librarian?" she warbled around her false teeth. "Do you mind taking me up to the 5th floor?"

"I'm already helping someone else," I said apologetically. "It might take a bit."

"Oh." Her face fell, clearly disappointed.

My mind scrambled for another solution. "But I'll send the elevator back up once I reach our destination. You can use it yourself."

Her eyes brightened behind the frames. "Thank you. That would be wonderful."

It took me just a quick second to let a muted Iggy know she could let others use the elevator without me. Then the doors closed shut behind the prince and me, and we made our way into the catacombs.

I escorted Jack Frost straight to the vault in the back but lingered well out of range of the adder stone's freaky influence. Through the icy walls, I watched the prince go through the dance and rituals. Becoming bored, I randomly pulled a book from a shelf beside me. The small book was bound in white leather and had no title, so I had no idea what to expect as I cracked it open.

It ended up being the handwritten diary of some privileged fae. I read several excerpts, flipping around haphazardly, but didn't find anything of note other than what the person ate and the high school-like feuds she waged with her equally insipid friends.

"I guess someone had to write this all down before social media was a thing," I said.

A loud banging caught my attention. I glanced over my shoulder, realizing quickly it was the elevator bumping around. I hoped the old lady made it to the fifth floor okay before skipping to the very last pages of the book.

I read a passage where the writer was really ticked off. *How dare they mock me. I am Carabosse, daughter of Queen Mab! When I come into power, everyone who has ever dismissed me will regret it.*

"From what I understand, lots of people regret your leadership," I told the book. I was about to read more when Jack Frost exited the vault.

"You ready to take on the throne?" I asked as Jack Frost sealed the vault behind him and walked toward me.

"Ready as I'll ever be. I just have to get the ritual exactly right, or I could perish. No pressure."

"You're going to nail it. You seem like the kind of person who's lived through a lot worse."

He glanced down at my hands. "Did you read about that in there?"

I lifted the book up. "You recognize your sister's diary?"

He nodded. "She always wrote in the same unicorn-hide journals."

I stared at the tome with fresh revulsion. "Is it common for books to be made from unicorns?"

"Not at all, but Carabosse always demanded the best for everything in her life, no matter the cost to others."

I wrinkled my nose in disgust as I shoved the book back on the shelf. "It's a double shame, then, because she didn't write down anything worth recording."

Jack shook his head as we walked back toward the elevator. "She very rarely had an original thought, mostly letting others fill her head with awful ideas."

"I take it you two didn't get along?"

"She was the older sibling, an only child for almost ten years before I came along. She saw me as a threat to her rightful place on the throne."

"But you didn't take the throne," I pointed out.

"Of course not. I never dreamed of challenging her birthright, but unfortunately, Carabosse always treated others as if they were miniature versions of herself: selfish, manipulative, and waiting to betray you."

"Fun family dynamics."

"You don't know the half of it."

The heartwood came into view, the elevator doors shut tight.

Jack Frost frowned. "Where's the elevator?"

"I just need to bring it back down," I muttered, worried he might see me as incompetent. "Another patron was using it while we were down here."

I placed a hand on the heartwood and found the elevator on the first floor, bringing it back down.

Jack flashed me a look of approval as the elevator arrived and the doors opened. "Sounds like you're getting along with everyone."

"More or less." The doors closed and the floor beneath our feet lurched only slightly as it shot upward.

"Does that mean you plan to stay on as librarian?"

I flushed. "Yes."

"Excellent. When did you make that decision?"

"About fifteen minutes ago when the dwarves finished their presentations."

He raised an eyebrow. "Those must have been some epic toy designs."

"You don't know the half of it," I said, throwing his words back at him.

He chuckled as the elevator doors opened on the first floor. "I think I'm going to enjoy visiting you here at the library."

"And I'm going to enjoy seeing you too." I was about to give him a deep bow when a faint rumbling in the distance caught my attention.

Jack heard it too. "What's that?"

"I don't know," I said, striding past him. "But I'm going to find out."

Jack stayed on my heels as we jogged to the front entrance. The rumbling grew louder until it clearly became a series of shrieks and roars. My heart sank when the bridge over the moat came into view, and I found Agatha throwing herself against the cage, clearly agitated.

"Agatha!" I yelled, stomping outside into the sun.

The dragon flung her head back, sparks crackling from her mouth as she intended to let forth a streaming of flames.

Jack grabbed me by the shoulder and pulled me back. "Be careful. She's upset."

"But why?" I asked, more to myself than him.

"Because she's the unstable beast that killed your grandmother," Henry interjected. I hadn't noticed him leaning against the doorframe, still guarding the entrance as he waited for Jack Frost to finish his task.

I was about to tell him I didn't believe Agatha murdered Clio when the dragon belched out flame. Fortunately, she'd not aimed it at us, but up the path toward the rim.

"No, Agatha!" I cried out. "Stop it!"

Agatha clacked her teeth, chastised. She shied as far away from me as she could in the cramped little cage, chagrined.

"What's gotten into you?" I demanded. She shied, tucking her horned head underneath her talons.

Henry narrowed his eyes at her. "You better go back inside and lock up the library. I don't trust this dragon, even caged, but Yggdrasil will keep you safe."

"Okay," I said, reluctantly recognizing the wisdom in his words. "But what about you and the prince?"

"We'll take a wide berth around her cage," Henry said.

"We'll be fine," Jack Frost added.

Even so, I watched the two of them safely make their way across the moat and up the path. Agatha continued to cower in her cage. She lifted her head up once, making me flinch, but she quickly lowered her head as if rebuked by my reaction.

I waited until Henry and Jack had made it up the rim and out of sight before pointing a finger at her. "And to think I stood up for you. Henry's right. You should be hauled away for your own good."

Agatha whimpered and settled back down, despondent. I ignored her pitiful cries as I closed the front entrance behind me.

CHAPTER 25

I WAS STILL FUMING over Agatha as I returned to the library. How could my instincts have been so wrong about her? I tried to remind myself that my grandmother had also been fooled by the dragon. Even Yggdrasil had allowed her inside the library.

I needed to calm down, but I had to dismantle the elevator first. I approached the heartwood with purpose.

Wallace rounded the corner just as I put my hand on the wall. He held a dustpan tilted upward so as not to spill the contents onto the floor.

"I'm glad you got rid of that nuisance!" he said.

"Me too," I said, thinking Henry couldn't drag Agatha away fast enough.

"He's gone too far this time," Wallace continued to complain. "You should ban him from the library."

I paused in confusion. "Him? Agatha's a girl."

"I'm not talking about that blasted dragon, although I'm equally grateful she's finally locked up. Best throw away the key with that one. No, I'm talking about Krampus's lackey, Egan.

He burnt one of the chairs." He thrust his dustpan at me to show it full of soot with a bit of charred wood sticking out of it.

I squinted at the evidence. "That's not possible."

Wallace stomped around a bookcase. "Then tell me how that happened."

I followed him to a tiny alcove which housed a table and chair. At least, it used to. The table was mostly intact, if scorched, but the back of the chair had seared clean off, leaving blackened ash around it.

It was the exact spot where Egan had been sitting the last few days.

Bewildered, I surveyed the sooty mess. "I thought Egan was an air elemental."

"Oh, he's an elemental all right, but wind doesn't burn," Wallace said. "The little bugger was furious when he saw you take Jack Frost into the catacombs. He plopped down right there and smoke came out of his ears. I told him fire was forbidden in the library, but he kept right on fuming."

I frowned. "Didn't he leave with the dwarves?"

"No. He grabbed the elevator after it returned upstairs. Pushed the old lady out of the way to get it too. She left in a huff, I tell you that."

My heart skipped a beat as a horrible realization took root in my head.

"I've got to check something," I said, darting for the elevator. Wallace grumbled in my wake, but I didn't pay him any attention as the doors shut behind me.

Once back in the catacombs, I called for Egan, but no one answered. I strained my ears but didn't hear anyone but myself.

I ran toward the shelf that housed *The Taboo Magic of Disease Management*. I prayed I'd find it in its normal place, but instead, it lay open on a table not far away from the elevator. Someone had opened it to the page on scirrhous.

Specifically, open to the spot where the book said a fire elemental could explode like a bomb.

I swallowed to prevent bile from clawing up my throat. I'd heard the elevator while waiting for Jack Frost but ignored it. Someone could have easily snuck in and out of the catacombs during that time.

And Egan worked for Krampus. Krampus had terroristic tendencies. Couple that with rumors about someone bombing Jack Frost's coronation, and all the puzzle pieces fell into place.

Maybe I was wrong. Maybe I was jumping to the wrong conclusion. I wished I hadn't let Henry leave with Jack Frost. I wanted to give him this information so badly. He'd know what to do.

But I only had Wallace. I took the creaky elevator back upstairs and found the hob sweeping up more ashes.

"Egan wouldn't hurt anyone, would he?" I asked.

"Of course not," Wallace said, so quickly that my pulse slowed a little.

Wallace ruined it by adding, "He's too sickly to do anything. The man only torched the table because he was blazing mad, and his ire seemed completely focused on the prince."

"But why?" I demanded, clinging desperately to the idea that my imagination was running wild. "Jack Frost is a fair ruler."

"It's not about the prince's fairness. It's about the company Egan keeps. Princess Carabosse was much cozier to Krampus's ideology. She looked the other way when he and his buddies committed crimes against humanity. The prince is different, though. He's lived among humans, even has a half-human child. Every fae predicts that the days of feigned ignorance in the Southern Court are over."

My heart sank. "Unless they can stop the coronation ceremony."

Wallace didn't pick up on my tone, still flicking his broom around. "In order to do that, they'd have to do something drastic."

"Like set off a bomb?"

That question finally caught Wallace's full attention. He stopped sweeping and met my gaze. "Why would you say that?"

I explained everything to the hob: the rumor about the possible bomb at the coronation, the misplaced book downstairs, and how Egan might have slipped downstairs to read it.

"We're not just blowing this all out of proportion, are we?" I asked, clinging to one last hope.

"No, we aren't," Wallace said. "Before Clio died, Egan often came here on his own. I don't get involved with the patrons if I can help it, so I'm not sure what they consulted about, but the last time he left the library, he was furious about something."

"He must have been trying to convince her to go to the Forbidden Tomes." My thoughts raced a mile a minute. "Did Egan visit the library around the time Clio died?"

Wallace lifted one knobby hand to his face in horror. "The same day, if I remember correctly."

Chills went up my spine "What if Agatha hadn't been the one to kill Clio? What if Egan did because he was furious at Clio for not letting him into the catacombs? And once Clio was gone, Krampus came here with Egan hoping I would be naïve enough to take them both down to the Forbidden Tomes. When that didn't work, Egan came alone, hoping to persuade me into letting him down there before the coronation."

Wallace paled the more I dove into my theory. "It does make a certain sense."

"We have to warn someone about Egan!"

"But how? We can't skitter off to the Stronghold office like I did when you showed up at the library. They're too busy providing security for the coronation, which is happening as we speak."

"Then we have to go to the coronation itself."

Wallace shook his head. "The guards there will never listen to us. I'm just a lowly hob with no standing in Court, and you're even less than that as a human."

"But I'm the Librarian of Atlantis."

"*Temporary* librarian," Wallace emphasized with scorn. "You have commitment issues, remember?"

"I'll have you know I decided this morning to commit."

"Fat lot of good it does us right now."

I slapped my hand against the heartwood. "Maybe Iggy can give us some advice."

It took me a few minutes since I had trouble concentrating, but I pulled all the elevator components apart and stored them properly away. Once the elevator disappeared, Iggy's full spectrum of emotions blossomed inside my head, from frustration to panic to outrage.

"I guess that means you've been listening to the conversation too," I said aloud. "But what can we do? By the time we finish arguing with the fae guards about the problem, Jack could be dead."

The tree sent me waves of encouragement, which I didn't know how to interpret, until I felt the library shift somewhere in the distance. I glanced around the walls, floors, and windows, but didn't notice any movement.

"Iggy's rearranging the library somewhere," I told Wallace. "Do you see anything?"

Wallace also craned his head this way and that but looked just as perplexed as me until his eyes settled on the hallway.

"There!" he said. "The front entrance."

We trotted in that direction. Wallace had impeccable vision because I didn't see it until we were halfway down the hall. Iggy had reopened the large doorframe, expanding it to twice its size so that the normal hexagonal room became almost became like a porch. Most of the wall branches folded back in on themselves, except for a few thick boughs which waved across the moat.

Iggy led us straight back to Agatha. The dragon heard us coming and jumped to her feet.

Wallace halted before leaving the building. "Why did Yggdrasil lead us out here?"

I blinked as I entered the sunlight. "Iggy never believed that Agatha killed Clio. I guess this confirms it."

"That doesn't help us with Egan."

"Maybe. But maybe not. Agatha hates Egan."

At the mere mention of his name, Agatha hissed, sparks flying from her maw. She bared her teeth the way a dog might on the end of a chain.

As I crossed the bridge toward her, Wallace called out, "Do you think it's wise to get close to her when she's like that?"

"She's not going to hurt me." Then, addressing Agatha instead of the hob, I said, "You knew about Egan, didn't you? You must have seen him leave right before I came out with Jack Frost."

Agatha let out a war cry, sending shivers down my spine. I went back over all our interactions. Besides our first meeting at the library—which, in retrospect, the dragon seemed more curious about me than anything—Agatha had only ever gotten aggressive around Egan. It dawned on me that might be why Egan had always traveled to and from the library with Klaus's dwarves. He'd sought safety in numbers.

Agatha had been trying to tell us that Egan had killed Clio all along.

"I wouldn't stand so close to the beast if I were you," Wallace called out nervously. "She made those exact same noises when I found her over Clio's body."

I glanced back at Wallace in alarm. "Did you witness Agatha murder Clio?"

"No. I heard all the racket and discovered that Clio had re-opened the front entrance to let the nasty dragon inside, as was her habit. The dragon stood over the charred remains of our beloved librarian. I'd only assumed she'd done it."

"But now we know better," I said, relieved to have that mystery solved. "How did Agatha behave at the time?"

"The dragon flailed about in a terrifying fit, shrieking like a cornered animal. I thought for sure my days were numbered when she lurched toward me. But at the last minute, she sniffed the air and whipped around in the other direction. She flew like a madman up the trail and over the ridge." Wallace shook his head. "The dragon had lost complete control of herself."

"No, she wasn't losing her mind," I said with a hitch in my throat. "Dragons have a keen sense of smell. She must have smelled Egan's scent around Clio and run toward the fairy ring after him. She was hunting her murderer."

Wallace went even more pale over that.

Agatha jumped up and down in excitement as much as she could in her confined quarters. Her actions cemented my theory.

I grabbed the bars of Agatha's cage and stared into her yellow eyes. "If I get you out of here, will you lead us to Egan?"

Agatha let out a booming shriek that echoed in the empty sky above us.

"Even if you wanted to let the dragon loose, which is a horrifying idea," Wallace said, "you can't. The cage is too sturdy for us to break."

I glanced back up at Yggdrasil's towering branches. "For us. But not for Iggy."

Wallace raised a skeptical eyebrow as I marched back across the moat so I could connect to the library. "How are you going to accomplish that? The cage is outside of Yggdrasil's reach."

"We'll see about that." I walked up to the nearest root and crouched to place a hand on it. Iggy's encouragement swept over me in a wave so powerful, it made me gasp.

"You think we can do this, don't you?" I asked her.

She beamed confidence.

"Okay then," I said, closing my eyes and concentrating as if I were at the heartwood. "Let's do this."

Iggy and I bonded as one, numbing myself to the point where I didn't know where I ended and the tree began. I sought out all her nearby roots, feeling how they twisted and plunged their way into the earth to keep her grounded.

I prodded the largest one and yanked it upward. The boughs high above me swayed as the colossal trunk leaned slightly off-center.

I felt through Iggy, rather than saw with my own eyes, that Wallace held onto the doorway for dear life. "What are you doing?" he cried out as the earth shook beneath us.

I didn't have the energy to answer, stretching that root out toward the moat. I hoped it would span across the chasm and to the cage because dislodging another stabilizing root might shake too much of Iggy's foundation.

Wiping the sweat from my brow, I finally opened my eyes to guide the thick tendril to its destination. The root unraveled, stretching as it coiled outward toward the eager dragon in the metal cage.

The root's tip stopped just short of the bars.

I grimaced, coaxing a strained Iggy to stretch a little more.

She complied, trying to shield me from the pain it caused her. The tree's branches shook even more.

"You'll topple the tree!" Wallace screamed.

But the root finally reached the cage, wrapping tightly around the bars like thread through a loom.

"Please," I whispered as Iggy and I yanked at the cage simultaneously with our magic.

Metal wailed in protest. Shooting pain wracked my body. Iggy screamed in my mind. Boughs as heavy as bowling balls swayed dangerously above me.

But it was enough. Three metal bars snapped wide open, allowing Agatha enough clearance to squeeze through.

Iggy and I immediately let go, the enormous root rebounding as it snapped across the chasm and back into the ground. It plunged deep into the earth, anchoring the trunk just as it tilted dangerously in my direction. As the root settled, Yggdrasil held herself upright once more.

As I gasped for air, something bonked me on the head. Wallace had lit up his glowy hands, grabbed a nearby stick with his magic, and smacked me with it.

"Are you daft?" he yelled as I rubbed the knot sure to form there later. "You could have killed Yggdrasil."

Before I could respond, something swooped down from above him and gave him a similar bonk. Wallace cried out in surprise as a thin branch waved an accusatory leaf at him.

"As you can see, Iggy wanted me to help Agatha," I said dryly.

Said dragon ran across the moat and nearly plowed me over with her weight. She blew hot breath in my face, nuzzling me like the world's scaliest cat.

"You're welcome," I told her, "but we're not done yet. Can you help me find Egan?"

Her mighty roar made my ears ring.

CHAPTER 26

RUNNING UPHILL AFTER A dragon literally took my breath away. Already exhausted from my magic use, I nevertheless had to ignore my burning thighs and keep up with Agatha. She zipped ahead like a captive jungle cat finally let free. I would have lost sight of her if not for the fact that she stayed on the trail and had to take breaks to sniff occasionally to ensure that Egan had stayed on course.

Wallace remained behind at the Library of Atlantis, wishing me the best of luck. He said he would let everyone know that Agatha had led me to my death if they couldn't find me later. So glad he had my back.

In all fairness to the hob, though, there wasn't a whole lot he could do. I highly doubted my own usefulness as Agatha paused near a fairy ring with snowflakes wisping out of it, leading presumably to the Southern Court.

"Let's . . . think about this . . ." I huffed as my feet dragged toward her. "We need a plan . . . to catch Egan. How about we . . ."

Before I could finish my jarring sentences, Agatha jumped through the glowing stones and into the snowscape.

I paused to catch my breath. It was tempting to just let her run on ahead and rip Egan to shreds. If he really did kill Clio, he probably deserved it.

But that would not only be irresponsible, but the other fae might kill Agatha in the process. She was Clio's supposed murderer, after all.

I stepped through the fairy ring after her. "Agatha, get your scaly hide back here before—"

The temperature dropped as a sharp whistle of something slicing toward me cut off my sentence. The spear that had been gliding toward me would have skewered me if Agatha hadn't blocked the blow.

"Stay back, beast!" a voice shouted.

I peered out from behind Agatha's snarling stance to find two fae dressed in crystalline armor, the sheen bright as if made from fresh ice. The pair wore silver kettle helms on top of their heads, making it difficult to determine their gender, although they were obviously guards. Both held spears with a hammer on one end and a blade on the other. The larger of the two had been the one to slash at me, the edge pointed in my direction.

The smaller guard shrank backward, terrified with Agatha growling at them.

"Wait!" I cried, coming out from around Agatha. I kept close to her not only to keep the fae from killing her but because she radiated warmth that I needed in this arctic environment. "Don't hurt her! She's under my protection."

The larger guard scowled. "Who are you?"

"I'm the Librarian of Atlantis," I said, willing my teeth not to chatter as I folded my arms over my chest. "We've come to warn you about—"

"That dragon is a menace," the larger guard cut me off. "It killed your predecessor."

"I know you think that, but—"

"Step aside before it hurts you."

"If you'd listen—"

But the guard wouldn't listen. He tried to strike Agatha again.

The dragon took great exception to this, snapping her jaws so he skittered back two steps.

We were at an impasse. We had to get away from the guards and find Egan.

A sudden blast of trumpets cut through the air, faint but probably loud wherever they'd originated from. I glanced over the guards' shoulders toward the sound and nearly fell over at the sight before me.

We stood in the middle of a gigantic stone courtyard. A magnificent castle made of pure ice rose from the ground. It looked too fantastic to be real with hexagonal towers bunched together in clusters. Blue flames lit windows and doorways, twinkling like stars. At the front was a gated entrance made of stalactites like the open mouth of some giant sea-faring monster.

The larger guard continued to swipe at Agatha.

With amazing reflexes, Agatha whipped her tail, whacking his spear so hard that it launched out of the guard's hand and landed far away. He stared down at his empty hands, stunned.

The trumpets sounded again from within the castle, followed by the muted applause of hundreds of people. The coronation ceremony was underway.

Agatha heard it too, shifting her focus from the surprised guard to the noise. She sniffed the air and then roared, her wings slapping out beside her as she crouched low to take flight.

She paused for a split second, glancing at me as if to say, *Are you coming?*

I couldn't believe I was doing this, but I threw myself onto her back. I barely had time to grab her neck before she flapped her gigantic wings and took off.

I was riding a flying dragon.

I held on for dear life, thankful at least that I had ridden a horse bareback before. But that was paltry training for hanging on to such a powerful creature three stories in the air. Scales dug into my clothes as the courtyard zipped by below us. Agatha headed for the open gate.

More guards in crystalline armor scurried like ants to take positions in front of the gate. The icicle stalactites also came down at a rapid pace, attempting to block our entry.

"We're not going to make it!" I screamed.

Agatha disagreed, roaring so fiercely that the vibrations shook my very bones. I could only hold on tight as she drew her wings in and swooped down toward the narrow gap at a sharp angle. I thought we were going to die as we hurtled on a collision course with the guards and gate.

Right before Agatha crashed into the ice, she let out a stream of fire that sent the spear-wielding guards dodging for cover. It didn't melt the stalactites, but it did knock off chunks of their tips, giving us room to slide underneath before the gate slammed shut.

Inside, a cavernous hallway held icy walls glittering like gems. It allowed Agatha enough space to flap her wings, knocking aside one guard who tried to stab her. As we gained a bit of elevation, we zipped past shouting kettle helmets below in a dizzying blur. On the far side, guards tried to close the largest set of double doors I'd ever seen to prevent our entry, but Agatha was too fast. The guards barely had time to sound a horn, announcing the threat as we veered into the throne room.

We'd made our dramatic entrance into the coronation ceremony.

The glass-like ceiling of the gigantic throne room was held up by icy cylinders, down which flowed waterfalls spilling into artful pools on the floor. A carpet of moss cut through the center of the room, bordered by black roses with wicked thorns. A throng of gorgeously dressed fae—decked in long ball gowns, suits, flora, and animal skins that meshed modern styles with primal roots—filled both sides of the aisle, standing room only. A huge dais of ice lined the back wall so everyone could watch the ceremony no matter their vantage point. Jack Frost danced on that dais in a glow of pale blue light, legs sweeping and arms dipping as he chanted to his people.

" . . . I will honor and protect the fae with my last dying breath," he was saying. "I swear it upon the lives of my ancestors and the powers of the Old Realm, upon a fate worse than death . . ."

He was in the middle of the ritual. One false move, and he would die.

All fae heads swiveled in our direction, their faces growing horrified when they realized a dragon had flown into the room. Agatha ignored them, sniffing the air.

Henry suddenly appeared to the left of Jack Frost, uncloaking from his invisibility to wave furiously at me. He opened his mouth to shout but didn't speak, presumably not to interrupt the fae prince. But he mouthed some choice words, most of them of the four-letter variety.

Everyone else shuffled and squirmed, unsure (or terrified) of how to proceed without harming the prince. Even the guards quietly tiptoed toward us, spears raised but not daring to strike for fear the dragon would break the eerie stalemate.

My heart pounded so loud I was amazed the whole room couldn't hear it. I squeezed Agatha's neck. "Please keep still," I begged in a whisper.

Agatha might have stayed calm if her nostrils hadn't picked up a scent. Her eyes suddenly darted to a bunch of fae on the left side, closer to the dais. She tensed, searching for a particular person.

Egan's wispy blond hair stood out against the brightly colored fae next to him, otherwise I might not have spotted him. He removed the rubber stopper of his cane, revealing a pocketknife-sized blade, which he stabbed into his infected leg. He didn't so much as flinch as he dipped an index finger into the wound and began drawing on his exposed leg in blood, lips moving as he spoke beneath his breath.

He was preparing to explode.

To her credit, Agatha didn't screech. She didn't roar or snap her jaws or make any noise at all. Like an owl spying a mouse in the grass, she simply dove toward Egan.

The fae around Egan fortunately had quick reflexes. They darted out of the way, a few winged ones even taking to the air as the others spilled onto the moss carpet. Only Egan was left behind, staring up as an ominous red glow emanated from under his skin.

Egan flashed us a deranged smile as we closed the distance. He opened his mouth to speak, but only fire shot out of it. It soon consumed his entire body as if he'd doused himself in gasoline.

Agatha landed right on top of him as he detonated, sending shock waves in all directions. The dragon rocked backward, throwing me off.

I landed hard on the ice, knocking the wind out of me. Pain wracked every fiber of my being as the world shook.

Disoriented, I tried to gather my bearings. My dull senses slowly came back into focus. Muffled cries increased in volume. Needles shot through my right side, which had borne the brunt of the impact. Blobs of dark shapes dashed past me. I blinked to jump-start my vision.

Egan had completely self-destructed. The only evidence he had ever existed was an ominous black star on the ice, outlined by hairline fractures in the thick flooring.

Agatha lay not far away, slumped over on her side like a sick horse. Her belly was also scorched, the scales cracked and broken in the same star-shaped pattern. She'd taken the brunt of the blast. I was amazed she survived intact at all.

Then again, she was so still, I couldn't tell if she was actually alive.

I scrambled to get to my feet. Agatha needed my help.

"Halt in the name of Queen Mab's champions!" A sword sliced right in front of my face. I gasped, my gaze following the line of the metal to its wielder.

A fae encased in sheer black armor hovered above me. He appeared as if someone had dipped him into a vat of ebony ice. The breastplate wove directly into the gauntlets and greaves like one single piece. It even connected to the base of the long-faced helmet, which exposed no skin but sported spiral horns, giving him the freakish appearance of a skeletal wildebeest. The only speck of brightness was the sword which he held close to my throat.

"Who are you?" he demanded in a booming, deep voice.

I'd read of Queen Mab's champions. They were rumored to be the fiercest fae warriors who protected the queen with their lives.

My speech failed under his intimidating sword. "I-I . . ."

Four more champions in the same exact armor appeared behind him. They approached Agatha with weapons drawn and hands glowing with unnatural light.

I found my voice. "Don't hurt her!" I yelled, trying once again to stand.

The champion with the sword shoved me back down with his forearm. My hip slammed painfully onto the ice. He slid his sword even closer to my throat.

"Not another step," he ordered, a dark promise in his tone.

I should have cowered beneath him. He was just looking for a reason to kill me.

But then one of his fellow champions blasted Agatha with a fireball. She responded with a weak cry. She was alive, but the limp twitch of her tail indicated she wouldn't be defending herself any time soon.

"She saved you from a fiery death!" I cried out.

"That dragon tried to murder the prince!" the champion countered.

Jack Frost. I'd forgotten about him. I glanced up at where he'd been performing the ritual, but a strange fog had formed on the dais. I couldn't see anything up there.

"Is Jack okay?" I asked.

"That's 'my liege' to you," the champion snapped. "No matter if he lives or dies, his assassin must be slain."

As if on cue, another champion struck at Agatha's tail with a spiked mace. It crunched on impact, sending iridescent scales flying.

Agatha wailed.

My heart throbbed. I couldn't let Agatha, who had just taken down my grandmother's killer, die in front of me.

I acted more on instinct than any thoughtful plan. I slid backward on the ice, using a foot to bat the sword away from me. That bought me a few seconds of surprise as the sworded champion jerked backward. I leaped to my feet, ignoring the throbbing in my right side, and ran for the dragon.

"Stop!" the champion yelled behind me.

I didn't stop. I never looked back, focused only on getting to Agatha. I knew I couldn't be faster than him, not with my hobbled pace. I expected at any moment to feel his armored hand yanking me back, or worse, the slash of his sword across my back.

Miraculously, neither happened. I didn't contemplate my good luck, pushing forward with all my might as the champion with the mace lifted the weapon for another strike. I dove straight into him, wincing as I collided with cold, unforgiving armor.

At least my target crashed down on the ice first. I managed to roll off him and stumble my way toward Agatha, arms held out wide as the other champions closed in on us.

I pressed my back against Agatha, her scales scratching my back. "Please," I begged as all five champions formed a tight circle around me. I stared upward at their faceless helmets. "Don't kill her."

In response, the sworded champion raised a hand, the ebony-gloved tips bursting into small flames. The fireball thrower. He swung his arm back like a baseball pitcher, focused on me.

It was futile. I was going to die with Agatha.

CHAPTER 27

I WAITED FOR MY life to flash in my mind, but apparently that wasn't in the cards for me, not even when faced with imminent fiery death. I didn't want to witness my violent end, but I was too petrified to even close my eyes.

Fortunately, that's when the fireball-throwing champion fell to the ground.

Or at least, that's how it looked. He didn't just collapse like he'd had a seizure. He didn't stumble either. He appeared to be almost yanked backward, as if an invisible force had tossed him there. He tried to get up, but he jerked to one side as if struck.

The other champions broke rank to help their comrade. One of them suddenly doubled over, as if punched in the gut. The mace dropped out of his glove, and a second blow also sent him to the ground.

"Show yourself!" another shouted, frantically searching around.

A disembodied voice replied somewhere in front of me. "I will if you back off."

The sworded champion got back to his feet and rallied the others. "We're under attack! Formation!"

The five champions quickly regrouped with the sword wielder in the lead and the others flanked out in pairs behind him. They faced me, but their eyes shifted to and fro looking for their real target.

Something pulled my arm. "Get up," that same disembodied voice growled.

I accepted the help. "Thank you, Henry," I whispered, trying not to choke on the relief of having him here with me.

A plaid shirt appeared in front of me. Henry kept me at his back, shielding me against the champions. "When did you decide you had a death wish, Rose?" he hissed back, an angry tremor in his voice.

"When I discovered Agatha didn't kill—"

I didn't have time to finish my explanation as a sharp command cut through our conversation.

"Everyone freeze!" an authoritative female voice shouted.

The champions became like icy black statues, their limbs not moving even an inch. Henry also stiffened beside me, bent over in a slightly awkward position to keep me safe.

Even I couldn't move. I tried to lift a hand, take a step, even close my mouth which hung slightly ajar. My body refused to comply. Thankfully, I could still take small breaths as the wind swirled on the dais above us.

The fog swirled, cutting down the center to reveal a gorgeous woman wearing a shimmering dress that clung to her hourglass figure. The blue and black fabric gleamed and shifted, almost like water running downstream. A crown of thorns sat atop her hair, somehow not getting tangled into deer antlers jutting out either side. Her sharp cheekbones only added to her stark beauty. She stepped off the dais toward us, and ice slabs emerged under her feet, floating in the air without supports. Her icy magic alone clued me in to her identity.

But what really gave her away was her fierce sapphire blue eyes, the same as her son Jack Frost.

Queen Mab was not alone. A massive stone gargoyle glided beside her, landing on the ice floor just as her toes touched down. With fangs and leathery bat wings wide enough to encompass his bodybuilder physique several times over, the gargoyle looked ready to hunt. Despite his nightmare-inducing appearance, something about his facial structure seemed familiar, but I couldn't quite place him.

Mab surveyed the scene with a regal grimace. "When I release you, no one will go anywhere until I'm satisfied. Understood?"

Something lurched in my stomach. I knew I would have to obey her command, even if I wanted to run away screaming. Queen Mab had the ability to control people with her words.

She waved a hand. My muscles instantly relaxed. Henry stirred in front of me.

So did the queen's champions. The sword wielder bowed deep. "Queen Mab, the woman hiding behind Stronghold's sasquatch is the one who brought the dragon. She is a traitor to the Court."

"She's not a traitor," Henry fired back. "She's the Librarian of Atlantis."

Mab focused on him. "Let me see her."

Henry fought against complying to her demand. "Rose didn't mean to hurt anyone." He turned to face the gargoyle. "Tell them, Gabriel."

I gasped. Gabriel Alston? Now that I examined the gargoyle closer, I could see the resemblance to the gigantic Stronghold CEO, but it still made my head spin.

Gabriel fixed Henry with his steel gray eyes. "Let Ms. Baldwin speak for herself," he said simply.

Henry grimaced but finally moved aside, leaving me vulnerable to the haunting scrutiny of the fae queen.

"Are you indeed Clio's granddaughter?" she asked.

Shaking, I gave her a deep bow before answering. "Yes, and the Librarian of Atlantis."

She raised an eyebrow. "That hasn't been decided yet."

"I intend to take the job."

"It remains to be seen if I will allow you to have it."

A murmur rose in the courtyard. Glancing over my shoulder, I found that while many of the fae had fled from the chaos, a decent crowd gathered near the massive double doors, watching events unfold like a bad soap opera.

Mab studied me from head to foot as if I were an unwanted pest. "Can you explain why you interrupted Prince Jack Frost's coronation with a bloodthirsty dragon?"

My heart raced. "Is Jack—I mean, the prince alive?"

"Answer my question."

My brain kicked into overdrive, searching for a way to explain as quickly as possible. "I came to stop an assassin from killing the prince. The dragon had his scent and could track him down more quickly than I could alone."

Mab glanced over at the prone dragon, who whined softly not far away. "Isn't this the same dragon who killed your grandmother?"

"No, she didn't."

The sword-bearing champion took offense. "You shall address her as 'my queen.'"

Mab rounded on him. "My champions will only speak when spoken to. Understood?"

They all straightened, clicking their heels together in unison as if they'd done so a million times before. "Understood," they said as one.

I swallowed hard. If I thought the champions might kill me before, it was nothing compared to this feeling that Mab could make me jump off a cliff without laying a finger on me.

She focused back on me. "If the dragon did not kill your grandmother, who did?"

This was it. I had to convince her of the truth. I steeled my spine.

"The elemental Egan did, my queen."

Henry did a double take. "What?"

"He wasn't a sylph that can manipulate wind like Stronghold presumed," I told both him and the queen. "His element was fire." I pointed out the scorch damage, both on Agatha's belly and the ice floor. "He blew himself up. That's what's left of him. The dragon didn't come to kill anyone but Egan. In fact, she saved a bunch of fae by throwing herself on top of him."

Another rumble went through the crowd, this one more intense. "That's absurd!" one angry fae even shouted out.

Mab suppressed the crowd with an upturned hand, then frowned at my evidence. "What do you think, Gabriel?" she asked the gargoyle at her side.

He also studied the scene. "It does appear that something besides the dragon exploded at that spot. However, no fire elemental can self-destruct with such force."

"Not under normal circumstances." I hesitated for only a second before plunging ahead to reveal my culpability. "But Egan read a book in the Forbidden Tomes. It granted him the ability to channel his magical scirrhous of the leg into a kamikaze explosion."

Mab lips curled in a sneer. "You allowed an unvetted fae into the catacombs?"

"No, he slipped in on his own. I swear!"

"A likely story!" the same angry voice from the crowd demanded as he pushed his way to the front. "Or maybe you led him to the book and are now covering your tracks?"

Krampus peered down his nose at me, even across the distance, as he made his accusation against me. He'd traded his fur-lined robe for one made of deepest black, almost like a living ink blot. The cloth matched the sheer malice in his flashing yellow eyes.

My hands shook so badly I had to ball them up into fists at my side. "Don't you dare blame me for this. We all know you want to kill Jack Frost."

A loud murmur arose from the finely dressed fae huddled behind him.

Krampus's twisted rage should have melted the ice below his hooves. "How dare you implicate me in this wicked scheme? You're the one who brought that wretched dragon here, not me!"

"He has a valid point," Mab said.

Henry, who looked like he could murder Krampus with his bare hands, spoke up. "He's the one who brought Egan to the Library of Atlantis on the very first day it reopened. He—"

"Stop interrupting," Mab said with a harsh snap.

Henry clutched his throat, his lips moving but unable to speak. Gabriel tensed at this but stood by his queen's side.

Unable to contain my fury, my voice rose. "But what Henry said was true. Krampus showed up with Egan on my very first day as the librarian. Krampus himself tried to manipulate me into allowing *both* him and Egan into the Forbidden Tomes."

Mab turned her measured gaze to Krampus. "Is this true?"

"Yes," Krampus admitted, "but the temporary librarian did not allow me access. Nor did I ever return to ask again."

Mab whipped back to me. "So how did Egan get into the catacombs?"

"I-I left the elevator open for other patrons while the prince went over his ritual. He must have snuck down when we had our backs turned and accessed the book he needed."

Mab shook her head. "A competent librarian wouldn't have ever let that happen."

My face flushed. I couldn't think of any way to defend myself.

Mab regarded me cooly. "Do you have any concrete proof that Lord Krampus was involved with Egan's scheme?"

I exhaled, defeated. "No."

"Then I cannot place any blame on his shoulders. You, on the other hand, flew past the guards on a dragon with a reputation for murdering fae. At the very least, I must deal with the threat at hand." She gestured toward her dark-armored champions. "Destroy this beast."

"No!" I screamed. I tried to run toward Agatha.

Mab halted me with a word. "Stop."

I froze in place. The champions marched past me with weapons drawn toward poor whimpering Agatha.

"Please," I begged the queen. "You can't do this."

Krampus sneered in derision. "This human-raised renegade is showing her true colors, caring more about her co-conspirator than her own flesh and blood."

"Agatha didn't kill Clio!" I cried out. "Egan did."

"How convenient, blaming someone who cannot defend himself," Krampus said. "You—"

"Who is leading this interrogation, Lord Krampus?" Mab asked, a sharp bite in her tone.

He cowed for the first time. "You, of course, my queen."

Mab stared at him for a few beats before returning back to me. "How can you be so certain that Egan, and not the dragon, killed your grandmother?"

"I don't have any direct evidence," I admitted. When Mab looked ready to cut me off, I rushed ahead. "But it makes sense given how Agatha has acted. She's had a lot of opportunities to hurt the patrons of Atlantis, but she's only ever directly gone after Egan."

Mab did not seem convinced. "I thought the dragon attacked you in the library."

"It only appeared that way," I insisted. "She was just curious about me, probably because of how much I looked like Clio. Yggdrasil also trusts Agatha. The tree let the dragon perch in her branches outside of my apartment window."

"The tree also allowed Egan into the library," Krampus smiled smugly.

I held out my hands imploringly to Mab. "I swear with absolute certainty that Agatha will not harm me. How else could I have flown on her back?"

Mab considered this. "There are only two logical explanations for that. Either Agatha did not kill Clio, as you proclaim, and thus would not harm you. Or you did indeed conspire with the dragon to hurt my son."

I winced at this implication. Henry also made his displeasure known by trying to put himself between me and Mab again.

"Stand back, sasquatch," Mab hissed at him. When he froze in place, she added, "You appear to have grown quite attached to this human."

"Rosalind's not an ordinary human," a new voice proclaimed. "She's a fae, one of us."

All heads whipped around to find Jack Frost entering from the rear of the dais. His skin was pale and sweat matted his brow, but he strode forward with confidence. Relief washed over me, not only because Jack Frost had survived the attack, but because no one could pin his death on Agatha and me.

"You should be resting," Mab scolded him. "The ritual took a toll on you."

The prince hopped nimbly down the floating ice slabs Mab had conjured to reach the ground. "It's nothing a healer couldn't fix. Besides, I'm needed here."

She gave him a disapproving look. "I may be your mother, but I'm also your queen and more than capable of rendering judgment."

"It's not judgment I'm here to issue. It's facts. If Rosalind had conspired with the dragon to kill me, I'd already be dead."

"And how do you know that?"

"Because the dragon was already caged when I visited the library this morning. It would have been much easier for Rosalind to ambush us at the library, where Yggdrasil can defend her. Why wait until here, at the coronation ceremony, where she's never been before?"

Gabriel nodded in agreement. "This plot reeks of someone who does not want Jack Frost to take over the Southern Court." He let his steel gray eyes linger on Krampus, who tried to blend back into the fae crowd, before adding. "Rosalind's only known about the fae's existence for a week. She has no stake in trying to assassinate the prince."

Queen Mab mulled over this. "You both have a point. It is very unlikely either Rosalind or the dragon had anything to do with Egan's self-destruction. And without any other evidence, we must assume he was acting alone."

Gabriel scowled once again at Krampus, but I just wanted to sit down on the floor in relief. Agatha and I would be spared.

"That leaves only the matter of the Library of Atlantis." Mab shook her head. "It is with a heavy heart that I must announce the permanent closure of its treasured halls until further notice."

A cry rippled through the gathered fae at this announcement.

All the previous butterflies in my stomach came back in full force. "But I'm willing to become the librarian."

Mab peered down her nose at me. "You are clearly not fit for the position. I worried as much when I allowed someone of your stature into the role. I can see now that my instincts were well founded."

My heart sank at the thought of losing contact with Iggy. Just when I'd found my true calling, it was going to be ripped away.

Jack Frost looked at his mother in bewilderment. "Why shouldn't Ms. Baldwin take the role?"

"You weren't here, so I will forgive your ignorance on the matter," Mab answered. "But she allowed Egan into the Forbidden Tomes, where he accessed the magic to explode like a bomb during the coronation."

"A regrettable mistake, true," Jack said, "but she's still new to the library. She has yet to learn all the ins and outs of its secrets."

"Which could have gotten you killed," Mab said, the fear of a parent losing her child underscoring her voice.

"But I didn't because Rosalind came here on a dragon to save me." Jack Frost put a hand on her shoulder. "You didn't witness what happened from my vantage point. That elemental was going to explode, killing not only me but anyone within a certain radius of his destruction. Countless lives would have been lost if Ms. Baldwin hadn't shown up when she did."

Mab brushed his hand aside. "Even if I consider that a point in her favor, there's the issue of her upbringing. She doesn't know enough about our ways to make any sort of difference to the fae."

"She did for me," Jack said. "I would not have been able to perform the sacred vow without access to the Library of Atlantis. Who knows how many fae would disregard my authority without it?"

Gabriel grunted in agreement. "There are many fae factions who have told me personally they would not accept the prince in the Southern Court without the ritual."

"Be that as it may," Mab said. "This is a one-time situation. She can't possibly fulfill all her librarian duties."

"Beg your pardon, my queen," a voice tittered from the crowd. "But we would speak on the librarian's behalf."

A trio of fairies with their gorgeous butterfly wings separated themselves from the crowd. I recognized them instantly in their elaborate dresses of silk and intertwined flora that I'd helped them research at the library.

"We met her at the library this week!" Twinkle (or was she Twilight?) exclaimed.

"She helped us make our dresses," her fairy friend chimed in.

"She was ever so helpful," the last one added.

"So she can help with a few scroll searches," Krampus spoke up again, heads once again whipping around in his direction. "So what?"

Gabriel narrowed her eyes at him. "Be silent or—"

Mab cut him off with a wave of her hand. "Let him speak." Gabriel reluctantly stepped back.

Krampus stood straighter at this invitation. "It takes more than writing in the Grimoire to become the Librarian of Atlantis. A muse helps others find out who they are meant to be, and she has shown absolutely no mastery of that talent."

"I beg to differ," a booming voice interrupted.

The crowd parted to reveal Klaus, his own full-length red robe a bright contrast to Krampus's dark one. He didn't walk alone. A ring of dwarves stood behind their leader, physically backing him up. You could have knocked me over with a feather when Brock, of all dwarves, emerged beside Klaus, his shy daughter in tow.

Krampus flashed his pointed teeth at his brother. "What do you know of this matter? You only visited the library once during her tenure."

"True," Klaus agreed jovially, "but my dwarves spent a lot of time there this week." He gestured for Brock to speak.

The red-bearded dwarf projected his voice. "My daughter Cindy here has been wanting to become an engineer all her days, but she couldn't find the courage to make her dream come true. Only with Rosalind's help over this last week was she able to speak up and prove to her peers that she has what it takes to join our ranks."

"Hear, hear!" the dwarves rumbled in support.

Klaus addressed Queen Mab. "It would be a great shame to lose the library when we have a muse of Rosalind's talent to lead it." He turned to Krampus to emphasize his last point. "With all her inspirational powers at her disposal."

Jack Frost also added his loud endorsement. "Ms. Baldwin may be green, but she has great potential. Yggdrasil chose her for a reason. We need the Library of Atlantis."

This time, I swear I heard more than the dwarves chime into the accompanying "Hear, hear!"

Queen Mab scanned the cheering crowd. I was close enough to hear her whisper to Jack. "It seems I have little choice."

"She's a solid choice, and quite frankly, our only option," Jack replied softly.

Queen Mab gave him a dubious glance but then raised her voice for everyone to hear. "It appears Rosalind Baldwin has high endorsement indeed. I hereby decree her our new Librarian of Atlantis."

Furious, Krampus balled up his fists and slunk back into the crowd, just as a rousing cheer followed the queen's declaration.

Queen Mab turned her back to the crowd, her voice quiet once again directed only at her son. "If anything goes wrong with this, I'll hold you personally responsible."

"I'll gladly take the blame," Jack said as she strode back up toward the dais. I worried he might be upset about this responsibility until he winked at me as he walked past on his mother's heels.

Henry could move again once the queen left the room. He rounded on me instantly. "I can't believe you!" he said, beginning a lecture.

He was interrupted by a rush of dwarves, who pushed him aside in order to congratulate me. I glanced around in bewilderment, finding Klaus giving me a hearty thumbs up.

As hands pounded me soundly on the back, it finally sunk in. I was officially the Librarian of Atlantis.

EPILOGUE

N ERVOUS DREAMS FILLED MY sleep, nothing concrete, just a lot of abstract thoughts that kept me tossing and turning all night. I finally gave up after dawn and stumbled to the apartment kitchen.

Today was the first day of the Library of Atlantis fully reopening to the fae public. It had been a week since Jack Frost's coronation, and the library had been closed the entire time for me to prepare. Wallace had taught me the rune sequence to reactivate the fairy rings around the island. I'd restarted as many as I could find, as my sore legs now attested, but there had to be more out there nestled in the wilderness.

Today, anyone from those portals could come and visit the library. I'd have a full house for the first time.

I strode into the kitchen to make tea. For the third time in so many days, I wished the cabinet with the tea kettle wasn't located on the other side of the sink. I could have shoved it into a closer cupboard, but it also made organizational sense where it was. In fact, I'd be happy if I could just swap it with another space containing the pots and pans.

Then, in a stark "no duh" moment, I realized I could.

Carefully kneeling so as not to overstretch my stiff joints, I placed a hand on the cabinet containing the pots and pans. Closing my eyes, I drew upon Iggy's magic. I pushed this cabinet's contents away and drew the tea kettle toward me. I could feel metal kitchenware flying behind the closed doors.

Then, once everything had settled, I opened the cabinet and found the tea kettle sitting right where I'd asked it to be.

I reached for it, then hesitated. I'd never rearranged anything in Clio's apartment. This place had always seemed more hers than mine, and I hadn't wanted to disturb anything.

Iggy must have felt my misgivings because she sent a beam of confidence toward me. It radiated through my core, filling even my cold toes with warmth.

"Thanks, Iggy," I whispered to her. She was right. I wouldn't disrespect my grandmother by making this place my own. I wouldn't change everything because I loved certain aspects of her style. But this was truly my home now.

Home. I'd never thought of any other place besides my parents' old house in that way before. That was Jason's now. This was mine.

And I loved it. Too bad Jason could never really know about it, but at least he thought I was safe and sound taking an office job, even if it was with a military contractor.

I spent the morning cleaning up the kitchen to get rid of my nervous energy. I had no idea what to expect when I opened the front entrance, not how many people would (or would not) come, not what kind of requests I would fulfill, nor the things I would learn. It terrified me.

More importantly, I couldn't wait to start, which is why I needed mindless tasks to keep me occupied until the library opened.

Finally, I went downstairs to the hallway. Wallace had already begun sweeping. I waved but he harrumphed in response. I would have offered to help, but it would only offend him. He considered all janitorial tasks at the library his sacred duty.

Mine was to help all those who entered.

Steeling myself in the front entrance, I put both hands on the ropey branches that made up the wall. I was ten minutes early, but I figured I could at least get some fresh air before the day began. Besides, Klaus's dwarves had promised they would be here this first day.

As the thick ropey vines that made up the wall parted, though, it wasn't Mikhail, Cindy, or even Brock that greeted me. Instead, it was Henry, dressed in his normal plaid shirt and extending something out toward me.

Flowers. A bouquet of gorgeous pink, white, and red dahlias accompanied by ferns.

"Congrats on your first day as the Librarian of Atlantis," he said with a flourish.

My jaw dropped, stunned. Henry had come back to the library the first few days after the coronation, but after determining that Agatha provided me more than enough protection with Egan dead, Stronghold had put him on another assignment. I hadn't seen him since, and I'd told myself I didn't miss him at all.

That lie bloomed across my face as a furious blush. "Wh-What . . . ?" I couldn't form a whole sentence.

When I didn't take the flowers, Henry grinned. "This is exactly why I volunteered to come. I've finally made you speechless."

"Oh," I said, realization helping me regain control of my vocal cords. "Gabriel ordered you here."

"Not Gabriel. Melissa," Henry corrected. "She asked for someone from the Stronghold office to welcome you on your first day. She also wanted me to remind you that you can pop into the Salem fairy ring during office hours whenever you want."

Ah, that made more sense. By taking on the job, I was officially on Stronghold's payroll. I'd already signed the absolute mountain of paperwork to make it official.

"As long as she doesn't have another form for me to sign. I don't think my hand has recovered enough to grip a pen yet."

"Good thing I'm just bringing you these." Henry pushed the bouquet toward me again.

"Melissa's got wonderful taste."

Henry's smile slid into a frown. "Are you saying I'm not capable of choosing flowers for a lady?"

My eyes widened. "You picked them out?"

"Of course," Henry grumbled, pulling the bouquet back toward himself. "I thought about getting roses since it matched your name, but these seemed better somehow. If you don't want them—"

"No," I interrupted, snatching the bouquet. "I do want them." I didn't tell him that I'd never been a huge fan of roses. Too many thorns.

A silence stretched between us. I coughed. Henry shuffled from side to side.

I tried to ease my embarrassment the way I always did, through useless knowledge. "Do you know these flowers' meaning?"

"Good luck?" he guessed.

I shook my head. "Dahlias are symbols of commitment since they bloom after other flowers die off. Ferns represent magic."

"A very fitting combo for you. I just thought they looked pretty . . . like you."

That statement hung in the air almost like a tangible thing. My brain short-circuited, trying to process the fact that the grumpy sasquatch found me pretty.

A low rumbling sounded in the distance, mercifully ending this awkward conversation I wasn't quite prepared for. Both Henry and I glanced up to watch Agatha fly over the rim straight toward us.

Henry put himself slightly in front of me. He still seemed wary around the dragon, despite everything that had happened.

Agatha landed with a thump and proceeded to nudge Henry aside to make excited mewls toward me.

"What's got you all worked up?" I asked as she nuzzled her snout into my shoulder.

Henry glanced past her up the hill. "Probably all those fae coming toward the library."

I followed his gaze and wished I hadn't. An absolute horde of bodies were coming over the ridgeline, like lemmings marching to shore. There was no break in between them as they bunched in rows of three to five. They weren't all dwarves, either, given their varying heights. And once they started coming, they didn't stop.

"Are those all patrons?" I asked.

"Yes," Henry said before turning back to my paling face. "Are you okay?"

"That's a lot of them. More than I anticipated."

"You're gonna be fine."

Agatha barked out a fierce agreement.

I relaxed. They were right. I was ready for whatever challenge came my away.

"I can handle this," I said, and I meant it. I could already feel Iggy growing excited at the prospect of so many people visiting the Library of Atlantis. The tree could finally fulfill her purpose. I'd be right there with her, doing the work I'd been born to do.

I'd finally found the place where I belonged.

From author DM Fike: Thank you so much for reading Rosalind's story! My local library was a near and dear place to me growing up. It may not have been a sentient living tree, but I have many fond memories of the librarians who shaped me into the reader and writer I am today.

If you have the time, please consider <u>leaving a review for this book</u>. As a small independent author, each review helps me continue writing more books.

If you want to read more about Rosalind's adventures as a magical librarian, check out the next book in the series:

Secret of the Fae Library

You can also <u>sign up for my newsletter</u>, where I often give away free stories about my book's characters. I love to hear from my readers so I hope to hear from you soon!

MAGICAL MIDLIFE MOM SERIES

Curious about other characters Rosalind meets in this story? Read about Melissa's magical journey!

Single mom Melissa Hartley discovers that the fae exists in the worst way possible: through her teenage daughter. Follow along as she protects her child from an ancient fae prophecy. If you like witty mother-daughter banter, magical adventure, and a slow-burn romance, check out this **complete** fantasy series!

BOOK 1: MOM OF THE CHOSEN ONE
BOOK 2: MOM ON A QUEST
BOOK 3: MOM IN SHINING ARMOR
BOOK 4: MOM'S LAST STAND

ABOUT THE AUTHOR

DM Fike wanted desperately to join the X-Men growing up. Barring that, she would have enjoyed riding a unicorn or at least meeting a fairy. Since none of that happened, she decided to write books about everyday people discovering magic through a series of epic adventures. She's currently living out her own happily-ever-after with her husband and two wonderful children in Oregon.

More places to keep in touch:

Website: dmfike.com

Email: dm@dmfike.com

Facebook: facebook.com/DMFikeAuthor

Amazon: amazon.com/author/dmfike

BookBub: bookbub.com/profile/dm-fike

GoodReads: goodreads.com/dmfike

Instagram: instagram.com/dm.fike

OTHER BOOKS BY DM FIKE

Magic of Nasci Nature Wizard Series

Legends of Llenwald Series

SPECIAL THANKS

Writing a book is one thing, getting it out to the world is another. Many talented people gave this book the professional care it deserved. Sandra Schiller and Jennifer Marshall always give me early feedback on my stories, of which I'm eternally grateful. I am so lucky to have Lori Diederich (pen name Lori Drake) as my editor. She loves and understands the nuances of my stories and always makes great suggestions to improve each book. Thanks to Kelley Scarrow, Sarah Metcalf, and Carrie James for catching a lot of pesky grammar errors that slipped past everyone else. Samantha Marshall also provides much needed emotional support in my writing journey.

One final shoutout to my husband Jacob Fike, who lends both his time and artistic skills to making each of my books better. I couldn't do this without him. Love is indeed a choice we make every day.

Printed in Great Britain
by Amazon

62823245R00180